I PUSHED MY [WAY THROUGH THE]
CROWD TOWA[RDS THE BAR.]
ACTON'S VOI[CE, LOUD AND]
OVERBEARING, [RANG OUT]
UNMISTAKABLY ABOVE THE
SURROUNDING RACKET, LIKE A
HUNTSMAN'S HORN ABOVE A
BAYING PACK OF HOUNDS . . .

Tony Acton. I hated him. The very sight of him made me feel sick. That cheeky schoolboy's grin, that slight but energetic frame, that lean and handsome face with its blue eyes and pale skin, its noble brow, its dark gypsy curls. I hated him so much it was like a fierce flame which burnt itself into every thought and filled every breath I took with sharp and acrid smoke. I hated him so much I was going to kill him.

NEIL TIDMARSH

FEAR OF THE DOG

A SIGNET BOOK

SIGNET

Published by the Penguin Group
Penguin Books Ltd, 27 Wrights Lane, London W8 5TZ, England
Penguin Books USA Inc., 375 Hudson Street, New York, New York 10014, USA
Penguin Books Australia Ltd, Ringwood, Victoria, Australia
Penguin Books Canada Ltd, 10 Alcorn Avenue, Toronto, Ontario, Canada M4V 3B2
Penguin Books (NZ) Ltd, 182–190 Wairau Road, Auckland 10, New Zealand

Penguin Books Ltd, Registered Offices: Harmondsworth, Middlesex, England

First published 1997
1 3 5 7 9 10 8 6 4 2

Printed in England by Clays Ltd, St Ives plc

CHAPTER ONE

The women were in party gowns and unseasonal suntans. All the men were wearing dinner jackets. The place was packed, brightly lit, buzzing with laughter and live jazz and raised voices. Waiters were pouring champagne as fast as anyone could drink it, and the air was thick with cigar smoke and expensive perfume. But nothing could mask that faint, animal aroma – a compound of fear and exhaustion – which lives in every gymnasium.

What looked like a boxing-ring had been erected on a platform in the middle of the floor.

I pushed my way through the crowd towards the sound of Acton's voice. Loud, spoilt, overbearing, it rose unmistakably above the surrounding racket, like a huntsman's horn above a baying pack of hounds. Then there was a sudden break in the press and there he was, talking to Stanley the journalist.

Tony Acton. I hated him. The very sight of him made me feel sick. That cheeky schoolboy's grin, that slight but energetic frame, that lean and handsome face with its blue eyes and pale skin, its noble brow, its dark gypsy curls. I hated him so much it was like a fierce flame which burnt itself into every thought and filled every breath I took with sharp and acrid smoke. I hated him so much I was going to kill him.

At that moment I didn't know I was going to kill him; I knew I wanted to kill him, but it wasn't until later that night – after the party – that I decided I was actually going to do it. Would I ever have taken the decision if it hadn't been precipitated by Acton's request? Who knows. But the desire was there. It was simply looking for a trigger, waiting for such a catalyst. That, I suppose, was why I had gone to Acton's party in the first place. That was why I had said yes when a man I hated had asked me an apparently innocent favour.

I lay awake half the night, in the darkness and the silence, turning the idea over and over and round and round. He deserves to die, a voice insisted. You're going to kill him. And you're going to get away with it. Is that possible? Yes, it must be. You'll find and execute the plan which guarantees it. He deserves to die. You're going to kill him . . . And over and over and round and round.

Three o'clock in the morning and I was still awake. I got up and went through the curtain separating the tiny space where I slept from the vast space where I worked. It was very cold and very dark, and when I switched on the light my eyes flinched from the sudden brightness and from the chaos it revealed.

The studio was a mess. A jumble of books, papers, paints, abandoned work, half-finished work, work which would never be finished. Tins stuffed with unwashed brushes and broken pencils; lidless jars of set glue, hardened varnish, evaporated thinner. Unwashed plates, cups of coffee, takeaway tin-foil dishes, crushed beer cans, empty wine bottles.

It hadn't always been like this. A year ago, six months ago, I'd still been in control.

A magazine spread itself at my feet. It was weeks old, some Sunday newspaper's colour supplement. Acton's face leered up at me from the front cover. I bent down and picked it up. Yet another profile of 'London's most exciting and successful young art dealer'. This one penned by Stanley the journalist. How many had there been since his gallery moved out of the Portobello Road and into Cork Street three years ago?

I looked closely at that picture. The photographer had done a good job. No lines of cruelty or corruption were visible on that apparently smooth face. There he sits, hands in pockets, perched on a stool in the gallery, amused, arrogant, successful. Relaxed but dynamic, draped in an elegantly unstructured woollen suit by some Italian whose label the whole world can pronounce. And behind him, hanging on the white wall, an obscure and tragic representation of antlered beasts being slaughtered by unseen huntsmen. A vast, dark, moonlit canvas. One of mine, as it happens.

I flicked through the magazine to the article. I'd read and re-read it a hundred times over the past few weeks. It had up-to-date news on the Wyndham Lewis coup and on the plans for New York. My eyes caught an off-the-record comment from myself, quoted without permission: ' "Tony Acton looks and lives like a young Roman emperor", said Nicholas Todd, an up-and-coming young painter from Acton's increasingly impressive stable, "complete with fawning court and an absolute power he's only too willing to abuse." '

I dropped the magazine back on to the floor and went into the alcove fitted out with the necessaries – cooker, sink, fridge – which I called a kitchen. An uncurtained window looked out at the blank cliff-face which was the rear of a long row of terraced houses in the next street. Not a single light shone in a single window – perhaps I was the only human being awake in the whole world. I looked down into the back gardens separating us. At this time of night they were no more than pools of darkness, prowled only by feral cats and bad dreams.

I know him well, I thought, but not well enough. I'll have to study him. I'll study him as closely as any hunter studies his prey, as closely as the man addicted to rod and line studies the living, eating, breeding habits of the fierce pike or cunning perch, the curve of bank, the weed, the exact flow and depth and temperature of the water it favours. I'll study him until I know him as well as the gamekeeper knows the fox.

I stared down into the black back gardens, trying to focus on shadows real or imagined. Trying to think clearly, logically. How long did I have? His move to the States was planned for the week after next. And he intended to stay there until the new gallery was up and running. How long would that take? A year? Two years? Ten? So I had a fortnight. No, even less than that. Next week he had that trip to Madrid booked. Checking out some Spaniard who sculpted dinosaurs from industrial waste or something.

Less than two weeks.

And then I made the mistake of thinking about Diana Artemis. Had she gone to the party on the simple off-chance that I'd be there too? I had made it a rule some time ago never to think about Diana Artemis. Never. It was a good rule. Such rules should not be broken. Even as I pushed the question to the back of my mind I knew that there'd be no sleep that night.

I switched on all the lights and turned up the heating. I loaded up a brush and tried to do something with the big canvas propped up in the middle of the floor. Which wasn't much. It was cold in there – it's always cold in there, even on a summer's day, and this was the early hours in February – but that wasn't the problem. That wasn't the problem at all.

In the end I gave up. I made some coffee and turned my thoughts back to the party. Back to Acton's request. With a sudden shock it occurred to me that perhaps it wasn't as innocent as it seemed. Perhaps he was playing

4

a subtle game of his own. Perhaps I wasn't the only one planning secret moves. Perhaps he had anticipated me and was planning some sort of pre-emptive step . . .

Well, I wasn't afraid. I'll take you on, I thought. I'll turn it to my advantage. I'll beat you at any game you want to play . . .

The jazz had grown louder and the air hotter and heavier as I had crossed the floor. Then Acton had turned to face me, as if he'd known I was approaching. He was grinning. I could feel the restless energy coiled up in that slight frame; even the elegance of his dinner jacket couldn't hide the threat of it. If he was surprised to see me, he wasn't showing it. I wondered if I was hiding my hatred just as effectively.

'Like the headgear, Nicky?' he asked in greeting. A wreath of gilded oak-leaves was resting on his dark curly hair, brushing his temples. 'A present from Stanley here. He nicked it backstage at the National when he was interviewing some knighted thespian.' He raised an eyebrow at Stanley. 'Or so he says. But we've got Nick here to thank for the idea, haven't we, Stanley?'

' "Roman emperor".' Stanley laughed drunkenly. He waved his glass vaguely at the crowd around us, spilling champagne on the bare wooden floor. ' "Fawning court. Abuse." '

'But which one?' Acton asked. He looked at me, still grinning. I couldn't tell whether my comments in the article had amused or annoyed him. Not that I gave a damn either way. 'Good Augustus or evil Nero? Clever Claudius or crazy Caligula?'

'No, no, no,' pronounced Stanley, struggling bravely for coherence. 'I see you more as a Renaissance prince. A . . . a . . . a Medici. Or a Borgia.'

'Patronage, poison and perversion,' I said. 'Is that what you mean?'

'A court full of clowns and assassins . . .' Acton mused. 'Which are you, Stanley? And what about Nicky here? Which is he?'

'A court full of courtesans,' Stanley leered. 'Courtesans, Tony. Where are they?'

'Which reminds me, Nick, the women will want to say hello.' He took my arm and turned away from Stanley. 'Besides,' he added cruelly, 'I've had enough of this old fart.'

Stanley's bottom lip quivered and his stooping figure drooped even more. I felt sorry for him. He was pompous and he was drunk but he didn't deserve the humiliation. Alone of all Acton's hangers-on, he had never really hardened himself to Acton's insults. Why did he keep coming back for more? 'I say!' He raised his voice. 'I must tell you what Jamie – Lord Gowrie – said to me last week, when I was dining with him at Sotheby's . . . in the directors' dining-room . . .'

'No, Stanley.' Acton was already walking away. 'You can bore someone else with that story.'

I followed him through the crowd. It was growing thicker and louder by the minute. Soon there'd be no room to move. Acton scattered greetings as he crossed the floor, hands reached out to shake his or clap him on the back. Then we were face to face with Greta, his Polish wife.

'Darling Nicky.' The four syllables of those two words fell heavily from Greta's Central European tongue as I bent to kiss her cheek.

Greta was small and blonde and blue-eyed, with a voluptuousness she did nothing to hide. She and her companion – someone I hadn't seen before – were wearing almost identical black dresses, very short and very tight. Golden tans.

'Look at them,' Acton said in mock or probably sincere disgust. 'Like a pair of tarts having a competition to see who can show off the most bare flesh.' He laughed unpleasantly. 'See you later, Nick.'

An angry frown creased Greta's brow. Her lips parted, she took a deep breath, but before she could say anything he was gone, his back turned, his laughter fading into the crowd. She watched him disappear, still frowning.

There was something slow and heavy and Slavic and gloomy about Greta at the best of times, which people who didn't know her put down to stupidity or to a less than confident grasp of the English language. In fact there was nothing wrong with her English – it was near-perfect, as was her grasp of German, Russian, French and half a dozen other languages. And she certainly wasn't stupid. Before she married Acton she'd been a professional student, one of those serious and passionate intellectuals who are a speciality of Central Europe. She had a degree in philosophy from Warsaw University and she'd read papers at the Sorbonne and Freiburg. Everyone who underestimated Greta came to regret it, sooner or later.

'He does not understand.' She sounded puzzled. 'This dress is a post-feminist concept. I have explained it to him but he does not understand.'

Her companion laughed. 'That's probably just as well, honey.' She had an accent as obvious as Greta's, but it was American, a slow Southern drawl. Prahbly juhs duhz wayul, herny. Unlike Greta, she was tall and thin, sharp-faced and red-haired. Her eyes were brown, but sharper and shrewder than Greta's. There was a sense of speed and energy and experience about her which I couldn't imagine in Greta.

'So who wins?' She was talking to me. I turned to face those sharp brown eyes.

'I'm sorry?'

'The tarts' competition,' she laughed. She was amused by Acton's comment. 'The most bare flesh.' Bayuh flayush. 'OK, Greta wins if we're judging by sheer acreage, but I think I have the edge if we're looking for percentage of the whole. Don't you agree?'

Greta turned back to us and put a smile on her face. 'Nicholas Todd, meet my friend Andrea Alvarez.'

I took her friend's hand. Long brown fingers encrusted with gold and jewels. It felt warm but very dry, hard and thin like something left out in the sun for too long.

'Nicholas Todd? But I know your work.' She grimaced. 'A bit tortured, isn't it?'

It was my turn to laugh. 'So you're an art critic?'

'No, no,' Greta explained unnecessarily. 'Andrea is in London on holiday. Her husband is being horrible . . .'

'Ex-husband, honey, ex-husband.'

'Her ex-husband is being horrible about the divorce, so she has come to London to forget all about it.'

'I'm sorry.'

'Sorry? You shouldn't be. Mr Alvarez divorced me, but my attorney came back from court with the old boy's boxer shorts in his hand. So I'm over here to spend some of the bastard's money, OK? No broken heart under this gal's titties.'

She looked at Greta and both girls began to laugh, giggling like a pair of schoolgirls wearing make-up for the first time, heads together, scarlet nails raised to scarlet lips. Their champagne jiggled and danced in glasses smudged pinkly around the rim.

'Nicholas doesn't approve,' Andrea chuckled. 'He thinks we look like a couple of tarts having a good time.' More laughter.

Over her shoulder, on the far side of the hall, I saw Diana Artemis. She was standing quite still, listening seriously to a young man in a white dinner jacket holding forth about something at great length. Diana Artemis. There she was. As thin and as pale as ever. Black hair, white face, blue eyes. Pale shoulders. Pearls and a simple dark green dress of great elegance. She looked beautiful. Something like vertigo tugged at my senses then I looked away, afraid that she might turn and catch my eye.

'Oh dear, we have upset him,' Greta sighed. 'Poor Nicholas, he has gone so pale.'

Diana Artemis. I shook my head. Let it go. 'So much the better to complement your fine suntans.'

'So charming,' Andrea purred, sipping her champagne. Behind her southern ease I was aware of a strong and alert will. A predatory will. She looked at me, slowly shaking her head. 'Why does such a charming artist paint such disturbing pictures?'

I felt a hand on my shoulder. 'Come on, Nick. You don't want to spend all evening with the little girls.'

Again I saw Acton's wife's eyes narrow and her frown return. But again he was too quick for her, sweeping me away before she had time to reply. He put his arm around my shoulders as he drew me apart from the crowd. I suppressed a shudder, seeing in my mind's eye the shudder of a cow's flank as a fly lands on it.

'I'm glad you came, Nick. After everything . . . You know. I'm glad you decided . . .' He sighed. 'Listen, Nick, how would you fancy a week in the country? You know, a bit of fresh air. Away from all this.'

Say nothing. Wait until you know what he's after.

'You see, Nick, I have a bit of a problem.' His voice was warm, confiding. 'You know I'll be in Madrid next week? Well, the Kennedys – the old couple who look after our place in Kent – the gardening, cooking, cleaning, all that kind of crap – they're off on holiday for two weeks tomorrow. Florida. I ask you. Do I pay them too much or what? You know what they said? We want to see Disney World before we're too old. Would you believe it? They're already a decade or two older than I ever want to be. And Greta – she insists on coming to Spain with me. Can't put her off, stupid cow. Thinks I'm having it away with a flamenco dancer or something. Which means, of course, that there's no one to look after the old palace next week. You know, no one to feed the animals, fight off the burglars, keep the toilet seats warm. Know what I mean?'

I knew what he meant.

'So how about it? A week to yourself, get away from it all. Go on, spoil yourself.'

'Why me?' I said. 'Surely someone else . . . ?'

'I've asked everyone else. George, Sonia, even old Palmer. Sonia said she'd do it, a week ago, but she's just pulled out. Has to go to Athens. Told me ten minutes ago. Please, Nick. You're the only one left.'

I shook my head.

'Come on, mate. Give yourself a break. It isn't the Outer Hebrides. Kent, you know. An hour down the motorway. You'd be doing me a very big favour.'

'OK. Yes. Why not?' Whatever my subconscious might have been working on, my initial conscious reaction was no more than that.

'Great!' He thumped my shoulder. 'We're flying out Sunday afternoon. We'll be back by lunchtime the following Friday. Come over for the weekend. Saturday morning? We'll show you round. You'll know where you are by the time we take off on Sunday. OK?'

I nodded.

'Thanks, Nick. I really appreciate it.' He was already backing away into the crowd. 'Drop by the gallery tomorrow. We'll sort things out. Directions and that.' Then he was gone.

It was hot and crowded in the gym. There was hardly room to move and the noise of laughter and shouted conversation was a deafening roar. I scanned the crowd for waiters and familiar faces, seeing neither. There were never many artists at Acton's parties; most of his guests were customers or hangers-on. Behind me I could hear the interior designer who had 'created' Acton's Cork Street gallery telling everyone about her latest piece of cosmetic surgery. Ahead I could see Klaus, Acton's wealthiest German customer, sulking as he watched his teenage boyfriend flirting with a researcher from Christie's.

The party had reached that stage where you had to shout to make yourself heard. Conversation was impossible. In front of me a group of girls was laughing and screaming as they tried to sign their names on an old man's shirt front with lipstick. The old man had very long hair and a goatish grin and he wasn't putting up much of a struggle.

Then, quite suddenly, a wave of cheering and applause spread out through the crowd. Two figures were climbing into the boxing ring. They were completely encased in padded robes and wicker masks, and each carried a polished bamboo stave between gloved hands. They stood to attention in opposite corners, facing each other, waiting for the silence which followed the cheers and applause. Then they bowed.

A woman giggled, but it was the only sound in the whole gymnasium, and it was a nervous sound, betraying the very tension and excitement it had tried to deny.

I heard a sudden intake of breath from behind each mask. Then both figures rushed forwards with their weapons raised above their heads.

'Ee-yah!' One cry bellowed from two pairs of lungs as they met in the centre of the ring. Their staves crashed together and locked, quivering, above heads which were now pressed face to face, mask grinding against mask.

Then they broke free, only to crash together again with increased fury. They slashed and thrust at each other, charged and jostled, hacked and parried, yelled and grunted. Bare feet stamped on the canvas-covered boards, wood crashed on wood.

The crowd was no longer silent. The hall echoed with cheers and applause, jeers and laughter. Any moment now they'll start throwing things into the ring. And this is just an appetizer. What is the main dish? I suddenly felt as empty as the glass in my hand. I don't want to watch this. Shall I get drunk? Or simply leave?

'Of course, Acton's parties are just another ego trip for him,' poor Stanley had said the last time I'd seen him sober. 'Another platform where he can be sure he's the centre of attention. He loves to play the generous host. It gives him the adulation of a crowd. A crowd he can humiliate.'

I decided to leave. I'd almost reached the entrance hall when a voice from behind made me jump. 'What's eating you up, Todd?'

It was barely more than a deep growl. I turned round. It was Patrick's, the head of a team of picture restorers Acton used from time to time. He was a big man, very fat, very bald, massively bearded.

'I've been watching you for the last few months. The last year. You look like you've got something gnawing away at your gut. And you're so sick and so desperate you're going to tear it out, even if it kills you. Yes, Todd. You can't fool me.'

He was sitting on his own in a corner, his immense mass sprawled across and almost hiding the chair which barely supported him. A dish of grilled prawns was cradled in his lap. His blunt, fat fingers cracked them open one after another and fed them greedily into his bearded mouth. His dinner-jacket was filthy. He looked coarse and clumsy, but I'd seen those same fingers cleaning and caressing badly-damaged old masters with the delicacy and deftness – with the love, even – of a mother with her baby.

'So what is it, Todd? What's got you twisted and squirming? Eh? Let me guess. It's Acton, isn't it? Eh?' He laughed. It wasn't a pleasant laugh. It was full of an ugly relish. He reached down to pick up his glass from the floor and drank noisily. 'Yes. Obvious, isn't it? What's he done, then? How did he get to you, Todd? You, of all people?'

I didn't answer. I stared down at him as he, still chewing on the prawns, grinned up at me. 'I remember, when Acton first took you on, I remember thinking he'll never fit in. Remember what you were like then? Pleasant, decent, good-natured. A very nice young man, just the sort my poor disappointed mother hoped I'd be when I grew up. Not Acton's type at all. Talented, yes, of course. Brilliantly gifted. But that goes without saying if Acton thought you were worth the punt. And now look at you. Now you're just like the rest of us, aren't you? You're just another of Acton's twisted freaks.' He leaned forwards. 'And what's more, I hear you've lost that talent somewhere along the way as well. Rather careless, don't you think?'

His eyes flickered away for a moment as he leered at a couple of girls giggling past. 'So how did he do it, Todd? How did Acton bring about this amazing transformation? Eh? How did you come to catch that most deadly of anti-social diseases, Actonitis? Oh, we're all infected, Todd. Look at us. Look at yourself. You look like you're dying of it. You've lost weight. You've aged ten years. Your hands are shaking. Are you losing sleep?

Is your hair falling out? Have you seen a doctor? A psychiatrist?'

I turned and walked away. I heard him calling after me, no longer laughing, bitter now. 'I'll tell you something, Todd. However you caught it, there's no way out of it. No cure. You'll just have to learn to live with it, like the rest of us.'

I left. As I walked out through the door I heard a woman scream behind me. Then a few moments of shocked silence. Then a sudden wave of laughter, male laughter. But I didn't turn to see what it was all about. I wasn't interested any more.

I could see the big glass doors at the other end of the quiet entrance hall and the dark street beyond, and cars going by with rain glittering in their headlights. The doors were half open and a breath of air swept past me. It felt cool and fresh. I walked forwards and out into the night.

It was dark and cold and wet outside. I drove home through the rain, my mind playing with patterns and possibilities, all groping their way towards a single end – the death of Anthony Acton.

Driving home – that was when I decided I was going to kill him. It wasn't the first time the idea had occurred to me. It was, however, the moment I realized I was actually going to do it. Somehow the whole thing seemed inevitable. The keys to his house – it was an irresistible opportunity. An opportunity which Acton himself, ironically, had provided.

It was almost midnight by the time I got back to the forgotten corner of Hackney where I lived. I parked in the road outside and sprinted through the rain up the steps towards the big front door. I fumbled with my keys in the darkness, half hearing a car door open and close behind me. High heels running across the road and up the steps.

'Nicholas.'

I knew that voice. I didn't need to turn round to know who was calling. I turned anyway. Diana Artemis was standing a yard away, just outside the shelter of the narrow porch, the rain streaming down around her.

'Nicholas,' she said again. 'We must talk. Please. We have to talk.'

I peered towards the roadside beyond, just making out the shape of her Alpha-Romeo at the kerb. I hadn't seen it in my haste to get in out of the dark and the rain.

'Why?'

'Please don't start that. You know why.' She took a step towards me but I didn't respond. 'You've been avoiding me for so long. It can't go on, Nicholas, I . . .' She stopped talking. Was she shaking or simply shivering from the cold?

I shook my head. 'I made my feelings clear the last time we spoke. You know what I think.'

'I didn't deny anything. Did I? I didn't try to shift the blame. At least I was honest. Isn't that worth something?' Her voice was quiet. It shook slightly. 'Why don't you answer my calls? Why don't you return my messages?' Was she crying, or was it just the rain?

I wondered when she'd left the party. I'd caught only that one glimpse of her. 'How long have you been waiting here?'

She didn't seem to hear the question. She raised a hand towards me. 'Please, Nicholas, can't we go inside? Just to talk?' Her hair was wet, soaking wet, curling and glistening around her face pale in the darkness. Was she crying?

'No.' I slid my key into the lock. 'There's no point.'

I felt her hand on my arm as I opened the door. It was

dark inside – yet again the bulb in the entrance hall had blown or been nicked by the squatters on the first floor. 'Please, Nicholas. I know it can never be what it was, but surely it can't be just nothing?' Now I could see that she was crying. She wasn't trying to hide it. 'Surely there's something still there. Surely? Tell me there isn't and I'll go away.'

I shook myself free and stepped inside. Diana didn't try to follow me. I thought I heard her say something as the door closed between us. I turned and crossed the hall towards the stairs. It was dry in there. But it was still very dark. And very cold.

At the far end of every art gallery in Mayfair, as far as possible from the street entrance and the general public, is a lift door. The lift connects with the owner's office – the inner sanctum of the place – on the floor above. Only the most privileged of clients make it through that door; only the most honoured of collectors are met there by the owner who descends from above to usher them into the lift and up into the holy of holies.

The office is not like an office – it is as silent and spotless as a temple. The walls are white. The carpet is white. There are only two items of furniture – a black leather sofa and a grey smoked-glass coffee table on which stands a clear glass vase bursting with white tulips in full bloom. The client takes a seat, the owner explains in hushed tones what they are about to see. Then, as if by magic, a door slides open on one side of the room and two black-clad assistants enter, carrying between them the work which this client – alone among all the clients in the world – is being allowed to consider. They rest it against the blank wall facing the sofa and depart, silent and respectful.

The works displayed here are never seen in the gallery

below, where the general public can come and go. They are reserved for this private ritual, for the eyes of those select individuals deemed worthy enough to appreciate them. So awe-inspiring, so reverential, so flattering is such a ritual that I have known it to sell a canvas covered in nothing more than a coat of red paint, sell it for more than most human beings would earn in half a lifetime.

Acton did not show me up to his office when I called in at the gallery the next day. (I didn't mind. Indeed, I had strong reasons of my own for feeling very grateful that I didn't have to set foot inside that sleek minimalist shrine again.)

He didn't even come down to see me. The beautiful blonde receptionist simply put me through to his extension. I stood there at the desk just inside the street door and he dictated the directions to his place in Kent over the telephone.

Just as I was about to leave, the street door opened and two figures came in off the pavement. I saw them and froze. Then I backed away towards the rear of the gallery.

It wasn't the visitors themselves – it was what they brought in with them. A small white terrier, no bigger than a domestic cat.

I have a pathological fear of dogs. Big ones, small ones, fierce ones, soppy ones, it doesn't matter. I'm terrified of them all. They give me cold sweats, the shakes, an overwhelming impulse to run away screaming. It's pathetic, I know. But I can't help it. I was born that way.

The couple approached the receptionist. I tried to creep out behind them but that damned dog was in the way. He stood just inside the door, peering up at the canvases on the wall above him like a true critic. Then he turned his back on them and for one moment I thought he was going to cock his leg at the wall. A valid critical gesture. But Acton's cool and beautiful guardian fixed him with an icy glare and he relaxed, shook himself and grinned at her cheekily.

'Tony in?' The dog's owner was a young woman with very short hair dyed very red. She was wearing leather trousers and a leather jacket. A fellow artist. Six months ago Acton had talked her into donating a picture for a charity auction, one of his regular publicity stunts. Presumably on the understanding that he would consider representing her. He was still stringing her along, as far as I knew.

'I'm afraid not,' the receptionist lied coolly. 'We aren't expecting him until tomorrow.'

'Oh.' The girl looked disappointed. In spite of her aggressive appearance, she was a friendly and innocent human being who didn't belong in Acton's world. Her work consisted mostly of beautifully stylized paintings of farmyard animals. Very sweet but not at all Acton's cup of tea.

Then the dog saw me. He began to snarl.

'Stop that!' The girl gave the lead a sharp tug. He stopped. 'Nicholas Todd! I haven't seen you for ages! No one's seen you for ages! Where have you been? What have you been doing?'

'I haven't been anywhere,' I said, keeping my eye on the dog. 'And, sadly, I haven't been doing anything.'

'You've lost weight, Nick. Listen, are you all right? You look like you need a holiday or a good meal or something. You look dreadful.'

'Thanks.'

'I haven't seen any of your work since your Field Sport series. That was fantastic. No wonder it was such a success. So powerful, so honest. Fantastic work. I've missed everything since then, though. I don't know how, I've been looking out for it.'

'You haven't missed anything because there hasn't been anything.'

'But that was over a year ago . . .'

'Have you seen this?' Her boyfriend had wandered off to look at the big canvas which dominated one complete wall of the gallery. It was the recently discovered Wyndham Lewis masterpiece which Acton had just sold to a Japanese outfit for a record sum. The find, and the deal, of the decade. 'So this is what all the fuss is about. Can't see it, myself.'

I looked at it again. Probably for the last time, as it was being shipped off to Japan the next day. The boyfriend was wrong. It was a magnificent piece of work. But he was just being cool. He looked as if he was going to a funeral – black suit, white shirt, black tie. The uniform of those who refuse to be impressed by anything short of an Old Testament miracle.

'Tens of millions of quid, I heard.' He shook his head. 'Ridiculous. Those Japs, they don't know what to spend their yen on.'

'How old is it?' the girl asked. 'Eighty, ninety years? It looks it. Why spend all that money on an old dead artist? Why don't they spend it on living talent? On someone who can appreciate it? On someone who needs it? Like you and me, Nick. Well, me anyway. You don't need it these days, do you, Nick? You're doing pretty well as it is.'

Was I? She'd said it: 'But that was over a year ago . . .' And in a year's time – what would they be saying then? 'That Nicholas Todd, a great talent once upon a time, the world at his feet, but he just dried up. The talent died.'

The dog sat down and put his head back and howled, a long, loud note of impatience and boredom.

'I think your dog wants a tree,' the receptionist smirked.

They left, the dog bounding out ahead of them, choking himself as he took the lead to full stretch. I watched them go. I lurked in the gallery to give the dog enough time to put half a mile between us and then I too left. It started to rain the moment I set foot on the pavement.

Friday night – the night before I was due to drive down to Acton's place in Kent – and once again I was still awake at three o'clock in the morning. This time I didn't even try to do any work. I found that magazine with Acton's photo on the front cover and sat down in the cold half-darkness of the studio to read Stanley's article for the five hundredth time. There was nothing else to do. I was just waiting now.

'Last month, a recently discovered painting by Wyndham Lewis was sold by the Acton Gallery of Cork Street, London, to Mr Yukio Haramaka of the Buruki Institute, Tokyo, for a sum known to be a record for twentieth-century British art and rumoured to be in excess of one million pounds. News of this painting and its sale has burst through the academic world of art history and the commercial world of the art market with an explosive devastation which Percy Wyndham Lewis, the self-styled Enemy, the editor of Blast, the founder of the Rebel Art Centre, the father of Vorticism, the one and only modern British painter of genius, would have deeply relished.

'Attempts to assess the fall-out are still being made by bearded brains in the book-lined studies of Bloomsbury and by Italian-suited calculators in the white galleries of Mayfair. The chatter will continue to animate seminars and private viewings for some time to come. But an overview of its significance is possible: there are, I think, three areas in which the event – the discovery and sale of this picture – is supremely important.

'First, Wyndham Lewis and his place in art history.

There has always been a case for Wyndham Lewis as the greatest British artist of the century; a case, however, which has never been generally accepted. Most reference books merely acknowledge him as the man who tried to introduce modernism to Britain, a few as the finest draughtsman of his generation. He has never been a household name. There are many reasons for this serious under-estimation. His works are disturbing. The man himself had a deeply disagreeable personality; abrasive, aggressive, antagonistic, proud of his self-created role of outsider, he ended his life half crazy and half blind. Such is the stuff of genius, but it did not endear him to the market makers or opinion formers of his time. Very few of his canvases from the 1920s have survived, and scarcely any pre-1914. In his later years he turned most of his energies to writing, and a painter who writes or a writer who paints never attracts the critic's undivided attention. These very factors add up to the indifference which has rendered this recently discovered canvas as good as invisible for over half a century.

'Be that as it may, this magnificent oil will change everything. It will re-write not simply the history of modern British art, but the history of the whole of Western art this century. It is a superb picture. Six feet by five feet, it is an almost abstract representation of what could be either a reclining human figure – tense and distorted – or an aeroplane in flight. Perhaps it is both. It is the finest known example of Lewis's character-istic "energetic angularity". It is a masterpiece of mod-ernism and its "machine aesthetic". In itself it is enough to confirm once and for all his pre-eminence in this country, but its date reveals him as a figure of towering international stature.

'It was painted in 1909, the date he returned from his seven years abroad which followed his graduation from the Slade. Now, it is generally assumed that modernism arrived late in this country, imported at second hand from the continent, with the founding of the Vorticist group by Lewis in 1914 as a pale imitation of Italian Futurism. But the staggering fact is that this painting predates Italian Futurism – Marinetti didn't write their manifesto until 1910. This painting has so many elements of Futurism at its purest and most mature – man as machine, the simultaneity of movement, the drama of flight, the destructive charisma of mechanical energy – that one has to conclude that, far from Wyndham Lewis imitating the Italian Futurists, the Italian Futurists were in fact imitating Wyndham Lewis. He must now be seen as a creator of modernism, a household name to stand with that of Picasso (Les Demoiselles D'Avignon, at 1907, predates this picture by only two years). The price it has commanded simply confirms this . . .'

I stood up and went into the kitchen and made some coffee. I walked around the studio, mug in hand, trying to keep warm. I stared up through the glass ceiling and out into the darkness of the night sky beyond. There were no stars, but the lights of a distant aeroplane were passing slowly overhead. Towards the east. Where was it flying to? Japan? I thought about the painting and its journey to Tokyo. Had it already arrived? Was it still on the way? Was it in the very aircraft I could see now? I watched until its lights disappeared beyond the rooftops and then I returned to the article.

'. . . The second significant element in this affair is that the picture was bought by a Japanese. Until recently, the Japanese were content to pay exorbitant sums indiscriminately for impressionists, post-impressionists and second-rate nineteenth-century views of country lanes. They were hardly trend-setters; their importance went no further than their cheque-books. Now, however, there is a growing sophistication, a developing taste, which will soon give them the authority to influence, if not dictate, market fashions and, ultimately, critical opinions.

'Which of course is exactly what has happened in this case. A large portion of Wyndham Lewis's critical restoration will be credited to the discriminating eye and cheque-book of Mr Yukio Haramaka, the director of the Buruki Institute, the fine arts collection of the all-powerful Buruki Corporation. Mr Haramaka graduated in History of Art from the University of Tokyo, studied in New York and has a doctorate from the Sorbonne. He deserves the rediscovered Wyndham Lewis. There are those who argue that it should remain in England, but its purchase is proof that the avant-garde is not foreign to the Oriental mind (if that was ever anything more than a fantasy of the Western mind), that the Japanese are as capable of "understanding" Western art as anyone else. It is a triumph for those who believe in the universality of art and in the superficiality of racial distinctions.

'The third significant point is that the deal marks the arrival of the Acton Gallery as a major player in the international art market. Anthony Acton, its founder and owner, was known as London's most exciting and successful young art dealer even before he moved his business to Cork Street from the Portobello Road three years ago. Since those Notting Hill days he has more than fulfilled his early promise, and it is no longer necessary to qualify such praise with the words "London" or "young" (though he is, of course, still in his thirties). He is an intriguing character around whom colourful stories are quick to flourish. Already it is difficult to distinguish between fact and legend.

'In appearance he is slight but fit looking, with short dark hair and pale skin. He has the smooth good looks and ready grin of a cheeky schoolboy. He favours elegantly baggy woollen suits designed by Italians whose names are more familiar to the modern world than those of any Renaissance giant. In speech and movement he is quick, restless, hyperactive. He attracts admiration and dismay in equal measure. "Of course, he's extraordinarily charming most of the time", said a former Portobello Road associate who didn't wish to be identified. "Extrovert, debonair. But you mustn't forget that he is utterly ruthless."

' "You have to admire his energy, enterprise and intelligence" said another, anonymous acquaintance. "But he's really just a spoilt child. When he can't get his own way he sulks for days or throws the kind of tantrum you wouldn't expect to see outside a kindergarten."

' "Tony Acton looks and lives like a young Roman emperor", said Nicholas Todd, an up-and-coming young painter from Acton's increasingly impressive stable. "Complete with fawning court and an absolute power he's only too willing to abuse."

'I have known Tony Acton for at least five years, and I must say that I have always found him . . .'

That was enough of that. I dropped the magazine back onto the floor. I didn't know whether Stanley's combination of insincerity and flattery made me want to laugh or throw up. What had he said on another occasion? –

'That Wyndham Lewis. How the Japs got an export licence I don't know. It's a bloody tragedy, a scandal, a British masterpiece like that ending up in Tokyo or Kyoto or wherever they've got it stashed away. None of those wimps in Whitehall would dare risk a trade embargo by denying an export licence. Bloody typical.'

Poor Stanley. Well, you'll enjoy writing Acton's obituary – no need to creep and crawl then. And I'll enjoy reading it.

CHAPTER TWO

It was still raining on Saturday morning when I drove out of London. The wet greys of the city gave way to the wet greens and browns of the fields and woods of Kent, but I was too preoccupied to notice the change.

Why me? Why ask me, of all people, to house-sit for him? He has good reason to be more than wary of me. He knows I have every reason to hate him. So what's going on? What is he planning?

Perhaps nothing. Perhaps a house-sitter is all he wants. Perhaps no one else was free and I really was the desperate, last-minute choice. Perhaps, with his egomaniac's complacency, he isn't in the least bit wary of me at all.

Perhaps, perhaps. The words thrashed to and fro like the windscreen wipers in the rain, clearing nothing.

Following Acton's directions, I turned into a half-hidden gateway off a narrow lane running down a wooded hillside. Sheep grazed in a gently sloping field on one side of a long curving track, a beech wood rustled dry leaves on the other. The track straightened as it descended and suddenly the house appeared from behind the wood.

I stopped the car and gazed down at it. I'd been to Acton's apartment in Holland Park many times but I'd never seen this house before. There it was, nestling in a fold of the hill's south-facing slopes. It looked very old. Stone-built, L-shaped, many-gabled. A walled garden and a stable block. Smoke slowly rising from tall chimneys.

Acton, I thought, you're in there somewhere. And

something in the way you live here makes you vulnerable. Some little detail in your day-to-day existence. I don't know what it is but I'm going to find it and use it to destroy you.

As I watched, a distant barking of dogs reached me on the breeze and the sound, sinister though faint, somehow eclipsed the beauty of the scene. I drove forwards again, slowly. Above the sound of the motor and the crunching gravel the noise of barking dogs grew louder.

And then a huge canine shape came hurtling around a corner of the building. My hands tightened on the wheel. Two more appeared in its wake, all three gathering speed as they tore towards me. They barked as they ran – tongues lolling, eyes narrowed – and then they were on the car. They didn't stop but threw themselves at me as though there wasn't a ton of metal and glass between us. I slammed on the brakes and got the window up just in time.

The world disappeared into a cramped panorama of frenzied animals. A nightmare of canine fury broke across the windscreen. Gaping jaws, snarling teeth. Bloodshot eyes rolling with mad vacancy or narrowed with violent anger. Nothing else was visible. The car rocked under the assault. The noise – barking, snarling, growling – burst through it like an explosion. Tongues and teeth smeared froth across the windows, paws scrabbled and thumped at the glass.

And then it stopped. Suddenly they were gone. Only one lingered, determined to have the last snarl. He rolled the whites of his crazed eyes at me and wiped his snout on the wing-mirror. I heard whistling and a shout – Acton's voice – and the monster sloped off.

I was shaking uncontrollably. My shirt was soaking and the steering wheel was slippery with sweat. I had been within a nerve's breadth of sheer panic.

There was a tap on the window. I looked up. Through the sheen of slobber and mud on the glass I could just see Tony Acton. I wound the window down.

'All right, Nick?' He held two dog leads, taut and twisting, in each hand. I could hear the animals panting and snuffling around at his feet. 'A bit of exercise. They need it, don't they?' Two of the unseen beasts began to snarl and snap at each other. He swore and tugged at their leads and the noise stopped. 'Follow the drive to the far side of the house, you'll see the garage. I'll be round the back, sorting the boys out. All right?'

I nodded. My mouth was too dry to speak. I drove on, past the front of the house, and found the adjoining stable block which had been converted into a garage. I parked between Acton's Jaguar and his wife's Porsche. Then I sat there and waited for my hands to stop shaking.

I was virtually hallucinating with terror. As I sat there I had a weird vision of myself as a fisherman who sets out, full of confidence, to hunt the great white shark, and miles out to sea looks down into the cold water and sees the huge and sinister shape of his enemy slide slowly by beneath his boat – a terrifying shadow, huge and as white as a corpse, sliding through the dark water under the tiny boat – and suddenly realizes that he is completely alone, in the middle of the vast ocean, miles and miles away from the safety of dry land.

Behind the house, on the other side of a vast lawn, the dogs' kennels and a big exercise area had been fenced off against a high boundary wall. Acton was in there playing with them. They were gambolling around like puppies now but their size and their build and the exhibition I had just witnessed showed they were killers.

They were big, muscular animals – solid bodies, thick necks, heavy heads, flattened faces. Grey and black fur,

28

brown around the eyes and muzzle. They looked like wolves on anabolic steroids.

'All right, then?' Acton grinned. He was wearing jeans and green wellingtons and a short coat of the very smartest, smoothest brown leather. 'I don't usually let them run around like that unless I'm on my own.' Was that supposed to be some kind of apology? He called to one of them and it stood up on its hind legs against him, its front paws on his shoulders, tail wagging. He staggered a bit under the weight while the dog slobbered all over his face. 'Aren't they great? I love them all. My boys. Love them. Beautiful, aren't they?'

I swallowed. 'What are they? What breed?'

'Himalayan mastiffs. All from the same litter.' He stepped away from the dog and it fell back on to all fours. He threw a ball and it went chasing off to the other end of the enclosure. 'Come on in and say hello. It's OK. They'll be fine once they get to know you.'

One of them spotted me and approached the wiremesh, stiff-legged and growling.

'I think I'll stay this side of the fence, thanks.'

'That's no good. You've got to win their trust.' The dog began to bark. Acton swore at it and the noise stopped. 'He thinks you don't like him.'

'I don't. And he doesn't like me.'

'You don't like dogs?' He sounded amazed. 'Why not?'

'One moment they're licking your hand, the next they're tearing your arm off. They shit on the pavement. They bark all night. They screw each other in public. They sniff each other's arses . . .'

Acton shook his head. 'You don't like dogs,' he repeated. 'I feel sorry for you.' He opened the high gate in the wire and stepped out of the enclosure, padlocking it behind him. He stood there, nodding lugubriously and watching the dogs chasing each other in circles and barking with simple-minded delight. Then he smiled. It seemed to me to be the smile of a man who was pleased with himself. Pleased because everything, so far, had gone to plan. It was a smile which told me he had planned my reception exactly as it had happened and was more than satisfied by my reaction to it.

On the other hand, I reminded myself, it could simply be the smile of a man who was lucky enough to appreciate and be appreciated by man's best friend.

Tony Acton, London's most exciting and successful young art dealer. Our paths had first crossed four years ago. Only four years? It felt like a whole geological age or more.

At that time he was operating from the Portobello Road. It was just before his move to Cork Street but he was already a well-known figure, a character around whom notorious myths and legends were beginning to gather. The known facts were that he had been born and brought up in London, had studied at art school in Paris and worked as something in the art world in Rome; he had returned to London on the deaths of his wealthy parents and had worked for some months at one of the more famous auction houses before setting up on his own in Notting Hill.

As for the legends, there was one typical story about his time at the auction house. Apparently, someone had come in one day with a dusty old leather-bound volume, to ask about its value and how to sell it. Acton took one look at it and told him it might fetch up to two hundred pounds in their next sale of second-hand books. Which is exactly what happened. But the volume was in fact an album of engravings by Joshua Reynolds, very valuable – in a sale of prints and drawings, they would have sold for between fifteen and twenty thousand pounds. Acton had realized this straight away. At the book sale, of course, the engravings went unrecognized, and he bought them himself for exactly two hundred pounds. When he sold them a year later he made more than seventeen thousand pounds on the deal.

Mind you, I've heard the same story (or variations on it) about other dealers, before and since. So perhaps it's only an example of Tony's myth-gathering charisma (or perhaps such practices are more common than we think). And to be fair, I'd never heard Tony boasting about the episode, which he certainly would have done if it really happened.

There was no doubt, however, about the equally scandalous way he operated in the Portobello Road. This was indeed something I heard him boast about on more than one occasion once he'd moved to Cork Street. His own words:

'I wasn't representing artists in those days, of course, just renting out gallery space at sixty per cent of all sales made. Artists were queuing up to rent space. You gave them an agreement to sign – a licence to screw them into the ground – and they gave you a huge deposit against expenses. Four out of every five artists were crap, you knew they were never going to sell enough to make the show worthwhile, so you simply cancelled it without warning and without reason. No one got their deposit back. You could tell them it barely covered the expenses you'd already incurred in preparing for the exhibition. Of course, there were no expenses. The money that came in, you wouldn't believe it, it was so easy . . .'

You'll understand that for the artist it was all a terrible gamble. A gamble I was prepared to take at that time, because I was broke and desperate. I was working hard but I wasn't getting any exposure, I wasn't making any sales. I was running out of time, money and hope. In many ways it was my last chance. I'd given myself three years to make something of myself as an artist, and only six months were left. I clubbed together with two equally desperate art school graduates and we approached Acton with the deposit we'd somehow scraped up between us.

Acton insisted that we each brought in a representative piece of work when we all came to the gallery to sign the agreement. Once an assistant had collected the deposit and the signed agreement, Acton appeared and looked long and hard at each work in turn. It was obviously a little ceremony of his. We knew that he was appraising the work to decide whether a show would be worthwhile, and he knew that we knew. It was a pure ritual of power, and I could tell that he was enjoying himself.

He stopped in front of the first piece of work. 'Interesting', he said at length before moving on to the second. 'Very interesting' was the verdict there. Then he came to my piece, and he barely glanced at it. He didn't bother to comment, but flicked the most expressionless of glances at me as he left to go back to whatever he had been working on before our arrival.

Afterwards, I could tell by the way my partners looked at me and spoke to me that they thought I'd screwed up the whole deal for them. They were keen to launch a whole charm offensive against Acton to keep him sweet, but I managed to talk them out of it. I guessed, rightly, that it could only be counter-productive; the more people suck up to someone like Acton, the more pleasure he takes in kicking them in the teeth. I was getting the measure of him early, just as he was getting the measure of me.

The show went ahead. Right up to the last minute we didn't know whether it would, of course, but that was how it worked. It was nerve-racking, to say the least. It wasn't until we were pouring wine for our guests at the opening party that we knew Acton wasn't going to cancel. The relief was enough to make us feel we'd won the lottery, even before we'd sold a single picture.

It was a good show. One of my partners sold almost half of her work, the other just over half. I sold all my pieces. The lot. I couldn't believe my luck. It was my first experience of the Acton touch, I suppose. I didn't make much money – after Acton took his cut, there was enough left to repay what I'd borrowed for the deposit and a number of other debts – but it was enough to justify the last three years and to encourage me to carry on.

It was one of Acton's last Portobello Road shows. Soon after that he moved to Cork Street and became a dealer proper. On the face of it, a dealer simply represents the artist in the market-place. He exhibits the artist's work and finds collectors to buy it. He doesn't buy the pictures himself, he just takes a commission on the ones he sells. He does buy pictures sometimes, of course – from an owner or another dealer, if there's someone else he can sell it on to. But only if the mark-up he makes on it is bigger than the commission he'd otherwise get. And the usual rate is fifty per cent.

Most people are amazed to learn that for every picture sold, the artist gets only half of what's paid for it. But most people don't appreciate just how powerful a dealer can be. How he can make an artist's career, make him wealthy and successful beyond the dreams of merchant bankers. How the best ones have a back door into the big institutions which invest in art as they invest in stocks and shares. How they control the tastes and chequebooks of the immensely wealthy individuals who collect art as the ultimate hobby. How the private collector sees the dealer helping him to build and maintain a collection as both priest and psychoanalyst, as someone to be trusted with his innermost hopes and fears let alone with every last penny of his fortune.

And right from the start it was clear to everyone in the business that Acton was destined to be one of the best.

I wrote to him soon after the move, reminding him of the show and inviting him to see more of my work with a view to representing me. It was almost a year before I heard anything; a secretary phoned to say that he would indeed like to see my work in progress – when would be convenient? I wasn't surprised at the delay – I was surprised there was any response at all. By that time artists were fighting each other to get into his gallery. The queue would have stretched from Cornwall to Cork Street and back again. He could take his pick.

When he turned up at the studio a few days later, he gave the work on display only the most cursory attention. I could tell straight away that it was the artist, not the art, who was under scrutiny. It was as if he had already reached a verdict about my ability as a painter, and was searching for something else within me. For what, exactly? Even then, I had the uncomfortable, half-conscious feeling that he was looking for the appropriate weakness, for a potential for corruption. Or perhaps something which would merit his efforts to corrupt?

'What did you do before . . . all this?' he asked, indicating the creative squalor around us. In those days the studio was truly squalid. It stank of poverty and despair. It was strange to see this immensely elegant and sophisticated figure in the midst of it all. That day Acton looked to me like an alien from an advanced civilization who had crash-landed on a primitive planet.

'I studied. The law.'

'Really?' He laughed, incredulous. 'So you're a lawyer?'

'Not exactly. I have a degree in law, but I was never a lawyer.' I suddenly felt strangely ashamed, telling all this to the cool, immaculately dressed, well-groomed near-stranger standing there like an exotic tropical creature amidst the gloomy mess of my studio. As if it was some sort of dirty confession, as if my choice all those years ago had let the side down, his side, the side that represented professional success, wealth, status and all the other trappings of apparent respectability. I could have had it too, but I'd let them down, and now here I was with nothing. 'I didn't finish my articles. I barely started them.'

'But you turned your back on the law. You walked away from it because you wanted to paint.'

I shrugged. 'And because I would have made a terrible lawyer. It wasn't much of a dilemma.'

'But this is excellent. Excellent.' He laughed again. At the time I thought it was the Gauguin-like stereotype which he found amusing, but perhaps it was the suggestion that my decision had indicated a potential for transgression, an ability to ignore or go beyond laws or rules of any kind. Or perhaps a lawyer was an irresistibly perverse target for him, in the way that the devil is attracted to the purest souls. 'A lawyer. Excellent!'

Suddenly he was no longer the cold, serious, untouchable super-dealer. He was all charm, that now-familiar blend of confidence and enthusiasm. He put an arm round my shoulders, a curiously intimate gesture which he somehow managed to pull off.

'Listen,' he said. 'I might as well tell you. I think your work is fantastic. You can tell at a glance. I saw it as soon as you showed me that piece a year ago, you know, before the show. The other two pieces, well, to be honest there wouldn't have been a show if your two partners hadn't had you to carry them. But that piece of yours

. . . I bought it myself, did you know that? Yes. I got that one. I wasn't at all surprised the show went so well for you. And you're just a beginner, really, I can see that. What you might be capable of doing, in a year or two's time . . . Well . . .' He laughed again. 'I think we should make that journey together, Nick. Don't you?'

I didn't know whether to believe him. I still like to think that he was telling the truth, rather than just softening me up as he must have softened up everyone he enticed into his court, to attend his royal presence.

'Your work is great, Nick, and you . . . well, you look like a decent, well-behaved young man, but I'm sure you have great potential as well.' Those were his parting words that day.

So he took me on, and my star rose with his. It was incredible. For five years I'd been living in poverty – real poverty – and then, all of a sudden, I had paintings selling for four (and even five) figure sums apiece. A break like that can really warp you. It's difficult not to crack on that kind of turn-around.

There's nothing noble about poverty. It is not good for the soul. It backs you into a corner and makes you fight dirty. It scares you, and leaves you scared for the rest of your life. Sudden success isn't good for the soul, either, especially if someone like Tony Acton is behind it. To come out of that corner like a rocket, with suddenly all the money and recognition you ever hoped for, it's difficult to remember who you are and what you ever believed in.

I followed Acton round to the front of the house, up the steps and in through the wide front door.

'How old is this place?'

'Seventeenth century. Built for an ironmaster from

the Weald, after he'd made a fortune casting cannon for Dutch and English privateers.'

The entrance hall was almost as big as the garage, with a double staircase going up to a gallery. A vast Bokhara rug had been rolled back from the ancient flagstones, and five open crates – the type used to transport paintings – stood in the middle of the floor. Pictures were stacked three or four deep against the walls. The walls themselves were bare except for dozens of square and rectangular patches where the pictures had been hanging.

Acton waved at them as we passed. 'They're off to a bank vault in London for the next eighteen months. I can't leave them hanging around in an empty house while I'm sorting the Yanks out, can I? An empty house in the middle of nowhere.' His voice echoed around the stripped hallway. 'One or two of yours here somewhere.'

I followed him along a corridor, catching glimpses of dust-sheeted furniture, rolled carpets, shuttered windows and emptied shelves through every open door we passed.

Eventually we came to a room which was still being lived in. A comfortable room – low ceiling, oak beams, leather furniture, logs burning in an open fire, big French windows looking out across the lawn to an ancient wall overgrown with moss and wisteria, the wooded hillside beyond.

Greta Acton and Andrea Alvarez (what was she doing here?) sat in front of a television blaring with some Saturday lunchtime dross which neither of them was really watching.

'More repeats,' Andrea sneered at the opening credits of some high-action drama. 'This cop show was running in the States twenty years ago.'

Greta looked half asleep. Rousing herself, she peered at the screen. She was short-sighted but for some reason she never wore glasses. 'Daytime television is simply the media's subconscious attempt to deconstruct itself.' That slow, heavy, Slavic voice. 'Via the analytic syntax of perpetual repeats. Would you agree?'

'Don't know, honey.' Andrea was smiling now the show's macho star had appeared on the scene of the crime. 'But that guy is the only stud in Hollywood who can look cool in a perm twenty years on.'

Acton dropped his coat over the back of a chair. He crossed the room without saying a word and turned off the television.

'We were watching that.'

'No you weren't.' He went and stood by the big window, looking out over the wet lawn and the wintry trees, his back to everyone in the room.

Greta scowled short-sightedly at him. Andrea gave her a comic grimace. 'Never mind.' She laughed softly, waving a bottle of wine they were sharing. 'At least there's plenty of booze left.'

It was very hot inside the house. The central heating was full on, the air quivered over the radiators. Andrea was wearing jeans and a yellow t-shirt. She was sitting back on a sofa. She had taken off her shoes and tucked her legs up beneath her; one hand stroked her bare feet with a lazy, self-conscious sensuality. Painted fingernails, painted toenails, gold bangles on a tanned and bony wrist. Greta was also barefooted. She was wearing some sort of leather mini-skirt. She sat down beside her American friend, still scowling, crossed her bare legs and tugged at her leather hem.

'He has been showing you his babies?' she asked.

'Of course,' Acton answered for me. He turned away from the window. His expression was surly and withdrawn. Taking the bottle from Andrea, he filled two glasses which appeared from nowhere as if in a conjuring trick. He gave one to me. The bottle was empty. It occurred to me he didn't want the wine particularly, nor was he being a considerate host in giving me some – he simply wanted to take the wine away from the women as he'd taken the television away.

'And you still have both hands left, Nicky? I cannot stand them. Great ugly, vicious monsters. Ugh.' Greta shivered. 'I will not go anywhere near them. And neither will the Kennedys. Mrs Kennedy is terrified of them. And with reason, I say. They won't let anyone near them but Anthony. Anthony is the only one they trust.'

They trust Anthony Acton? Proof that dogs are the most stupid creatures on earth. Trust him? I surprised myself by almost feeling sorry for them.

'Nick isn't scared of them. Are you, Nick? No. They'll be in good hands next week. Nick'll soon make friends with them.'

My heart lurched. So I'm dog-sitting as well as house-sitting? This is news. Bad news. Nightmare. I took a good swig of the wine and sat down.

Andrea smiled at me. 'Where did you get to on Wednesday night?'

'I had to leave. My car turns into a pumpkin at midnight.'

She laughed, one hand now in the pile of thick red hair pinned up on top of her head, raising her chin to show off her bare throat and slender neck. 'That's no way to meet Prince Charming.'

'Why, did you meet him?'

'I'm still looking, Nicky. I'm still looking.'

'What's for lunch?' Acton demanded. 'I'm starving.'

Greta looked away. 'Why ask me?'

'It's gone one o'clock! Where's lunch?'

'In the deep freeze, of course, with all the other food Kennedy left for us. If you want to eat, you go and get it. If you take it out now, it might just be thawed by the time we have to catch that plane tomorrow.'

Acton swore. 'What about that quiche? Didn't she make a bacon pie or something just before they went away?'

'We finished it last night. Remember?'

Acton glared at his wife. I could see him wondering whether to stir this all up into a full-scale row. Andrea caught my eye and grimaced, raising her eyebrows in comic apprehension.

He strode across the room and snatched his coat from the back of the chair. 'Come on, Nick.'

Greta turned the television back on as we left the room. Its volume shot up and crazy studio laughter chased after us along the corridor.

In the kitchen Acton hunted out half a loaf of bread, some cheese, margarine and cold ham, sullenly and silently. He began to hack the loaf with such savage clumsiness that I took the knife from him and sliced the bread myself. He took a couple of cans from the fridge and we sat munching sandwiches and drinking beer for some moments before he spoke.

'Don't worry about the dogs, Nick. They're as harmless as kittens.' He laughed but it was still a sullen laugh. 'As long as you keep them well-fed and happy.'

'And if I don't?'

'Well.' He laughed again. At last he was beginning to unwind. 'In the Middle Ages the Mongol Khans used to keep a pack of Himalayan mastiffs. They were the Khans' favourite method of execution. If they got hold of someone they particularly disliked, a defiant Chinese king for instance, they'd strip the clothes off him and thrash the dogs to a fury with them. Then they'd set the dogs on him. The scent, you see. Dogs would tear him apart. And they'd half-starve the dogs for a day or two beforehand, of course, just to give their killer instinct that lethal edge . . .'

He was trying to frighten me. I tried hard not to let him know he'd succeeded.

'Are there any Chinese kings you want to kill, Nick?' Still laughing, he looked me straight in the eye. 'Well, now you know what to do if there are.'

I returned his gaze, saying nothing.

'I saw Henry Booth last week,' he said, changing the subject. 'He's still very keen to get you hanging on Norris Harding's wall. Don't keep him waiting too long, will you? He's beginning to sound a little bit impatient.'

Henry Booth was a director of Norris Harding, the merchant bank. He was building up a corporate collection of modern British art for them, with Acton's help. I'd seen their City premises and it was most impressive already – a Bacon in the boardroom, a Freud in reception.

Then he gave me a different look, and I knew he was going to ask a favour. 'Listen, Nick, that auction I did for that animal rights charity last year. It was such a success, we're thinking of doing another one. But I can't ask Eileen to do another canvas for us. Not that she needed much persuasion in the first place. And that donation didn't do her any harm, far from it. Her work's really taken off since it had all that coverage. But you know how it is. It simply wouldn't be fair on her, and besides, we need something fresh.'

He kept his eyes on me as he spoke and smiled his most charming smile. 'So, how about it, Nick? It is all in a good cause. And the stuff you were doing last year could have been commissioned for it. I'd have asked you the first time but, well, you know how things were then. And Eileen, she does do such a, shall we say, "sweet" picture, doesn't she? The punters need kicking off with a bit of sweetness but now I think they're ready for the real thing, don't you? Truth, suffering. That's what charities are all about. That's what gets everyone digging deep in their pockets, isn't it? I know what your pictures say, Nick, and this is a great chance to get the public to listen. To listen and, more important, to respond in the most practical way. It's a great opportunity for you, Nick.'

'I don't know,' I said. 'I don't know if I can do it.'

'What do you mean?'

'The last few months, I can't . . . I just haven't been able to work. I've tried, but it comes out wrong. It doesn't come out at all.'

He shrugged. 'You'll be all right. You'll come out of it. I'm not asking for a definite decision. Just think about it. All right?'

He hadn't listened. Perhaps I should have said, No, you don't understand. Whatever I might have had, talent, ability, whatever, I can't find it anymore. It's gone. But I didn't. I didn't expect him to listen, even though he should have done. It was his job, after all. His business. I wouldn't have said anything if there hadn't been a professional obligation to do so. I wasn't after sympathy or advice.

So I said, 'OK. I'll think about it.'

'Please do. That's all I can ask at the moment.' He drained his last can. 'Thanks, mate.'

He gave me another look but this time it was one I couldn't read. 'You know, Nick, I'm glad we can talk like this. I'm glad we're here, you and me like this, being sensible, still friends. I know it might have been a bit rough but no damage done, and we've both made a lot of money, eh? No hard feelings, then?'

I looked at him, amazed. Did he really mean it? I couldn't speak but I held his eye and raised my glass and drank as if what he had said was a toast. I was drinking a toast, but my own silent toast, and it wasn't to his health.

'A man's got to be practical at the end of the day,' he said. 'All the rest of it, it doesn't really matter, does it? I knew you'd see that. After all, we're two of a kind. We've always seen eye to eye.'

Was he trying to provoke me? Was that what he wanted? I looked at him – Anthony Acton, relaxed, at home, cheerful – and would have sworn that it wasn't. But the very suspicion was enough to enforce an icy self-control.

'Come on.' He stood up, glancing down at the remains of lunch spread on the table. 'Someone else can tidy up this crap. I want to show you something.'

CHAPTER THREE

I followed him along yet another corridor and up a short flight of steps which ended in a door which was closed and locked. He took his keys from his coat pocket and opened it and I followed him inside. It was a long, narrow room with a sloping ceiling and I could tell from the view out of the windows that we were directly above the garage, on the upper floor of the converted stable block.

'My gun room.' The walls were lined with glass cases which were crowded with racks and racks of rifles and shotguns. Acton unlocked one of the cases and took out a pair of shotguns. He passed one to me. 'Twelve bore. Ever used one?'

'No.' I took it. The feel of polished walnut and tooled metal surprised me. There was something reassuring and attractive about its weight and balance.

'Don't worry. It's easy.' He opened a drawer and took out a cardboard box which rattled as he transferred it to a pocket in his leather coat. He took another box from the drawer and tossed it to me. I caught it. 'Cartridges.' He pulled a big green canvas bag from a hook on the door at the far end of the room and slung it from his shoulder. 'Come on,' he said, unlocking the door. 'Let's go and shoot the ass off some rabbits.'

We went down a steep and narrow flight of concrete steps which opened into the garage. The air was suddenly very cold after the tropical heat indoors.

'Sod it!' Acton stared out of the open garage door. 'It's raining again.'

I paused by my car, stood the shotgun up against a

ladder running along the wall and opened the boot. Acton saw that my bag was still in there. 'Leave your keys in the lock, Nick. Greta will take your stuff inside while we're out.'

I unzipped my jacket and threw it in the boot. I found the coat I used to wear hiking in the hills many years ago and put it on. Then I took my shoes off and pulled on a pair of wellingtons.

'This way.' We passed through a walled garden and out of a wooden gateway which opened on to a track along the side of a ploughed field. We walked in silence towards a bare, dark wood on the crest of the hill. The rain had settled into a steady drizzle but I didn't mind. The fresh air and the silence were marvellous.

'Bloody weather,' Acton said. 'Shit! Look at that. I can hardly move.' The mud was sticking to our boots in great clumps as we trudged uphill along the side of the field. He stopped to scrape the soles of his boots on the bottom strand of the barbed wire fence.

It was a strange sight: Acton in the country. He was still the same urban, urbane character I knew, looking for all the world like a spoilt star ballet dancer with his slim and energetic figure, his fine and delicate features. But there he was in the middle of a wet field with mud on his boots and a gun in the crook of his arm. Bizarre.

We began walking again. A lapwing flew up from the field, so close I could see the crest on the back of its head. Acton's right arm jerked but it was gone before he could even raise the barrel.

'I thought we were going after rabbits?'

'Please yourself. I'm going after anything that moves.' We trudged on. The dark wood was a few hundred yards ahead of us. 'You know,' he said, 'you're a lucky man, not being married. Believe me, marriage is hell. Stay well away from it. I quite liked Greta when we first got

45

married. Now she just irritates me. It gets worse every day; she nags a bit more, picks on me a bit more. And every day she looks more and more like a tart. I mean, you see what she wears, what she looks like. It's that bloody Yank friend of hers, bloody Andrea. She's a bad influence. My wife never went around flashing her tits and thighs like that before she met Andrea. Makes me sick. The pair of them.'

He shook his head and when we came to the edge of the wood he paused for a rest. He seemed impervious to the fresh air, to the sweep of the countryside, to the sound of the wind in the trees, sighing and tapping through the bare branches. I wandered on along an over-grown track between the grey trunks.

A few seconds later I heard his steps cracking bracken and squelching mud behind me. The branches closed in overhead, the brambles reached out across the path and the world was suddenly enclosed, private and dark. The sound of Acton's footsteps stopped and I turned to see what was holding him up.

He stood facing me five yards away, his shotgun at chest height, both barrels aiming straight at me. 'I know what you're up to, Todd,' he said. 'I can see right through you.' He licked his lips and swallowed. 'Your game's up.' He raised his weapon to his shoulder and aimed along the barrels with his right eye. We were close enough. He wasn't going to miss even if he fired from the hip.

My own gun wasn't loaded. Even if it was, he could have let fly with both barrels before my finger found the trigger. There was no point in rushing him. The brambles were too thick to dodge to either side of the path. I was caught like a rat in a drainpipe.

So that was that. At least it was very clear in my mind. All those questions had their answers. I looked up through the dead and dripping branches towards the sky. A wind was rising. The higher branches were dancing with it, the grey cloud scudded by in an unbroken mass. Big black birds flew high above the trees, flapping and wheeling, wings outstretched. 'The last red leaf is whirled away, the rooks are blown about the skies': where did that line come from, I wondered with a strange abstraction. I closed my eyes.

Acton started to laugh. I opened my eyes. He was still standing there but the gun was lowered and pointing away into the undergrowth. He was leaning forwards, laughing, incredulity all over his face.

'Bugger me!' he choked. 'You really thought I was going to do it. Didn't you? You really thought I was going to do it!'

I felt a burst of fury and renewed hatred explode through me. 'You stupid bastard! Even I know you should never – never! – point a gun at someone!'

'Only a joke, mate.' He broke open the weapon, so I could see that the barrels were empty. 'You can take a joke, Nick. I know you can. That's why I did it.'

'Not even if the gun isn't loaded!'

He was still laughing. 'Your game's up!' he repeated, delighted with himself. 'You should have seen your face! I bet you were saying your prayers, when your eyes were closed. Weren't you? You were saying your prayers!'

I shook my head, my fury ebbing with the relief. 'You bastard.'

'All right, mate,' he said. 'All right.' He came forwards and took my arm. 'I won't do it again.'

The sweat which had poured off me in the last few minutes was turning cold in the chill air. 'OK.' I wiped the rain from my face with a trembling hand. 'Forget it.'

The trees soon began to thin out. We could see the far side of the wood ahead of us, a green field showing through between the dark trunks. Acton stopped, his shotgun still broken over the crook of his arm, and took two cartridges from his pocket.

'Load up,' he whispered. 'This is where the fun starts. That field through there is swarming with rabbits.' He slid the cartridges into the barrel and snapped the piece shut. I copied him. We moved off again, Acton taking the lead, his weapon ready in both hands now. We came to the edge of the woods and peered out at a wide green field. The wood bordered it on two sides, a thick hedgerow on the other two. The grass was long and thick, and gleamed bright and heavy with the rain. Acton crept forwards. 'Keep your eyes skinned,' he whispered.

A slight ditch separated the wood from the field. Acton lurched across it and immediately I saw a pointed brown shape jerk up from the long grass twenty yards ahead of us and scud away to the right. Acton saw it too. He raised his gun and fired. The animal rolled a yard to one side, as if kicked off course by a giant invisible boot, but picked itself up again and began limping towards the nearest hedgerow. Acton ran after it, and I ran after him, but the creature had stopped moving by the time we reached it. It lay on its side in the wet grass, still alive but bleeding heavily. Its eyes were wide with terror, still bright, not at all clouded. Its whole body trembled and its front legs pawed the turf. It had only one hind leg. The other had been blasted away.

'All right!' Acton was suddenly very excited. 'All right!' He pointed the shotgun at the hare and pulled the trigger. The air was thick with gunsmoke. I could smell it, acrid, burning. It drifted away on the wind and when it cleared I could see that the body lay a few yards further away from us. The second barrel had blasted its head to nothing.

Acton was grinning broadly. He stepped forwards and

snatched it up. 'This is more like it, eh?' He laughed, holding the body high, then dropped it into his canvas game-bag. 'Don't worry, there's plenty left for both of us. Rabbits all over the place here. They're so bloody stupid you can't miss them.'

I felt numb. 'They aren't rabbits,' I heard myself saying. 'They're hares.'

'Hares, rabbits, who gives a shit? They'll all be stone dead in a minute anyway.' He began to run back towards the wood. 'Come on, we'll hang around in the trees and they'll come out again, they're so bloody stupid.'

We returned to the edge of the field and crouched side by side in the shallow ditch. Acton reloaded with feverish speed, hardly taking his eyes off the long grass to do so. 'There! Over there!' He rose, pointing. 'Your turn! Go on!'

I stood up. Two long tawny ears pointed up from the greenery twenty yards away. I raised the shotgun to my shoulder. The ears swivelled, a head appeared beneath them, a tiny glittering eye blinked at me and then the animal was off, leaping and dashing towards the nearest hedge. I aimed along the barrel and saw its hind legs kicking away. But I couldn't pull the trigger.

'Shoot! Shoot!'

The hare zig-zagged as it ran across the field. I followed its flight with the point of the gun, my finger tight on the trigger but I couldn't shoot. With one last kick and leap it disappeared into the hedgerow.

'Shit! Bad luck!' Acton shook his head. 'You've just got to blast away. Don't wait until you've got a perfect shot. It isn't a rifle, you don't need a perfect aim. And you've got two barrels, remember. You can afford to waste one of them.'

We settled down to wait again. Acton pulled off his leather gloves and blew on his fingers. The drizzle had almost stopped but now it was very cold. 'Should have brought a hip flask,' he muttered, 'and a pair of binoculars.'

Nothing moved in the field. There was an occasional rustling and creaking from the trees behind us, and the movement of a solitary bird flapping in the far hedgerow but no more hares in the long grass.

Acton looked at his watch. 'It'll be getting dark soon. We'll give it ten minutes here, then we'll walk all the way round the field and see what we can raise.'

Five minutes later he stood up and I followed him along the ditch to the hedgerow. 'I don't know where they've gone. There's always loads of them. I've usually got the bag stuffed by this time.' He patted the canvas sack, hanging heavy and darkly stained at his side.

'Perhaps you've killed them all.'

'Nah. They breed faster than you can shoot them. They're at it all the time.' He laughed. 'Last year I caught a couple of them on the job, gave them both barrels while they were at it. Never knew what hit them. Great way to go, eh?'

We walked along beside the hedgerow, Acton scanning the grass all the time. I could feel his impatience, the excitement held in check as tightly as his gloved hands gripping his shotgun. 'You can almost tread on them sometimes. They jump out at your feet even before you know they're there.'

At that very moment a hare sprang from the long grass only a yard or two in front of us and in its confusion began to run away from the hedgerow. The thunder of Acton's shotgun was deafening and immediate.

The hare lay stretched out in the grass, very still, its eyes closed. It must be dead I thought. Acton can't have missed. He bent down and even as his hand reached out, the animal jumped to its feet and kicked away from us. Acton leapt on it, somehow seizing it in both hands, and rolled in the grass with the animal thrashing in his grasp. He got to his feet, laughing and muddy, the hare wriggling in his hands but firmly held.

'It must have been stunned. The shock. Well, I've got you now, you little bastard, haven't I?' The animal thrashed wildly, convulsed and contorted itself, and Acton grunted as he fought to hold it still. 'Ouch! The little shit scratched me! The claws on the beast. It's a monster!'

It squealed with fear and the sound became a loud and prolonged scream of distress echoing horribly around the empty field. Then it went limp in Acton's hands.

'Let it go,' I said. 'Kill it or let it go, for God's sake.'

'Kill it? Let it go? No way!' He bundled the still form into his game-bag and buckled the flap down tight. I'd hoped the poor creature had had a heart attack but the bag began to bulge and wriggle and for a few seconds it seemed to have a life of its own before the movement ceased. I tried not to imagine what it was like in there: the darkness, the enclosed space, the smell of man, the smell of the blood of its own species, the corpse of its own brother or sister.

'Come on, I'm bloody freezing,' Acton said. 'Let's go home.' We cut across the field back towards the woods. I let Acton walk in front of me. I watched his leather-coated back and felt the weight of the gun, loaded and ready, in my hand. No, I thought, wait. Wait and be clever.

In the woods a blackbird broke away from a bush to one side of the path and fluttered into a tree. Acton swung his gun up and blasted at it, a random shot just for the hell of it. Even when the report had died down, the sound of pellets falling among the trees could still be heard, but so could the blackbird's alarm call as it flew to safety. He had missed. 'Get you next time, birdy!' he shouted, laughing, and discharged the second barrel among the empty branches. Another crash of thunder, the patter of another shower of lead rain.

'You can do some shooting next week if you like, while we're away.' We trudged back across the ploughed field. It was getting dark and a mist was rising from the fold in the hill below us where the house stood. 'On your own. Any time. Just help yourself to a gun and cartridges.'

We came to the gate in his wall and he unlocked it. We walked across the lawn round to the back of the house. Two dogs were lying on the ground in their enclosure and came bounding up to the wire as we approached. One of them barked and two more appeared from the kennels against the far wall.

'All right, boys. All right.' We came up to the wire and the dogs began to bark and bound about, very excited, leaping up against the fence. Acton very carefully unbuckled the game-bag. I could see the scratches across his right wrist. They were more than scratches, long cuts which were still bleeding. He groped around inside the bag and brought out the dead hare. The dogs were running around the enclosure in a frenzy. Acton re-fastened the bag, took a step backwards and hurled the carcass into the air as hard as he could. It sailed up over the wire fence and plummeted down towards the dogs. They had snatched it in their jaws and were fighting over it even before it hit the ground.

Acton unlocked the gate and edged into their enclosure while they were occupied. He unbuckled the game-bag again and brought out the live hare. I could see it trembling in his hands as he set it down, almost gently, on the wet turf. Then he sprang back out of the enclosure, swung the door to and locked it.

For a few seconds the hare sat motionless on the grass,

paralysed with fear, then it sped off along the side of the fence, running fast, running blind.

'Come on, boys,' Acton hissed. 'Come on.'

Two of the dogs were still fighting over the first hare. A third was making the most of a scrap they had dropped. The fourth had won nothing and he was the first to see the small brown shape bowling along the edge of the enclosure. With a snarl of fury and delight he was after it. And then the other three were in on the chase.

It was all over very quickly but not quick enough. It was all over before I had time to turn away. I felt sick. I walked back towards the house, leaving Acton to savour every last detail. He was too engrossed to miss me.

I took a bath and tried, for once, not to think about Tony Acton. I tried, but failed. The water was hot, the bathroom full of steam, there were clean towels and dry clothes waiting for me, but I could not relax. I was too angry and too sick, and I was still feeling that way when I got out of the bath.

My bag was on the bed, where Greta or whoever had carried it up from the car had left it. It was a big leather sack. I unzipped it and reached inside. Then I froze. Someone had beaten me to it. The bag had been unpacked and re-packed. Everything was neatly folded but not as I had done. Everything was back in the bag but not in the order I'd packed them. Someone had searched my luggage. Why? What were they looking for? What did they think they'd find? And who'd done it? Greta, while I was out with Acton? Acton, while I was in the bath? Andrea?

At that moment there was a knock on the door. Acton leaned into the room, holding out a glass of scotch. 'Celebration – Greta isn't cooking tonight. Get that down you, Nick, then get some kit on. Then we'll be off for the best lobster bisque this side of the Channel.' He grinned at me as I stood there with one hand inside the bag, and if he noticed any surprise or alarm on my face then he didn't show it or he found it very amusing.

We drove into Canterbury and dined at a seafood restaurant called La Mer Gourmande. Its lobster soup might well have been the best in the country but the evening was not a success. The two girls had dumped the tart image for a silk-and-pearls elegance which turned every head in the place, but that didn't help because Acton was in a deep sulk, a sulk which I was already associating with his wife's presence. They didn't speak to each other throughout the meal. If they so loathed each other's company, why was Greta going to Madrid with him? They were going to have an amusing week together.

Only once, when he saw the menu, did Acton pick up. 'Ah, veau de mer! That's shark! I'll have it, fins and all!'

'That's disgusting,' Andrea grimaced, laughing. 'Sharks eat people, don't they? If you eat a shark which has eaten another human being, doesn't that make you a cannibal?'

'Exactly!'

'It will be porbeagle shark,' Greta said. 'They do not eat men. Only haddock. And herring.'

Acton gave her a look of disgust and ordered the Dover sole.

The evening's only entertainment came from Andrea. She was determined to flirt with me, flirt outrageously. I played the game but I was very wary. I had the feeling I was being set up, I wasn't sure for what, but I was certain it wasn't just for a cosy foursome. For all their mutual hostility I could sense in Acton and his wife a shared interest, a vested interest, in Andrea's progress with me, an interest which they did their best to conceal and which had nothing to do with its entertainment value.

Perhaps I was being too wary. Perhaps it was just Andrea's predatory looks and her unexplained presence. But the luggage search had put me on edge again. I was suspicious of them all. If Acton could get his wife to search my luggage, he could get some man-eater to slip under my guard in order to have a spy in the enemy's camp. Perhaps they were in it together.

Acton drove home in silence. He hurled the Jaguar through the darkness and along narrow lanes and around tight corners at an angry speed. Andrea laughed at the fury of his driving and used the corners as a good excuse to press her warm body against me on the back seat, to steady herself with one hand on my knee.

'He will kill us all,' Greta muttered from the front, as stolid as ever but clearly alarmed. 'He drives so fast, the mad fool. Why he must drive so fast, I do not know.'

It wasn't late when we got back but I was ready to turn in. Greta, however, didn't know when to call it a day. Out came the scotch, out came the vodka, and out came a new board-game, Green Crusader or something, which she insisted everyone was playing.

Andrea caught my eye, grinned, shrugged and rolled a joint. She lit up and offered it to me. I shook my head. She shrugged again and inhaled deeply. 'Let's play,' she laughed. 'Let's save the goddamned planet.'

We rolled dice and dealt cards and pushed coloured counters around a map of the world's eco-regions, and within ten minutes Greta and Acton were at each other's throats.

'I cannot save the beached whale? Why not? I have thrown a six. I am on the blue square. Why not?'

'You haven't got the right card! You have to draw the Marine Biologist card!'

They were on their feet shouting at each other.

'You do not want me to win! You do not want me to score for the beached whale! You cheat!'

'It's in the rules! It's in the rules, you stupid cow! Read the bloody rules!'

They were yelling, red in the face, completely lost in the violence of their conflict. Andrea lay back on the sofa, laughing, insulated by her little cloud of pungent smoke. I got up and walked out. Out of the room, out of the house.

It was very dark outside and very quiet. It was Saturday night, but there were no sounds of traffic or drunken singing. London was a million miles away. The air was fresh and not too cold. At last I was on my own. I turned my back on the house and its lights and walked on blindly.

Slowly, as my eyes adjusted to the darkness, dim shapes became distinct and identifiable. Trees and shrubs, and the high wall at the far end of the lawn. And there was the dogs' enclosure. I was up against the wire fencing almost before I knew it was there. I could see, or thought I could see, one or two low black shadows prowling around in the darkness at the foot of the wall. Like dark thoughts circling the depths of a murderer's mind. I could hear them sniffing and panting. I imagined their eyes, their teeth . . . I shivered. Even then, when I could barely see them, I could feel an irrational terror stirring within me. I turned and walked quickly away.

And then it came to me. The plan. Suddenly it was there, in my brain, complete and perfect. The shock of it left me momentarily faint. My pulse raced, my mouth was dry, I was sweating in the cold night air. I stopped and took some deep breaths. The faintness passed. I shook my head but the plan was still there. I laughed. It was perfect. Acton was as good as dead.

I walked on. Let's see, let's see. Stay calm. What if . . . What if . . . I dissected the plan as I walked, considered it from this angle, from that angle. From every angle. There had to be a weakness. There had to be at least one fault which I'd have to work on, a mistaken assumption which could undermine the whole structure and bring it crashing down. But there wasn't. I took the pieces apart, examined each one and put them back together again. The more I thought about it, the clearer it became – what I had to do, how I had to do it. The whole thing was simple but ingenious, functional but elegant. Of course, it was dangerous – but once it was through I'd be in the clear. And Acton would be dead.

I was wide awake and full of energy. I couldn't go back to the house, not just yet. My shoes were soaked from the wet grass, my feet were damp, but it didn't matter. I followed a path round to the front and walked down the drive along the side of the wood to the narrow lane.

The moon came out, a thin crescent, and a few stars showed through breaks in the cloud. I walked uphill along the lane, feeling the countryside alive around me. I'd thought the night was still and quiet but it wasn't. The woods and fields were on the move with living things. I could sense it. The darkness was full of hunting animals, hiding animals, animals trying to kill, animals trying not to be killed. Living things blind to everything but the imperatives of fear and hunger and aggression. The air was stiff with it. The night amplified every sound in a way unimaginable by daylight. I felt as if I could hear every rustle, every beating wing, every scratching claw for miles around.

I walked and thought until I was too tired to walk or think any more. Then I made my way back to the house. All the lights were off and for a moment I thought I was locked out. But I wasn't. I passed through the hall and up the stairway without putting on a light. As I crossed the first landing I heard laughter, soft and low, from behind a closed bedroom door. A man's laughter and a woman's laughter.

I made my way up a second flight of stairs and along a passageway to my room. I locked the door behind me, as if turning the key would safeguard the secrecy of the thoughts in my head. I lay down on the bed. I was too tired to undress or turn the light off but those thoughts still kept me awake. I had walked off the excitement and euphoria but they had left behind a residue of anxiety and caution which kept my brain probing relentlessly at the plan. Probing for blindspots and inconsistencies. Why do you think the thing is perfect? Because I can't find any faults in it. Does that mean there aren't any faults in it? No. It just means I haven't found any yet.

I heard footsteps, soft but fast, in the passageway outside. There was a knock at the door. 'Nick?' Andrea's voice. She chuckled. 'Let me in, Nicky baby.'

I froze.

'I know you're awake. I've been waiting for you.'

I didn't move, I didn't speak.

'Come on, sweetie.' More soft laughter. 'It's cold out here. Don't you want to keep me warm?'

I tried not to think about that thick mane of red hair. The lithe body I had felt against me in the back of the Jaguar. That golden tan.

'Nicky, honey, let me in.' The amusement in her voice

had given way to impatience. She knocked again, louder. 'Nicky.' She was angry now. The door handle turned, rattled vainly against the lock. 'Suit yourself,' she hissed. 'You English faggot!' Then she was gone.

CHAPTER FOUR

Acton and his wife left for Heathrow at midday the next day. Andrea left earlier; exactly when or to where I didn't know – our paths crossed only once that morning, among the packing cases and stacked canvases in the hallway, and the look she gave me was more frozen north than deep south.

Acton spent the morning instructing me in dog care. He was anxious about leaving the monsters in someone else's hands, but trying not to show it. He opened a deep-freeze in the kitchen and I saw packs and packs of frozen meat, huge chunks of it, yellow-skinned, red-fleshed, white-boned. I couldn't tell what animal had donated it and I didn't ask. I didn't want to know. There was a big metal bucket full of the stuff standing by the back door.

'They need five pounds of raw meat a day, Nick. Each. Feed them once a day in the morning, any time before midday. You can weigh the meat out on those scales if you like, but it's easier just to fill the bucket up to the top. It's all the same. Do it every night, last thing, so it's thawed out come the next morning. There's a cleaver over there if any bits are too big and you need to chop them up.' He picked up the bucket. It looked very heavy. 'Don't forget. Fill it up last thing every night. Right up to the top.'

I followed him out into the garden at the back of the house and across the lawn. The dogs knew what was coming. A couple of them were trotting to and fro on the other side of the wire, their tongues hanging out, their eyes on the bucket. Two more were standing up against the wire, tails wagging, snorting with excitement. By the time Acton reached the gate they were in a barking frenzy, falling over each other to get at him. Acton, laughing, had to push and fight his way into the enclosure and across to a long metal trough into which he emptied the bucket. There was some snarling and snapping, then it was heads down and tails up.

Acton stepped back and beckoned to me. 'Come on in. I'll introduce you.' This was the moment I'd been dreading. Fighting against every instinct I forced myself to take a few steps forwards through the gateway and into the enclosure.

'It's funny,' Acton was saying, 'I got the first one as a joke, really. You know, the camp macho thing about a big brutal dog. But before I knew it I was hooked. Got three more, straight away. The whole litter. I'm planning to start breeding them soon. Bitches are difficult to get hold of, though. And bloody expensive. You wouldn't believe it.'

I didn't take my eyes off them. They were too busy with their trough to register my presence but I wasn't going to give them a chance to surprise me. 'Listen, dogs terrify me. Even the little ones. I can't help it. It's a phobia.'

Acton laughed. 'Rubbish! It's simply fear because they're so big and strange-looking. But you wait till you get to know them. They've all got their own identities, Nick. They're just like people. Pablo over there is the leader. No one does anything without his permission.'

The biggest of the dogs raised his head at the sound of his name, noticed me inside his enclosure, and began to snarl. Another dog, almost as big, tried to get at his leftovers. Pablo snapped at him and he turned sullenly away.

'That's Sal, Pablo's rival for top dog. One day he'll

push Pablo too far. I'd like to see what happens then. Over there's Max – he's completely subservient to Pablo, a real hero worshipper. And then there's Marcel – he's a perfect opportunist. He's lazy but he's clever – he'll exploit the tensions between the other three whenever he can. What you've got here is a basic pack. Fascinating, isn't it?'

Pablo Picasso, Salvador Dali, Max Ernst, Marcel Duchamp. It was surreal, all right. The animals looked like a cross between wolves and bears. In spite of the introduction it was impossible to tell them apart. They all looked equally stupid, equally brutal.

'A week with them, Nick, and you'll be a changed man. You'll love them. You'll want to take them home with you.' He laughed. 'Just remember to keep them well-fed and happy. Don't half-starve or thrash them, unless you want to kill a Chinese king. Chinese kings, Nicky, remember the Chinese kings!'

The food was gone. They had downed it in less than a minute. They bounded forward, eager for a game. I was out of there in a flash, clanging the gate shut behind me. Acton booted a brightly coloured plastic ball in my direction, hard, and the dogs came hurtling after it. Ball and dogs hit the wire fencing right in front of me. Like the All Black pack smashing into the opposition. I cowered. Acton laughed. The whole enclosure shook like a bamboo grove in a hurricane.

'You wait, Nick. By Friday you'll be in here with them, romping around as if they were your own kid brothers!'

I turned back to the house, leaving Acton to make his fond farewells in private. I hope he appreciated the gesture.

It was a relief to see Acton's Jaguar disappear round the curve in the long drive. I was alone at last in that big old house with its dust-sheeted furniture and bare walls. Their return flight wasn't due in until midday on Friday, which gave me five days to do what had to be done. Just long enough. I went into the kitchen, had some lunch and planned the rest of the day.

The first thing was to hunt out Acton's laundry basket. I found his bedroom at the far end of the passage off the first landing. I hesitated in the doorway. It was strange, I had no doubts about killing him, but there I was, decidedly uneasy about invading his private territory and poking about among his private things. Trying to ignore everything else in that bedroom, I tracked down the laundry basket and rummaged around among the dirty underwear and shirts until I found what I wanted. Luckily it didn't take long. There it was, the powder-blue silk shirt Acton had been wearing the night before.

To one side of the house, overgrown with creepers and ivy, were a couple of outbuildings, little more than ancient brick sheds with their doors and half their roofs missing. There was a woodpile in one of them, as I had hoped, and I soon found the second item I wanted. A length of well-seasoned timber about four feet long and about as thick as my wrist. Strong but not too heavy. I left it there for the time being.

Back in the house I telephoned Stanley the journalist. But there was no answer. I guessed it would ring and ring until closing time was called in whichever pub he was having his Sunday lunch. Never mind. I'd try again that evening.

There was nothing more to be done for the time being, so I pulled on my hiking boots, stuffed an Ordnance Survey map into my coat pocket and went out for a walk. I passed the dogs' enclosure on my way to the gate in the corner of the garden wall. Only two of the beasts were out. One of them – Pablo? Max? Sal? – was having a squat, dumping a steaming load on the grass by the fence. The other was sitting outside one of the kennels, licking his balls. They both sneered at me with ignorant disdain, but didn't make a fuss. Already they'd written me off as someone who wasn't worth growling at.

It was very cold; cloudy but dry. I took a path uphill through the woods behind the house, and within half an hour I was out on the top of the Downs. I followed the broad ridge for a mile or two until the woods gave way to open grassland. I sat down on the turf and looked at the map and tried to identify landmarks in the distance. Below me the view stretched for miles across the Kent and Sussex Weald, a rolling, wooded landscape patched with fields and hedgerows. To the south it flattened out into the beginnings of Romney Marshes, and beyond that I guessed the English Channel would be visible on a good day. The wind was strong and cold up there, but it was very peaceful. If I was going to have second thoughts about Tony Acton's fate, this was the moment for them. But there were no second thoughts. I was going to do it. I put the map away and began to retrace my steps.

It was growing dark by the time I got back and cold enough to make the warmth inside the house welcoming rather than stifling. I went from room to echoing room, closing shutters, drawing curtains, shutting doors. Cutting off parts of the house I wouldn't need. I put more logs and coal on the fire in the small sitting-room, then sat down with the phone and called Stanley. This time he was in.

'Yes?' Only one word but there was no mistaking Stanley's patrician drawl.

'Hello, Stanley? Nicholas Todd here.'

'Yes?'

'One of Acton's rising stars, remember? We spoke

before the last piece you did on him. And at the party last Wednesday.'

'I remember.'

'Well. It occurs to me there were one or two things about Acton I didn't tell you. The most interesting things, really.'

'Really?'

'Yes. One or two things I forgot to tell you. A shame. I'm sure you'd have found them fascinating.'

'And now you've remembered?'

'That's right. And I was wondering if you were interested.'

'That depends. Tell me what they are and I'll tell you if I'm interested.'

'It's more about Wyndham Lewis really.'

'Really?'

'The British Library has a pretty good collection of his correspondence. 1920s, 1930s, even some pre-1914. A number from 1909, even.'

'Really?'

'There's a good series of very early letters to Augustus John. They shed an interesting light on any work he might have done in that year.'

Stanley was listening carefully. 'Tell me more.'

'Come on, Stanley. You're the professional journalist. Do you want me to do all your research for you?'

'Hmm. Quite. Quite' he mumbled. 'Augustus John, you say? The British Library?'

'One more thing, Stanley. Whatever you find, don't publish anything before Friday. There's a lot more to it, and I'll tell you everything as long as you don't publish before Friday. You can buy me lunch when I'm back in town. But publish before then and my lips are sealed. You'll never know the whole story. Is that clear?'

'Hmmm.' Stanley was playing it cool but I knew he was very excited.

'Do you know the Eagle in Farringdon Road? See you there – what – half twelve on Friday?'

'Jolly good. Yes. Better be worth it, er, Nicholas, eh? Better be worth it.'

'It'll be worth it, Stanley. Just remember – one word in any paper before Friday and I won't be there. You'll be lunching on your own and you'll miss out on the story of a lifetime.'

I let my breath out, slowly, as I hung up. So that was that. Easy.

I was still very tense. I got up and stretched and helped myself to a large whisky. Then I wandered into the kitchen and fixed some supper.

Not long after the beginning of our association, Acton had approached me about a particular piece of work.

'I have a commission for you, Nick. Nothing very exciting, I'm afraid. More interior decor than fine art, to be honest. A client wants a series of pen-and-ink drawings for his study.' He paused and grinned, one hand stroking the silk of his tie. 'He has a rather specific requirement – he wants something in the style of William Holman Hunt. You know, the Pre-Raphaelite. What do you think? Interested? Don't worry about materials – paper, pens, ink – I'll supply them.'

I took the job seriously. I did a lot of research and took great care over the designs before I put pen to paper. And I got the job done on time. A few weeks later I learned that they'd been sold as original Holman Hunts.

I found that I wasn't shocked or upset but simply amused. I suppose I must have known what was going on from the moment I accepted the work. Why else would Acton have been so keen to supply the materials?

(The paper clearly consisted of unused pages removed from some nineteenth-century album.) Why else had I chosen not to sign or date any of the drawings? If I'd thought about it, I'd have realized it wasn't the sort of commission I should have accepted in the first place. But that was why I had tried not to think about it.

So when he asked me, six months later, to do a water-colour 'in the style of James Stark' I agreed, laughing, and we both knew what sort of game we were playing.

Acton had been engaged in this sort of business from the very beginning, and continued with it even when his legitimate business was booming and dwarfed that sort of sideline. I suppose it was against his nature to turn his back on a good money-spinner, even if he didn't need it. Above all, however, it amused him. He loved duplicity. He loved fakes and forgeries for their own sake. The fact that they were profitable was merely a bonus. The duplicity of forgeries excited him, and the excitement was almost sexual. Forgery turned him on.

And my motives? Well, I didn't need to do it for the money either. My own work was selling well. I had paid off all my debts. For the first time in years I actually had money to spend, and there was more coming in, lots of it if Acton was to be believed. On the other hand it did pay well, and when you've experienced real poverty as I had, there's no such thing as not needing the money. You always need it, no matter how much you have, you're so scared of being without it.

And there was also a sense of obligation towards Acton, pathetic though it may sound. My life had changed since he'd taken me on, and it would have seemed ungrateful if I'd refused to help him. There was certainly the fear that he would cease to help me if I refused to help him. He certainly hinted that the more I was prepared to co-operate in this sideline the more energy he was prepared to put into selling my own work. He made it clear that the two went hand in hand.

And it amused me too, at first. The trickery of it. The challenge of seeing if your own talents are capable of producing convincing work. The vanity of trying to prove that you can produce work as good as that of the masters of the past. And, not least of all, there was the purely academic fascination with the techniques of forgery. The more I practised this art or craft or science or whatever it was, the more interested I became in the methods of other practitioners. It became something of an obsession with me; I was like a teenage boy hooked on motorcycle mechanics.

Greed, weakness, fear, vanity. Perhaps these were what Acton was looking for in me when he called at my studio at the beginning of our association. Well, he certainly found them.

I remembered one piece of work – my John Sell Cotman – particularly vividly. Acton had turned up at my studio one day with a blank canvas under one arm and a painter's box under the other. The paintbox was almost two hundred years old; some associate had unearthed it in a junk shop. The blank canvas, and the wooden stretcher on which it was mounted, were just as old. I guessed the canvas had once been covered by a worthless or nondescript picture which one of Acton's assistants had deliberately removed by giving it a thorough wipe-down with a powerful solvent.

Acton explained his vague requirements: something English, early nineteenth-century, and unusual. I thought about it and decided on an oil by John Sell Cotman. Cotman, of course, is known as a master of watercolour; an oil by him would be very unusual, but not totally unknown (there's the magnificent 'Drop Gate at Duncton Park' in the Tate, for example). Besides,

Cotman had always been an inspiration for me. I liked the way he built up a picture out of plain but precisely organized blocks of colour. There's something very modern about the simplicity and austerity of his work; and there's something else as well – a frightening but fascinating hint at the despondency and melancholia which haunted him all his life and which ultimately tipped him over into madness.

Three factors make for a successful forgery. First, the painting must be convincing. Second, the materials used must be as old as the painting is supposed to be. Third, the painting must exhibit appropriate signs of ageing; once a picture is more than fifty years old, the paint is rock-hard, the varnish begins to lose its clarity, and the colours fade. The varnish, paint and ground all begin to crack as they slowly dry out and contract, and as the canvas tension changes with the atmospheric humidity.

As for the first factor, it remained to be seen whether I could paint a convincing Cotman, but I was confident. As for the second, Acton had furnished me with contemporary materials: the painter's box, the canvas and its stretcher. For the third, there were techniques which, if used carefully, could artificially produce the effects of ageing.

I began by examining the canvas carefully. Whoever had removed the original, dispensable painting had done a good job; I was sure that no traces of it would be visible even under ultra-violet light. And they had left the original ground (the treatment spread over the canvas to ensure that the paint takes to it). That was good, too. It meant that I wouldn't have to manufacture a convincingly authentic ground. But the old ground was laced with cracks, some of them quite severe. That was a problem. If I painted straight on top of it, the paint would go through the cracks and onto the canvas, which would betray the fact that the paint had been applied after the cracks had appeared. But I overcame that by filling in the cracks with a water-solvent glue.

I then spent a week studying the work of John Sell Cotman. I spent hours in front of the 'Drop Gate' in the Tate, closely examining his brushwork. Then I spent a couple of days sketching various designs, before settling on a view of wooded downland not dissimilar to that seen in the background of his 'ploughed fields' watercolour. Then I ground up my paints and away I went.

In the early days, Acton always liked to watch me as I worked on a forgery. He was like some sort of voyeur. His face would be flushed, his voice and movements agitated and excited. Breathing heavily, like someone watching a blue movie. And all the time he would talk of his past deceptions, like a man boasting of his sexual conquests.

'I learned a lot from picture restorers, you know,' I remember him saying. 'Many years ago I got hold of an eighteenth-century portrait of a rather severe looking young man. It was a very fine picture, beautifully executed, but it just wouldn't sell. In despair, I eventually took it to a restorer and asked him if he could do anything to make it more attractive. He promised me he could guarantee a sale, and sure enough the thing was sold within a week of its return. What had he done? Painted out the young man's frown and painted in a broad grin. Simple.'

He laughed and put his feet up on a bench. I worked away in silence, only half listening to him.

He went on. 'It's amazing what a restorer can find in a picture like that. I've had dozens of other examples since then. Old landscapes which no one would find interesting enough to look at, let alone buy, get sent off to the restorers. They clean away the muck of centuries to find . . . horses, sheep, cattle, whatever, exactly the kind of charming detail which has customers reaching for their cheque-books. Dull family groups of anonymous seventeenth-century merchants are found to have dogs or cats running around at their feet, and you can't go wrong with pets, can you? Sometimes, even, a picture goes to a restorer with the signature of a minor artist in a corner, and comes back with the signature of a major artist in its place. It seems that the one signature is cleaned off and the other is found underneath. Amazing, isn't it?'

He was there when I put the finishing touches to the picture. 'What do you think?' I said, putting down my brush and stepping backwards.

Acton peered at the picture. He was breathing heavily. His face was flushed. 'Let me see, let me see. Definitely British, definitely early nineteenth-century. A touch of Cézanne, perhaps, but too English, too early. So . . . my God, it's a Cotman! Not a watercolour, but an oil! An oil painting by John Sell Cotman! Brilliant! Very unusual, very valuable! That's brilliant, Nick, brilliant!'

I laughed in triumph, picked up another brush, and with a confident flourish added a signature I'd practised a hundred times to the bottom left corner.

With the addition of the signature I passed from the safe, legal territory of the copyist/pasticheur into the dangerous, illegal territory of the forger. There is, after all, no such thing as a forged picture; only a forged label. A picture of a sky is simply a picture of a sky; even a picture of a sky in the style of Constable is simply a picture of a sky in the style of Constable. But once a label is attached to that picture saying that it is indeed a Constable, then that constitutes a forgery.

Many famous forgers argue quite legitimately that they are not forgers because it is not they themselves who add that all-important label to their work. The lovable Tom Keating, for example, even went to the lengths of painting the word 'Keating' or 'Fake' on the bare canvas in lead-based paint before starting a picture in the style of Samuel Palmer or whoever. The lead paint, of course, would show up quite clearly under X-ray. The uniquely gifted Eric Hebborn didn't need to add a signature; his draughtsmanship was so brilliantly convincing in itself.

But I had neither the pride of Keating nor the genius of Hebborn.

We left the painting to dry for a couple of days, and then Acton was back to watch the varnishing. The 'Drop Gate' looked as if it had an oil varnish rather than a mastic varnish, and from its discoloration I guessed that Cotman had used a copal resin rather than amber or sandarac. So I made up an appropriate resin by dissolving copal in a fixed oil, carefully avoiding the usual organic oils which would betray their age or lack of it if anyone scientifically measured their light-deflecting qualities.

Once the picture was varnished, we had a convincingly Cotmanesque picture made from authentic early nineteenth-century materials. But it looked brand new. No one would have believed it was almost two hundred years old. So we left the varnish to dry for another couple of days, and then the fun really began.

First, I sponged the back of the canvas down with lukewarm water. This dissolved and dispersed the glue I'd used to fill in the cracks in the ground before starting the painting. Then I pre-heated the oven in my kitchen to just over one hundred degrees centigrade, and put the picture in to bake for a couple of hours. Acton had brought along a bottle of champagne and we made the most of it while we waited.

I took my Cotman out of the oven after exactly two

hours and twenty minutes. In that time it had aged by nearly two hundred years. Acton and I examined it carefully. The varnish and paint were rock hard. Both were laced with spider's webs of little cracks. The varnish had taken on a slight yellow-brown discoloration, and some of the colours had faded. Acton laughed with delight. It was all totally convincing.

I based my methods on the work of van Meegeran, a Dutch forger famous earlier this century for his Vermeers. He developed a technique of modifying the paint medium to ensure that it cracked and aged when baked. The modification involved the use of an artificial resin (which shall remain nameless here) when grinding up pigments and mixing paint. Van Meegeren was unmasked at the end of the Second World War, when he was charged with collaborating with the Nazis because he had sold a 'Vermeer' to General Goering; he found himself in the curious position of having to prove himself to be a forger in order to save his neck.

With Acton still laughing, I took the empty champagne bottle and tapped the surface of the picture a couple of times to dislodge a few loose, tiny flakes of paint. Just enough damage to suggest the wear and tear of centuries. Finally I took a handful of dust and muck from beneath a loose floorboard in my genuine nineteenth-century floor and brushed it into the fine cracks in the surface of the picture. Nothing that a decent restorer couldn't cope with.

The restorer who handled the picture after Acton sold it did an excellent job; he managed to reverse almost all my attempts to age the piece. His work – and my work – can be judged by any visitor to Washington DC, where the picture is now on public display. I won't say exactly which museum or gallery bought it. After all, it shouldn't be too difficult to find; it is the only oil painting by John Sell Cotman in the whole of the USA.

There was a telephone in Acton's kitchen so I made another call while I was waiting for the kettle to boil after supper. My own number this time – I wanted to check any messages on my answerphone. I clicked the little play-back device into the mouthpiece and heard the tape rewind on my machine so many miles away back in London. Then I listened to the messages. There was only one and when I heard it I wished I hadn't taken the trouble.

'Hello? Nicholas . . . It's Diana. I'm sorry to phone you. I know how you feel about it. But . . . I've been away recently . . . I've had time to think and . . . I don't know . . . I wrote you a letter . . . I . . . Have you read it . . . ? I wondered . . . Well. Read the letter. Please. That's all. I'm sorry, I shan't phone again . . . Take care.'

I replaced the receiver and made coffee and did the washing up. Then I sat down with the coffee and thought, I'm not going to think about it. Not even for a second. Thinking, Where did she go? And why? And who with? Thinking, Enough. Stop it. You're not interested.

On the back of the kitchen door hung my coat and in a pocket was a sketchpad, a pencil and some crayons. I put a chunk of meat from the dogs' freezer on to a plate in the middle of the table. I began to sketch it. Flesh, blood, bones, skin – an intriguing still life.

I had brought no other tools of my trade with me for the week. No brushes and paints, not even watercolours. On Friday I had finally abandoned the canvas I'd been working on for the past eight weeks. Nothing was happening with it. And it wasn't the first one I'd abandoned; I hadn't finished anything for over six months now. I knew instinctively that it was dangerous to try to analyse such a problem rationally – who knows what might come apart in your hands once you start tinkering, and who knows if all the pieces will go back together again? But I had to do something. I had the vague idea that a deliberately relaxed approach might work, if combined with a return to basics. Basics, of course, meant drawing, and drawing from nature. Organic forms – bones, shells, flowers, feathers, a curiously shaped tree root or fallen branch. Fruit, vegetables.

I tried to concentrate on the piece of flesh on the plate. I tried to lose myself in it. There comes a moment when you're not so much seeing the item you're drawing as feeling it. You can feel its shape, its proportions, its textures, and the feeling is transferred through the pencil to the paper. After half an hour that moment was still a long way off. I had some sort of representation of the thing but looking at it you couldn't smell the blood or taste the raw flesh. I screwed up the sheet of paper and threw it away. I stood up, slid the flesh into the empty bucket and then filled it to the brim from the freezer. Time for bed.

I threw enough coal on the fire in the living-room to keep it going until morning. And before I went to bed I listened once more to the message from Diana. It was uncanny to think of my phone ringing in an empty room many miles away, to think of Diana's disembodied voice speaking to the deserted studio, no one listening. Except me, and I was miles away, and the voice was a recording. I made sure it was wiped from the tape and then I hung up.

The previous October we'd hired a cottage on the banks of the River Severn somewhere north of Tewkesbury for a week's holiday. Diana and I. Just the two of us, in the middle of nowhere, surrounded by fields full of apple trees heavy with fruit, and horses grazing among the windfalls. Only last October. Less than four months ago.

We got in a week's provisions and forgot about the world. In the evenings we read books or listened to music or just talked. When the weather was fine we went walking on the Malvern Hills; when it rained we spent the day in bed.

Diana was happy. She was as quiet as ever but she smiled more, and laughed often. I really felt we'd left our ghosts behind, if not forever (of course, at that stage I hadn't realized just how many there were or what desperate exorcisms were required) then at least for one glorious week.

Only once did her frown return. We were standing on the summit of Midsummer Hill, resting from the climb and taking in the view. To the north, the peaks of the Malvern ridge marched away towards the blue shadows on the horizon which were the Shropshire hills. To the west, wooded valleys separated us from range upon range of Welsh mountains. The Cotswolds escarpment stretched along the horizon to the east, and to the south the Bristol Channel glittered in the distance. Below us, the fields and orchards of the Vale of Evesham and the Severn valley were spread out like a map.

I turned to Diana to say something and it was then that I saw that her frown had returned. I held back, waiting for her to speak.

'That view' she said. 'It's like standing on top of the world. It just goes on and on. And the detail. It's all there. Just look at it.' She turned to me, the breeze blowing her thick dark hair around her pale face, the frown deepening. 'Why don't we ever get a view like this of our own lives? If only we could look down every now and then and see the whole picture. Where we've been, where we are, where we might be going. No one would get lost or make mistakes, take the wrong turning and get trapped or tricked or disappointed. There'd be no confusion. No mess. No unhappiness.'

I watched the cloud-shadow scudding across the bright fields miles below us. I wondered if she was going to say any more, but I didn't try to encourage her. If she wanted to explain something, it was better to let her do it in her own good time. I wasn't going to press her or dig for an explanation. This wasn't the moment for it. But neither was I going to let her brood in silence.

'They say you can see eight counties from up here,' I said, trying to break her mood. I pointed to a medieval tower on the eastern slopes of the ridge a mile or two away. 'That's Little Malvern priory. In the Middle Ages, a young monk had an affair with a local woman. He was ordered to crawl up to the summit of Raggedstone Hill over there, every day, on his hands and knees, as penance for breaking his vow of chastity.'

'And did he?'

'Oh yes. He was supposed to say his prayers when he reached the top, but one day he was so tired and hacked off by the time he got there that he uttered a curse instead. He cursed everyone the shadow of the hill might ever fall on.'

'Ugh.' Diana laughed, shivering, as she looked south towards the peak of Raggedstone Hill. It had a dark, jagged outline. It looked bleak, even on such a clear day. Sinister and threatening. 'That's one hill we're not going to climb. Where's its shadow? Is it going to catch us?'

'It was all a woman's fault. Your lot were causing trouble even in those days. Nice to know some things never change, isn't it?'

She tried to hit me so I threw my arms around her. We were both laughing. She struggled but I held her tight. So she stopped struggling.

'This hill's one of the few places where the glow-worm survives,' I said. 'The guide-book says these slopes are alight with them at dusk.'

'Glow-worms? Oh, Nick, can we come back and see them? Can we come back tonight? What time does it get dark?'

That evening it rained so we didn't leave the cottage. But the next day – the last of our holiday – was clear and bright, and we found ourselves climbing up Midsummer Hill as the sun was setting beyond the mountains of Wales. And sure enough, from the gathering shadows all around us came little glimmers and flashes of unearthly pale green light. It was altogether strange and magical. Diana ran to and fro across the path, bewitched and laughing, chasing the little sparks of light as they flared and died here and there, but she couldn't catch them – she might just as well have been chasing the stars themselves. It was impossible to believe that mere beetles were responsible for such enchantment.

It was dark by the time we reached the top. The sun had set and the night had fallen. The rain of the day before had cleared the sky, and now it was thick with stars. We stood together at the top of the hill, silent but close, and looked up at the stars and down on the scattered lights of Worcestershire's distant farms and villages. It was a moment of pure happiness.

The next day we returned to London. I knew that happiness would not survive our return, but it gave me hope nevertheless. I believed that the holiday had given us a foundation on which we could build some sort of new beginning.

In a way I was right. Because our return to London was the beginning of the end for us.

CHAPTER FIVE

The next morning there was a thick frost which crunched underfoot as I crossed the lawn with the dogs' breakfast. The bucket was very heavy and my breath came in icy clouds. It felt cold enough for snow.

The dogs were ready and waiting. They were standing up against the fence, tongues hanging out, teeth gleaming. Snorting with expectation. The sight of them made me want to turn round and go back inside but I forced myself to walk right up to the wire. I stopped and put the bucket down. The dogs began to bark. The sound of it felt like putting your brain through a shredder.

I took a dripping chunk from the bucket and threw it up over the top of the fence. All four dogs leapt for it as it plummeted down towards them. I hurled another piece and another. More. One after another, scattering them widely around the enclosure. The dogs raced to and fro after them, snapping and snarling, chasing each other, fighting. Tearing at the flesh. Bolting it down.

I stopped when the bucket was half empty. I picked it up and walked away from the enclosure. At the gate in the wall I glanced back. One of the dogs was still eating, two were fighting over a last scrap, but a third was staring after me, puzzled. Sensing that something had changed but not sure quite what. I unbolted the door in the wall and walked out of the garden, into the woods. A chorus of furious barking broke out behind me on the other side of the wall as the animals finally realized that they'd been short-changed.

A few hundred yards into the woods the track opened out into a small clearing I'd noticed the day before. On a patch of bare earth beneath a fallen tree at the clearing's edge was a scattering of feathers and bones. I emptied the bucket onto it. It was better than burying the leftovers. Buzzards and foxes and badgers were sure to clear away the evidence just as effectively.

In the afternoon I had a look through the paintings stacked in the hall. I kept my coat on. There was a draught from Siberia blowing in through that 400-year-old doorway.

All the pictures were modern. Most of them were by artists Acton's gallery represented. But this was his personal property, his own private collection, a hobby quite apart from the business of the gallery. It was a good collection – the best piece from the early years of each artist. He had an undeniably brilliant eye for a work of art. The fact that he should have been taking such pieces out into the market-place and hustling the best deals for them, rather than snapping them up himself at bargain basement prices while the artist was in no position to complain, didn't worry him in the least. I don't think it was something he had ever considered.

I soon found one of my own. A green landscape – it was five years old and I remembered it well, I remembered painting it. But I had forgotten how good it was. That was a surprise, and not a pleasant one. I didn't want to be reminded of how well I could paint five years ago. I didn't know if I could still paint that well. I didn't know if I could paint at all. It was like looking at someone else's work, at the work of an artist you knew you could never hope to emulate. I didn't want to look at it. I turned it back against the wall.

I had my first (and last, as it happened) one-man show within two years of joining Acton's gallery. I remember the time vividly. I'd never known such excitement, euphoria, sheer incredulity. Half the pieces went during the private view alone. Acton stuffed the gallery with collectors and journalists. The collectors were generous; they had his assistants running around sticking red dots on the walls all evening. The critics were complimentary; not only did they write about me in the week that followed – they wrote with enthusiasm.

I'd been to many private views of such shows in the past, and always found them to be exercises in embarrassment and insincerity. I'd always assumed I'd hate my own, if and when I had one. In fact, I loved every minute of it. Every second. The show ran for a month and all that time I drifted around in a haze of unreality. It was as if I hadn't stopped drinking champagne since the first magnum was uncorked at the private view. I might have guessed that a massive hangover would follow.

Acton came to see me the day after the show closed. He was as delighted as I was. 'Read these,' he said, waving a file of press cuttings. 'They write like this and we don't even pay them? Incredible.'

He glanced around the studio and it occurred to me that he no longer looked as out-of-place there as he had almost two years earlier. It was cleaner and tidier, space and materials arranged more efficiently and purposefully. It had lost its atmosphere of squalor and despair. And there was evidence of my new-found wealth as well.

On one table, positioned to make the most of the light, was a group of Korean ceramics, celadon vases from the Koryu era. Eight or nine centuries old and exquisitely beautiful. The soft glow of their pale green glaze seemed to purify the air around them. Some of them were decorated with white and black slips applied in delicate, almost abstract patterns which resolved themselves into the shapes of bats, birds and plants only when you focused on them.

On a mantlepiece behind them was a row of ancient Egyptian ushabti, funereal figurines placed in the tombs of noblemen as stand-ins to do the manual labour demanded of the deceased at various stages of the after-life. They were a cheerful little clay gang, their colours still bright and their glazes still clear even after three thousand years in the darkness of some New Kingdom tomb. Some of them held a hoe in each hand and a basket on the back, ready and eager to do someone else's hard work for them, others carried the whips and wore the long robes of overseers. All were inscribed with the sixth spell from the Book of the Dead.

I hadn't yet bought a new car or a new home, but these were pieces such as I had seen in museums and had never dreamt I would ever be able to own. They hadn't been on open sale, but I was inside the business now, I knew where to go and who to talk to, and they knew I had the money to pay for what I wanted.

Acton was pacing the floor of the studio and still laughing. He opened the file of press cuttings and read at random. ' "Todd's Field Sport series represents the brightest (or should we say the darkest? At least let us say the most powerful) arrival in years." ' He snapped the file shut and tossed it to me. 'Congratulations! And now for a bit of light relief after all that hard work. I have a client who's looking for –' He stopped suddenly and turned to face me as if I had interrupted him. I had said nothing, but perhaps an involuntary gesture or exclamation had alerted him to my reaction. I knew what he wanted, and he knew straight away that I didn't want to do it.

The truth was that the sideline Acton and I were running no longer amused me. The novelty had worn off, and the technical challenge was no longer exciting – I knew I could do it, so it was no longer a challenge. The increasing success of my own work was beginning to make me feel more secure, and at last I was starting to realize that I really didn't need the money that badly. And yes, I was beginning to feel guilty about the whole thing. Now that necessity was no longer in the way, guilt could not be avoided. It was wrong. The whole business was dishonest. It was an abuse – of others' ignorance, of their trust, of one's own talents.

I suppose that at the back of my mind I had always told myself that yes, I will do it until I'm really established, and then I shan't need to any more. I'll stop. At the back of my mind I'd always assumed that Acton would find someone else once I'd reached that stage, that he wouldn't expect an established artist to help him in such activities. And yet here he was, only the day after the show had finished, the show which a whole file of press cuttings confirmed had launched an artist who now had to be respected . . .

'Tony . . . do we have to do this? . . . Now, after this? . . .' I held up the press cuttings. 'I mean . . .'

'What do you mean exactly?' He had frozen, his smile gone and his tone very cold.

'Well . . . it's not as if we need the money, do we? . . .'

'What's need got to do with want? Money is money, Nick, enough is never enough!'

'But . . . it's wrong . . . Don't you ever feel, well, guilty?'

'Wrong? Guilty?' His smile was back, but twisted with scorn. 'What are we, Nick? Boy scouts? For shit's sake.'

'No. I've had enough, Tony. You can find someone else. I'm not going to do it.'

'You bloody well are, Nick.' I could hear the suppressed fury in his voice. I tried not to register it.

'No way.'

'Now listen to me, Todd.' He leaned forwards, his face even whiter than usual, his features tight with anger. 'One hit show and you think that's it. Well, it isn't. I turned it on for you, Todd, I can turn it off again.' He wasn't shouting, but he was beginning to tremble with the effort of keeping his anger under control. 'You do what I tell you to do or you're out on your own, where I found you two years ago. And I'll make sure no one will touch you or your work.'

He breathed in and out deeply, stood up straight and turned away. He had been inches away from an explosion of uncontrollable rage. He saw the Korean vases on the table beside him, and their glow seemed to calm him down. He picked one up and examined it closely. 'Very fine,' he said quietly, nodding. 'I've seen few pieces to rival this one. Even from Sung-dynasty China.'

He turned to me. 'Just remember. I made you, Todd. And I can break you.' His hands parted. The vase fell, a blur of pale green light, and then the studio was filled with the sickening chimes of its impact, of its shards skidding across the floor. 'As easily as that.' And then he left, without looking down, his feet crunching blindly on the scattered remains of the vase.

He returned the next day with full details of his requirements. And I didn't even try to argue with him. He had dismissed my hesitations. He had made it clear that he would refuse to represent me if I refused to co-operate. And I was too weak to call his bluff, too scared of losing what success I had found with him to try and take it elsewhere. So I continued to co-operate, on that job and others. But not without a growing hatred of the fear and weakness within me.

Self-disgust ate away at me. I found it harder and

harder to work. My paintings became darker, tortured, more difficult. Each picture was taking me longer and longer to paint, the subject matter increasingly obsessive and introverted, and as soon as the long process of dragging this horror up from my inner depths was complete, I couldn't wait to get the monster out of my studio. And the irony of that was that they sold for higher and higher sums. I produced fewer and fewer pieces, but more and more money came in. Each one was snapped up from Acton's gallery as soon as it arrived. I don't understand the tastes of collectors. They must be masochists, every one. The more tortured, disturbing and obscure the picture, the faster they jump on it and the more they pay for it. It's weird – totally weird.

At four o'clock I put another log on the fire in the sitting-room and then I went upstairs to get the shirt I'd fished out of Acton's laundry basket. I put my coat on and took the shirt out to the woodshed and lashed it tightly around one end of the length of wood I'd selected the day before. Then I carried it across the lawn to the dogs' enclosure.

They began to snarl as soon as they saw me. I didn't stop at the fence but followed it round to where it met the wall. The dogs followed on the other side of the wire, barking, as angry and indignant as self-important diners who think the waiter is ignoring them.

The wall was at least seven feet high, with moss and ivy growing up it. It must have been a few centuries old but it seemed solid enough. A couple of yards further along, a covered water-butt stood against it. I climbed up on to the butt and then scrambled on to the wall.

The top of the wall was over a foot wide but crumbling at the edges and slippery with moss and leaf-mould. I edged along it until I was past the point where it met the wire fencing and I was over the dogs' enclosure. I held the length of wood like a sword, the shirt tied around the business end. In spite of the cold my right hand was ungloved for a better grip.

The dogs were milling around in a tight and agitated group below me. I looked down at them. They looked even stranger from up there, their grotesque proportions further exaggerated. They looked strangely foreshortened, their heads and shoulders even bigger, their legs even shorter.

One of them stood up against the wall. Stretching up towards me, teeth bared, growling. His eyes were narrowed and his ears flattened. He was hungry and he wanted to kill me – I could see it in his eyes. Suddenly he leapt up. His teeth snapped at the height of his jump, then he fell back on all fours, snorting and panting and wheeling around for another attempt. Then they were all at it. Jumping up the wall and over each other. Snapping at the air only a foot away from my ankle.

The wall was too high – just – but they were relentless. Their determination was chilling. They weren't barking – this was real business, not display – and the only noises they made as they hurled themselves up the wall at me again and again and again were grunts and snarls and snorts of ferocious determination. I wanted to back off. I wanted to run away to the house. But I stood my ground, thinking: I'm just as determined as you are, you bastards.

After a minute or two there was a lull. The dogs stood there, glaring up at me, barrel chests heaving, mouths open and drooling. I reached out, very carefully, and lowered the shirt-wrapped end of the baton towards them. One of the creatures, growling but curious, raised his snout and sniffed at it. The growling stopped. He sniffed again. Suddenly he seemed to relax. He wiped his snout on Acton's shirt, licked it, nuzzled it. His aggression had suddenly evaporated.

I tightened my grip on the baton and swung it to give him a tap on the jaw. For a second he looked stunned. Before he could collect himself I swung the baton again and gave him a sharper crack on the side of the head. This time its impact jarred my wrist. The creature exploded with fury. Barking, he leapt up at the retreating baton, fell, raced round and round, leapt again blindly. I caught him with a good crack on the ear as he did so. I watched him snapping blindly and madly at the dogs around him at the foot of the wall. They caught some of his madness and started barking. And jumping again. The noise was deafening.

Stay calm, stay calm. Once more I lowered the baton. A second curious dog, barks subsiding to growls, sniffed the piece of wood. Once more there was an amazing transformation. The dog nuzzled the shirt, licked it, buried his nose in it. Then another crack on the jaw, another explosion of rage.

I caught them all like that, one after the other. I didn't withdraw until the whole pack had been clouted with a club reeking of their master and sent into a mad fury. Frothing at the mouth, rolling bloodshot eyes, barking loud enough to burst their lungs. Then I got down off the wall pretty quick and left them to it.

It was going perfectly according to plan, but the results were terrifying. I was drenched in a sweat of fear. By the time I got back to the woodshed I was shaking with the cold, the tension, the relief. So far so good, but I didn't know if I could keep it up. The dogs were still barking at the other end of the lawn. The sound of it made me shake more violently. I hid the baton and returned to the house.

The telephone was ringing. I heard it as soon as I

opened the front door. It rang through the empty rooms and corridors and halls of that deserted house like a fire alarm. I tugged my boots off and sprinted to the sitting-room. I don't know why I didn't simply ignore it.

'Hello . . . ?' What was the number? I didn't know the number. There it was . . . 'Hello, 0122 . . .'

'Tony?' A woman's voice, puzzled, impatient. 'Is that Tony?' she asked, realizing it wasn't.

It was a voice I knew, a voice I knew very well. 'Diana, it's me, Nicholas . . .'

There was a pause. It seemed like a long time but it wasn't long enough for me to come up with anything with which to fill her silence. I was too busy listening to it, trying to guess at the thoughts and feelings behind it, waiting for her to say something. But she didn't. She rang off.

I began to call her back. I'd dialled half the number before I realized what I was doing and put the phone down. There's no point, I told myself. It's over. Forget it.

Already it was dark. Time to draw the curtains and put some more wood on the fire. I felt very tired. I had something to eat, took a bath, filled the tin bucket with gobbets of flesh once more, and went to bed.

It was very cold in the bedroom. The whole house seemed to be getting colder by the hour. I couldn't sleep. I lay awake for a long time, wondering whether to drag a mattress down into the warm kitchen.

A December afternoon, just over a year ago. Some smart Mayfair restaurant – I can't remember which one. Acton was holding court after some private viewing or exhibition at a rival gallery. The usual mix of Acton acolytes – a few critics, a few artists, collectors, hangers-on. The place was warm and crowded and noisy – everyone was in pre-Christmas high spirits.

We were discussing the work we'd just seen. No one thought much of it. I'd just made some ironic remark which everyone seemed to find highly amusing, when a girl walked in, looked around, and made her way over to our table. I saw her before anyone else did. They were too busy laughing. It was odd, really. I usually didn't say much at such gatherings and I'm the world's worst comedian. I was feeling rather pleased with myself and then this girl I'd never seen before walked in and I immediately felt ashamed of the cynical, superficial witticism which everyone had found so amusing. It was something about her. Some sort of innocence, I suppose.

She went round towards Acton's chair – he didn't see her until she was standing at his shoulder. It was noisy in there and she didn't look like the kind of person to shout across loud, crowded restaurants. Then Acton jumped to his feet, still laughing, and kissed her. 'Diana,' he said, introducing her to everyone. 'My little sister.'

I hadn't even known Acton had a sister. But I noted the family resemblance. They had the same slight, elegant build, the same dark hair, very pale skin, blue eyes. But I could see straight away that there were differences. She didn't seem to have her brother's arrogance, his colossal self-assurance. She looked quiet and serious, whereas Acton was an extrovert who laughed at everyone and everything. She was a few years younger than him, I guessed.

'What was the joke, then?' she asked as she sat down on the chair someone had pulled up for her. Someone repeated my comment, nodding towards me. Someone else explained it.

'Oh. I see.' She smiled with what could have been shyness but certainly wasn't amusement. She looked across the table at me. The glance wasn't meant to rebuke – it was simply a faint curiosity about the author of this cynical and sarcastic aside – but it was clear she didn't like cynical or sarcastic people. I felt a strange moment of panic – and a desperate anger – as she looked away. I'm not like that, I felt like shouting. Ask anyone. I hate cynicism and sarcasm as much as you do. I never say things like that. It isn't fair . . . Which was all true. But I said nothing.

I watched her as the party went on around us. She had her brother's sophistication, but a shyer, more reticent variety. She was wearing a simple dress of dark green wool, and big silver earrings and matching bangles, which emphasized the thickness of her hair, the delicacy of her features and wrists. Her lips looked scarlet against the paleness of her face.

I was entranced. It wasn't just her looks. It was the way she behaved. Her attitude to the crowd seemed to mirror my own. Sometimes she joined in, but most of the time she sat back and watched and listened, taking everything in, contributing only when it didn't mean cutting in on someone else or grabbing the limelight. She already knew some of the people there. Someone turned to her and said 'Diana, how's Iphigenia?'

'Getting excited about Christmas already, I'm afraid. I don't envy the babysitter tonight.'

'Iphigenia?' I asked. The woman who had asked the original question – one of Acton's assistants – had already turned away.

'My daughter.'

'Does she have a brother called Orestes?'

She looked at me, surprised, and smiled. 'Well done,' she said. 'Most people think I made the name up, or called her after some honeymoon island in the Aegean.'

'But in fact you're just a student of classical Greek

drama?' That sounded stupid. Or pompous. Or both.

'No. Her father's simply Greek.'

'Ah.' Only then did I notice the wedding ring on her left hand. 'How old is she?'

'Nearly seven.'

'Iphigenia. If I ever have a son, I'm going to call him Xerxes. Just so he can sign himself with the initial X. Mr X Todd. That would have everyone guessing, wouldn't it?'

That sounded even more stupid, but at least she laughed. 'Xerxes? What's wrong with Xavier? Or Ximedes?'

'Or Zephyrus?'

'That begins with a "Z".'

'Does it? Oh well.'

That was the end of the conversation. We were both laughing, both glancing at each other, both thinking of a thousand things to say next, but neither of us spoke. There was something there. We had established some sort of compatibility, and neither of us knew whether we were prepared to do anything with it. If we weren't then there was no point in talking. I don't remember who turned away first. I was inhibited by many things, by the image of a husband and a daughter somewhere out there in the world outside the restaurant, by her brother, by the very fact that I found her so attractive I was spellbound. That, I knew, was dangerous enough in itself without any other complications. And Diana? Well, she had ghosts enough of her own. No wonder we hesitated.

We didn't talk again that night. We seemed to spend the rest of the evening avoiding each other's eyes. And the following week, when I learned from Acton that she and her Greek husband were separated, had been for years, for longer than they'd been together as man and wife, were practically divorced, I began to wonder, now the danger had safely passed, whether I had avoided something which I'd miss for the rest of my life.

CHAPTER SIX

The next day was Tuesday. There was a morning mist so thick I couldn't see the length of the garden, let alone the wall around the grounds or the woods and hill beyond.

I carried the bucket across the lawn. The dogs must have heard me coming because there were already four dark shapes waiting up against the wire when the enclosure emerged from the mist. I couldn't see them properly but I could hear their snarls all too clearly – the only sound in that still, silent, cut-off world. I stopped when I reached the fence and began to hurl pieces of meat over the wire at them. I watched them chasing around the enclosure, four heavy shadows running in and out of focus through the fog. Their animation was weird in the stillness of the mist.

When the bucket was again half empty I carried it through the gate up into the woods and the small clearing. The damp mist had penetrated the wood and I could hear trees dripping around me. The patch of bare earth beneath the fallen tree was clear. That was a relief. Not even the bones from yesterday's meat had been left behind. Somewhere in the woods or deep beneath the hill were some very well-fed foxes or badgers. I emptied the bucket out on to the ground. Come and get it, Reynard.

The dogs started barking as soon as I came back in through the gate. The harsh noise shredded the silence of the mist. This morning they knew what had happened. Half-rations, the same as yesterday. They were still hungry and they knew who to blame. I ignored them and walked back to the house.

Diana and I bumped into each other at the gallery a week after that first meeting. I'd agreed to drop something off for Acton, and she was there when I arrived. I saw her through the plate glass doors before she saw me. She was leaning against the front desk, chatting to the receptionist. Was I fooling myself when I noted a nervous apprehension about her which said she was waiting for something or someone? And when I went in and she looked up, was I imagining the expression on her face – a mixture of relief, excitement and near-panic – which was enough to tell me who she had been waiting for?

I didn't, and still don't, think it was a coincidence – I'd never seen her there before – but we both pretended it was. In the first rush of excitement, before nerves or common sense or caution could deter me, I heard myself asking her what she was doing for lunch.

We didn't go anywhere special, just grabbed a snack at the nearest sandwich bar. It was her lunch hour, and she was already late. But every detail of the place seemed to take on an exotic, magical significance. I remember the bowl of anemones on the counter, the purple, mauve and scarlet glow of them; the smell of fresh coffee; the voices of the Italian youths chatting about the weekend's Inter Milan result as they served us.

We didn't talk about anything special either, but I couldn't remember a conversation I'd taken more delight in (even though it was an intense, almost anxious delight – there was nothing relaxed about it). It occurred to me that I hadn't smiled or laughed so much in ages, probably years. Diana smiled and laughed a lot too, and a little scarlet flush of nervous tension on each cheekbone seemed to suggest that she too wasn't used to being as cheerful and open as she appeared to be at that moment. We didn't talk about her brother, which might have seemed strange because at that time he was the only common ground between us. Perhaps we were trying to establish our own common ground, build links which had nothing to do with other people. We talked about her work; she was a copywriter in the marketing department of a big finance house in the City. We talked about the areas of London we lived in. We talked about our plans and preparations for Christmas, which was little more than a week away. And we talked about Iphigenia.

'Is she a good girl?' I asked.

'Oh yes. She's very cheerful and well-behaved. But . . .' Diana paused for a moment. 'I sometimes think she's too happy with her own company. She's too self-sufficient. She should have more friends . . .'

This was so obviously a cause of real concern for her that I didn't quite know what to say. 'There's nothing wrong with self-sufficiency,' I began, in an attempt to reassure her. 'It's the only foundation for honest relationships.'

She looked at me, nodding, serious for a moment. 'You mean, because it's a matter of choice then, not necessity?'

'Something like that.' I shrugged. For how often is one ever free to make a rational choice about the relationships which really matter? The irrational always seems to be a much more powerful force in such things. After all, whoever would rationally choose to fall in love? To step open-eyed and willing into all its liabilities and madness? But I said nothing. I hadn't wanted to strike a serious note in the first place, and I was sure I wasn't capable of the concentration necessary to see it through. Diana Artemis – the mere appearance of her – was too much of a distraction.

She was wearing a charcoal-grey trouser suit and a

cream silk blouse, beneath a rust-coloured woollen coat. Her hair was very dark and very thick, her face pale, her eyes blue. She was so beautiful. She looked so small and elegant, delicate yet not weak. I could see it all in her ankles as she crossed her legs, her wrist as she raised her coffee cup, her naked throat as she drank. So slender. I couldn't take my eyes off her. I found her so attractive I felt literally dizzy. Like a man on the edge of a cliff, about to jump off, caught between the joy of the impending free-fall, the call of the sunlight and warm water far below, and the voices which advised caution, common sense, the sanity of fear.

Somewhere beyond her friendliness, there seemed to be something guarded about Diana as well. In her case I guessed that it was more than just the natural hesitation and caution about what might be developing between us; it seemed to indicate something she wasn't prepared to talk about, something in her life or her past that she didn't want me or anyone to know. I sensed that it was most evident whenever the conversation seemed to be leading towards the question of her marriage and her husband. In fact, I was deliberately keeping the talk well away from that particular area. I was desperate to know more, but of course it wasn't my business, and if it ever became so then I was sure Diana would tell me in her own time and of her own free will.

'I can't believe I'm so late,' she said, shaking her head and laughing but making no move to go.

With a shock I realized that this conversation wasn't going to last forever. Desperate, I had a sudden idea. 'Does Iphigenia like animals? I mean, I go to the zoo pretty often, for my work, to sketch them, to see how they move, how they live together. Perhaps we could all go one weekend, a trip to the zoo, all three of us?'

She seemed delighted by the idea. 'Oh, she'll love

that. I'd love it. Yes.' Then she laughed again. 'For one dreadful moment, when you asked if she liked animals, I thought you were going to suggest buying her a puppy or a kitten or something for Christmas.' She smiled, and ran one hand back through her thick dark hair. 'I think it's a wonderful idea. I'll look forward to it.'

And so one cold day between Christmas and the New Year the three of us went to the zoo together. I met Iphigenia and was utterly charmed by her. She was very much her own person; she wasn't at all shy or nervous, but not bossy or a show-off either. She simply had what I thought was a healthy indifference to other people and their opinions. Not that she was selfish, far from it; when her mother told her I was going to draw the animals, she produced a box of coloured crayons and asked if I'd like to borrow them. Thank you very much, I said. I promised to look after them properly.

'I always feel a bit guilty at zoos,' I said. Diana and I were sitting on a bench outside the elephant enclosure. Iphigenia had wandered off on her own again to have another look at the ring-tailed lemurs. 'I know animals shouldn't be kept in cages, but I love to come and see them all the same.'

Diana didn't say anything. I turned and saw straight away that she wasn't listening. She was miles away. She was frowning and there was a thoughtful, serious, even slightly troubled look on her face which I was to learn was her normal expression in repose or when she was on her own. But as I watched, something in that look deepened and intensified until an expression of such utter sadness and desperation drifted across her features that I gasped in alarm. It was as if I'd been peering along a darkened corridor when a sudden shift of angle had sent a shaft of light down it to show a prison cell at the far end, a face behind the bars. Diana's face.

'What's the matter?' I exclaimed before I could stop myself.

She turned to me and the sadness and desperation were joined by an equally intense panic and agitation. Panic that I had managed to see what I had seen. I had a fleeting impression of doors slamming, of blinds being pulled down, of vulnerable creatures bolting for cover. Then her expression was, once again, no more than thoughtful, serious, perhaps slightly troubled.

'We'd better go and see what Iphigenia's up to.' She stood up, and I noticed her hands were shaking as she picked up her bag.

Neither of us spoke as we retraced our steps. A lion roared in the distance; a fierce, terrible, melancholy challenge, repeating itself over and over again. When we came in sight of Iphigenia, still face to face with the lemurs, Diana stopped and turned to me once again.

'There are always animals in your work,' she said. 'As prey, quarry. Not predators. I've heard your work described in terms of cruelty. But I can't see that. I see only compassion, sympathy, righteous anger.'

Iphigenia looked back over her shoulder, saw that we were following her, waved, and moved off again, skipping. We walked on.

'Do you know what your work reminds me of? There's something in the British Museum – an Assyrian frieze of a lion hunt, from the palace at Nineveh. Do you know it?'

I nodded. I knew it. I knew it very well indeed. Seeing it for the first time had been the greatest artistic experience of my life. I was staggered at her clairvoyance. At first I thought she was being underhand, that she must have heard her brother talking about me talking about it. But no – I had never discussed it with anyone. And no one had ever made the connection before. It was amazing.

'It's a cruel scene,' Diana was saying, 'but it's not a cruel piece of work. Honest, powerful, compassionate. But not cruel.'

The Assyrian king, Ashurbanipal, must have commissioned the artist for a relief carving to commemorate his prowess at lion hunting, the traditional sport of Assyrian kings. And that's what he got, in a very limited sense only, because it's obvious that it was the lions – their tragic agony – which really interested the artist, which really engaged his sympathy and skill. The king is reproduced as a mere cartoon, an empty convention, but the lions – the lions are real, you feel for them, their pain is terrible. You're on their side.

'I haven't seen them for a long time. But I'd like to look at them again. Perhaps – with you? Next weekend, perhaps?'

'Next weekend . . .' Diana frowned, and looked towards Iphigenia. 'Yes. I'd like that. But it will have to be just you and me. Not Iphigenia; it's her father's turn next weekend.' She took my hand. 'Thank you, Nick. Such weekends, when Iphigenia isn't there . . . they're hell for me. Seeing you will help.'

So that took us into the new year. And we saw each other most weekends after that, all three of us, unless Iphigenia was with her father. Diana and I had lunch together every week. In spite of everything, I think we were still trying to fool ourselves that what was developing was merely a friendship, because it was months before we slept together, before we admitted that it wasn't simply friendship and never could have been.

It's hard to describe the effect Diana had on my life. It was like some sort of miraculous rescue. It was as if I'd been living in a dark room and suddenly the curtains were opened and the windows thrown wide. A flood of light and fresh air. The compulsion to create dark and tortured images released its grip on me. My work paused, marking time as the possibility of a new direction began to emerge, promising a way out of an obsessive impasse and into something more celebratory, airborne, transcendental. Something I recognized as self-respect began to return. I felt the weakness and fear which had been eating away at me begin to fade and evaporate.

The affair seemed to have a similar effect on Diana. Intimacy first revealed her as someone haunted and withdrawn, as lost in some unknown obsession as myself. There were many unguarded moments when that shadow of sadness and despair returned. But I never questioned it again. I accepted it; I let it come and go without comment. I didn't want to push her for an explanation – I sensed that it would be dangerous to force her hand. All in good time, I thought. She'll tell me herself when she's ready.

But as the intimacy deepened and developed, she changed. She remained her essential self, quiet and serious, but she became relaxed, cheerful, less introverted. It seemed to be a release for her as well, a real exorcism even if I didn't know what ghosts were being exorcised. That shadow of sadness and despair became less and less frequent, until eventually it seemed to disappear altogether. I'd had no explanation for it; I learnt little about her marriage – her husband, Takis Artemis, was a wealthy second-generation Greek who owned a number of clothing factories around north London. She told me no more than that. But in the end I didn't think it mattered, because the shadow was no longer there.

That spring we all went away on holiday together. Myself, Diana and her daughter Iphigenia. We went to Spain – Galicia, the extreme north-west corner. Two weeks in an old whitewashed cottage which still belonged to a fisherman. It stood in a narrow rocky cove beside the Atlantic, a tiny but golden beach outside the front door and hills green with thick grass and oak woods at the back.

For two weeks we were a family. It was a strange experience, but a convincing one. I decided to wait until we'd been back a couple of weeks before doing anything about it; but after a fortnight of normal life the conviction was still there.

'I think we should get married.' It was Sunday afternoon, and we were taking a stroll along the South Bank. We'd stopped to look out across the Thames towards the Tower of London.

'Nick...' The reflections of a rapid sequence of hidden thoughts flashed across Diana's face as a series of fleeting expressions; first surprise, then joy, alarm and finally hesitation. 'What did you say?'

'Will you marry me?'

'Yes.' She laughed. 'Of course.' She hesitated, sighing. 'But...'

'But what?'

She didn't answer for some moments. 'I'm already married.'

'Is that a real obstacle? I mean, more than a technicality?'

Diana took my hand and walked on, looking straight ahead. She was thinking, seriously. 'I could ask for a divorce,' she said eventually. 'But... I know Takis wants Iphigenia to stay with him. I'm sure he would seize it as an opportunity for a custody battle.'

'There's no way he'd win, surely?'

She sighed again. 'Who knows? There's always a possibility, isn't there, with the law, if you know which way to push it? Which angle to take? You don't know Takis, Nick. He can be very dangerous. He's very sharp. He has power, influence, wealth. He's ruthless. He'll move heaven and earth to get his own way.'

'Are you sure about this?'

'Positive, Nick.' She stopped and turned to me again. 'I couldn't stand it, Nick. Losing her . . . the idea of it . . . it makes me feel ill. And Iphigenia . . . she couldn't bear it, I know. She'd hate it.'

'Her opinion would be decisive, surely?'

'I don't know, Nick. I'm just frightened. I'm terrified . . .'

We walked on again, in silence.

'Is it that Iphigenia wouldn't like it . . . you and me, married . . .'

'No, no, Nick. She'd love it. I know she would.' She sighed again. 'Listen, I do want to marry you. Believe me. I want it more than anything else in the world. But . . . but there are so many other things to consider . . .'

We said no more about it that afternoon. Indeed, we said very little about anything at all. It wasn't that either of us was sulking; she no doubt was too busy thinking things through – her anguish was genuine enough – and I simply didn't know how to help her with it. But by the evening she'd made her mind up.

'I've reached a decision, Nick,' she said. 'I'll ask Takis for a divorce. I owe it to the three of us.' She looked very frightened. We held each other tight. 'Wish me luck, Nick. Wish me luck.'

I spent the rest of the morning in the warmth of the kitchen, trying to read or listen to music on the ghetto-blaster I plugged in behind the freezer. But I couldn't concentrate. I kept on thinking forward to the afternoon when I'd have to get up on to the wall again, shirt-wrapped baton in hand. I could remember all too easily those snapping, frothing jaws, the mad, stupid eyes, the powerful haunches tensed to leap. What if one of them cleared an extra six inches this time? What if one of them grabbed the club? What if I dropped it? What if I overbalanced . . . ? I saw it all happening. I tried not to, but I couldn't help it. I had an early lunch and half a bottle of wine and decided to get it over with.

The mist hadn't lifted. The barking of the dogs came out of it to greet me even before I could see them. I collected the baton from the woodshed, crossed the lawn, scaled the wall. Rigid with determination. Not looking at the dogs, trying to ignore their terrifying racket. I concentrated on the wall at my feet, wet and slippery with leaf-mould, but aware of the angry milling beneath me. At last I had to look down at them. They were all staring up at me, heads raised, jaws open, bumping blindly into each other as they jostled for the prime position for attack.

I lowered the end of the club. The nearest one sniffed it, suspicious. I clouted him on the side of the head. Mad rage. Frantic high-pitched barking, snapping, leaping, as I quickly raised the baton. By now they'd started to jump up the wall. I was out of reach and they knew it but that didn't stop them – it just made them angrier and angrier. I hit out in a blind panic of fear and hatred, catching them on snout, ear, jaw, as they leapt up at me, as they tried to grab my ankle and drag me from the wall and tear me limb from limb. Smack, crack, thud. And then I left them to it while they were still mad for revenge and bursting with fury.

That was how I wanted them. I didn't hit them too hard, just hard enough to make them angry. I didn't want them hurt or frightened – they had to keep coming back for more. Not that anything could have hurt or frightened those animals. They'd have come back for more even if I'd broken their jaws and smashed all their teeth.

I stowed the club in the woodshed and stood in the doorway looking out at the mist. It was turning into rain, a heavy drizzle. Visibility hadn't improved. Darkness would come even earlier today. I could see the house and a little beyond it: a stretch of gravelled drive and a car . . . My heart lurched. A car parked out at the front. I could see it round the corner of the house. Visitors. Who were they?

I stepped back into the shadows of the shed. My first thought was to stay there until whoever it was grew tired of ringing the front doorbell and drove away again. But that wouldn't do. I had to find out who it was, how long they'd been there, what they might have seen.

I walked round the side of the house to the front. The car was an old Volvo, battered and muddy. There were two visitors. One was still in the driver's seat, the other – a girl, tall and slim, a big leather coat slung round her shoulders like a cape – stood at the front door. She heard my footsteps on the gravel and turned. It was Eileen Ward, the artist who had donated the picture for Acton's last charity auction. The rain had flattened her spikey scarlet hair and plastered it close to her skull. She smiled and waved. 'Hello!' She came forwards to the edge of the top step, leaving the shelter of the stone porch. 'Nicholas Todd! How are you?'

'Eileen.' I climbed up the steps towards her. 'You're out of luck, I'm afraid, if you're after Tony. He's away for the week. I'm house-sitting.'

'Ah.' She nodded slowly, disappointed. 'That's a pity.' She looked out, away from the house, through the mist and the rain. 'That is a shame.' Then she shrugged, turned back to me and smiled again. 'Oh well.'

I knew I'd have to invite them in. Come on in, out of

the cold, get dry, get warm, have some coffee. But I hesitated. I didn't need the interruption. I didn't want the disturbance. But there was no way round it. And there were things I had to know. How much had they seen? Did they see me out at the back? Did they see me with the dogs?

I heard the car door open and slam shut.

'What's the matter, Ellie? Where is he?' It was her boyfriend. He stood beside the car, hunched and shivering in the rain. I guessed the leather coat was his.

'He isn't here, Tim.'

'Where is he?'

'He's gone to Spain,' I answered. 'Madrid. He won't be back until Friday lunchtime.'

'Damn.' He frowned, the rain running down his face. 'Damn it.'

I suddenly felt sorry for them. 'Look, why don't you come inside? Get warm, dry out.' I took the house keys from my pocket. 'Have some coffee or something.'

'Well,' Eileen smiled, gratefully. 'That would be nice . . .'

'We can't, Ellie, we can't stop.' His voice was sharp with irritation. 'We've got to get back. Remember? We didn't really have time to come out here in the first place.' He turned back to the car and opened the door. 'What a waste of time.'

Eileen shrugged apologetically. 'Yes. Well. Thank you. I wish we could, but . . . Well. You know.'

'I'll tell Tony you called.'

She began to walk down the steps to the car, but paused on the last one. 'What's the matter with the dogs?'

'Dogs?'

'The barking. Are they all right?'

'Oh. Yes.' The dogs were still barking, louder than

ever. 'They're OK. They just get a bit carried away when I play with them. Don't want me to stop.'

'There could be something wrong. Would you like me to take a look at them? I have a sixth sense about dogs, you know. I used to work for a vet, some years ago.'

'No . . . no,' I managed, my brain scrambling in panic. I hadn't anticipated this. It could ruin everything. Everything. If she got anywhere near those dogs . . . At best she'll find out what I've been doing to them, at worst she'll be torn to pieces . . . 'They're fine. They get over-excited, that's all.'

'Are you sure? I'll check them out if you like. I know how Tony loves those dogs. It would be awful for you if anything happened to them while he was away. You wouldn't mind, would you, Tim?'

'All right. Poor things, they do sound disturbed.'

'Really, don't trouble yourselves. I'm sure they're fine.' Stay calm. Don't panic. 'They're probably just pining for him. Really. I'm sure they miss him.' Go away. Please. Just go. Get into your car and go away.

The moment seemed to freeze itself in time, Eileen standing at the bottom of the steps, a frown of concern on her face. Her boyfriend standing by the car, one hand still on the open door, head raised as he listened to the savage howling. The drizzle was now so continuous it seemed to hang suspended in the air.

Tim shivered. 'Come on, Ellie. It'll be dark soon. And I'm getting drenched.' And with that he climbed into the car and slammed the door shut behind him. I almost cheered with relief.

Eileen looked up at me. 'Don't hesitate to call us if you do get worried about them.' She opened the car door, but paused once again. 'You know, Nicholas, I'm beginning to get worried about you. You're not looking any better. You still look exhausted. Are you sure you're all right?'

I laughed. 'I'm fine. Really.'

'Well. Look after yourself. OK?' She got into the car and wound the window down to wave goodbye.

I waved back, watching the car pull away down the gravel drive. Its lights came on before it disappeared round the wood. It was already dark.

I let myself into the empty, silent house. Once I had dried off and made some coffee I found myself almost wishing that Eileen had accepted my hospitality. I liked her – her innocence, her friendliness. And I feared for her. Perhaps, as one of the few people who had seen into the very depths of Acton's true nature, I had a duty to warn Eileen and everyone like her. In case they ended up like me – not only victims of Anthony Acton, but willingly corrupted by him.

But of course there was no need to warn her. Soon – very soon – the whole world would be safe from Tony Acton.

That night a strong wind blew up over the Downs and came storming through the wood and around the house. It woke me in the early hours, and I lay there for some time, listening to the groaning of trees, the cracking of branches, the rattling of roof tiles. And as I slid off into sleep again, a new noise joined the edges of the storm's chorus – a howling and barking of savage, angry dogs. It scared me but it didn't keep me awake, so perhaps the sound came from my dreams and I was already asleep. Even there, there was no escape from that dreadful noise.

So that summer – last summer – Diana had begun divorce proceedings against her husband. The business dragged on for months. There were many meetings with lawyers, letters from lawyers, telephone calls to lawyers.

I could see it taking its toll on Diana, but whenever I tried to help she made it perfectly clear it was something she felt she had to handle on her own. So I kept well clear of the whole thing. And generally it kept well clear of me. Only once did it intrude on my day-to-day life, and that one exception was a bizarre encounter which struck me as utterly inexplicable at the time. One afternoon early that summer, I'd taken a break from the studio and gone to the pub across the road for a quiet beer. The pub itself had nothing much to recommend it; it was a spit and sawdust kind of place, and usually empty, but I liked it because it was good for a quiet drink on your own.

I hadn't been in there long when someone came and stood at the bar beside me. I didn't look at him, thinking it was someone waiting to be served. But then I noticed out of the corner of my eye that he had a drink already, and he was standing sideways on to the bar, facing me. I turned and looked at him. He was a good-looking man, tall and dark and well-built. He was wearing a dark suit. He had a gold bracelet round his wrist and gold rings on his fingers. He seemed tense and confrontational.

'Well, well, well,' he said, looking me up and down. 'So it's the boyfriend. My wife's boyfriend.' He nodded to himself. 'The man who wants to marry my wife.'

I realized with a shock that it was Diana's husband. Takis Artemis.

I had often wondered what he looked like. Diana had told me very little about him, and enquiries of my own had revealed nothing more than that he was a self-made man, worth a fortune, a serious tough guy who did karate and took great pride in being ruthless and successful in business. I hadn't noticed him when I first came into the pub, but he must have been waiting for me. For how long? Hours? Days?

'Whatever does she see in you, anyway?' He laughed and, reaching into a pocket for cigarettes, he seemed to relax. He lit up without offering the packet, inhaled, exhaled, squinted at me through the cloud of smoke. 'Well, whatever do you see in her, eh? Miss Iceberg.' He laughed again, a bitter laugh. He leaned forwards, lowering his voice. 'I mean, she isn't much fun in bed, is she? Oh, she does her duty all right. When she has to. But there's no enthusiasm, is there? No relish. No enjoyment. Eh? Let's be honest, my friend. Man to man. I know what she's like. I can remember.'

I said nothing. I didn't know what to say. My brain was a jumble of confused thoughts. What does he want? Is he going to get violent? Is he talking about Diana? He can't be. It doesn't make sense. And yet, perhaps . . .

But he wasn't expecting me to talk. He was staring through the smoke into the distance, remembering. There was an unsteadiness about him which suggested that this drink was not his first by a long way. I noticed for the first time the deep lines on his face which looked like scars of grief or bitter experience. There were flecks of grey in his black hair.

Eventually he spoke again. 'I'll tell you something, my friend. A little secret. I hired a detective soon after we were married, had her followed.' He shook his head, still staring into the distance. 'I've had hundreds of girl-friends, thousands, but Diana . . . She was so cold, so unenthusiastic, I was sure there was someone else. So I had her followed.' He drew heavily on his cigarette. 'But there was nothing. No boyfriends. No friends, really. And no girlfriends, either. You know, I was expecting that more than anything. I was almost certain she was gay. A lesbian. You know?' He sighed and stubbed out his cigarette. 'No. There was nothing. And that's it, I suppose. Some women just aren't interested. They just don't like it, and that's that. Nothing you can do about it.'

He seemed to have lost interest in me as anything other than someone who would listen to him talking about Diana. He was like a man in the grip of an obsession, hopelessly trying to exorcise it through speech. Perhaps that's why he's here, I thought. Not to check me out, not to start some sort of violent confrontation, but simply to talk about Diana.

'Well, I feel sorry for them. Them and their cold English inhibitions. English girls, they're all like that, aren't they? No sex, please, I'd rather have a cup of tea on the lawn with the vicar. Well, it's pathetic. I pity them.' A sneer replaced the puzzled frown on that ridiculously handsome face. 'And English men are just the same. If they were men, their women might be different. But they aren't. Are you? None of you have any balls. You'd rather have a jolly good game of cricket with your chums than a bloody good time in bed with some girl. Wouldn't you?' He laughed again and lit another cigarette.

And then, to my amazement, something in him collapsed. He leaned forwards on the bar and buried his face in his hands.

'I miss her so much. I've always missed her. What was wrong? I just don't understand. She didn't give, she didn't let me give. We were man and wife but I couldn't touch her. I just couldn't reach her.' There was a sob, and then a long intake of breath which became a sigh. And then silence before he wiped his hands across his face and took up a cigarette again. 'I loved her.' He shook his head. 'I wouldn't have left her. She left me, remember? I would never have left her, in spite of everything. Never. Why did she leave me? Why?'

He leaned back on his bar-stool and rubbed his hands over his face again. 'Oh, who gives a shit? Who gives a shit about her or anything?' Then he leaned forwards. 'Listen, my friend. Let me tell you something. A word of advice. Bitches like Diana, there's nothing you can do about them. The more you try, the more they fuck you up, and it's no one's fault but your own. A bitch like that, she finishes you off before you know it, and she doesn't even realize what she's done. You end up hating her. I hate her. Yes, my friend. I hate her now. I hate her so much you wouldn't believe it . . .'

I'd had enough of this. I put down my glass, picked up my newspaper and walked out.

'You'll end up hating her, boyfriend,' Takis shouted after me. 'You'll hate her so much you'll wish she was dead.'

CHAPTER SEVEN

Wednesday was clear and bright and sharp. The sky was cloudless and icy-blue, scoured by a wind which still had some bite left after its busy night. The sun was low and threw long shadows across the grass. The garden was littered with branches, broken flowerpots, twigs and odd scraps of paper left behind by the storm.

I fed the dogs from ground level again, hurling the meat up over the wire fencing. I watched them closely as they chased around the enclosure after the falling chunks. Three days of half-rations hadn't slowed them down. If anything it had given them a new edge – a fresh turn of speed and a desperate agility. There was no longer anything playful about the way they raced after the scraps and fought over them – food was now a deadly serious business.

I left them and carried the half-empty bucket up into the woods. Among the trees the storm damage was all the more obvious – a couple of conifers around the edge of the clearing had been uprooted and lay against their fellows at crazy, drunken angles. A reddish-brown shape slunk away from the patch of earth beneath the fallen elm as I approached. A fox. It had gone – disappearing into the undergrowth – before I realized what it was. Some of the meat I'd left the day before was still there. Perhaps the storm kept him away in the night, I thought. I imagined him lying low and hungry until it blew over and then coming out to feed in the daylight. Maybe he'll return to finish the meat as soon as I've gone. I emptied the bucket and withdrew to the far side of the clearing, crouching among the trees a yard or two into the wood, well-hidden but with a clear view. I watched and waited.

It was half an hour before he re-emerged from the undergrowth. He stood at the edge of the clearing for some moments, cautiously sniffing the air. Then he resumed his meal. He was a handsome creature, sharp and elegant in his red coat. Bushy tail, black ears, black socks, glossy black nose. It was strange, but watching this subtle and intelligent presence I felt none of the overwhelming fear and loathing which was my reaction to dogs. He ate his fill and then he slipped away. A shy and quiet shadow, so different from the loud, stupid, ugly, aggressive monsters which Acton kept as pets.

If they hadn't been so stupid and aggressive they'd have kept well away when they saw me climbing up on to the wall, club in hand. But they didn't. That afternoon we confronted each other yet again – me shaking with fear and sweating with concentration, the dogs barking, snarling, biting. Yet again they threw themselves at me in a murderous but futile frenzy; yet again I struck them on jaw, ear, nose – heavy blows which jarred my wrist and elbow. The focus of their aggression was changing – now they were falling over each other to attack the shirt-bound club rather than me.

The shirt was torn and beginning to disintegrate. It was soggy with saliva and froth and stained with mud and blood. I noticed this with satisfaction as I stowed the club in the woodshed. It meant that the dogs were channelling their hatred at the shirt, at the weapon used against them. Good. This was all according to plan. By now they would identify that shirt – its scent, its smell – with pain, hunger, violent attack, danger, hostility, frustration. Anyone or anything identified with it would be an enemy to be destroyed.

What I found when I went back into the house, however, was definitely not according to plan. I heard the music as soon as I opened the back door. An operatic aria. On disc, played very loud. And there was something else – it was very hot in there. Someone had turned the central heating full on.

I followed the music along the corridor and into the sitting-room. There was no one there. A compact disc boomed, there was a fresh log on the fire, but the room was empty. I went to the kitchen but there was no one there either. I went into one of the dust-sheeted rooms at the front of the house and looked out of the window. There, on the drive by the steps up to the front door, was Acton's Jaguar.

The sight of it hit me like a blow in the stomach. My legs felt weak, my head spun. I held on to the windowsill to steady myself. All the time Verdi pounded away in my head and I couldn't think. Forevermore I would associate that aria with disaster, panic, disintegration. Even now, whenever I hear it, my brow sweats and my hands shake.

I left the room and climbed the stairs to Acton's bedroom. The door was ajar. I knocked but no one answered. I went inside. It was empty. There was an open suitcase and clothes all over the bed. Only one suitcase, only women's clothes. The bathroom door was closed. I could hear running water and what sounded like Greta singing to herself.

Greta. So she'd come back early and alone. Why? Where was Acton? It didn't matter. None of it mattered. It was all the same – everything was ruined. The end of the perfect plan. There was no way I could complete it with Greta here. I'd have to drop it. Everything.

I went back down to the sitting-room. Pavarotti was still belting out of the hi-fi but I hardly noticed. I sat down and tried to get my thoughts together. What should I do? What could I do? Nothing. It was all over.

I sat there for some time, not thinking, not listening, doing nothing.

Eventually Greta appeared. She was wrapped in a big yellow towel, with her hair wrapped in another. She gave a gasp of alarm when she saw me. Clutched the towel tight. Then she saw who it was and giggled. 'Oh, it is *you*, Nicky.' She walked into the room grinning. 'You gave me a surprise, sitting there in the dark like that, so quiet.'

I hadn't noticed it get dark. I hadn't noticed Pavarotti fall silent. It wasn't until Greta put on the light that I realized how dark it had become. It wasn't until she spoke that I realized how much I'd become used to that silent house. The fire was burning low. I got up and put another log on it.

'And you still have your coat on.' Greta was trying to close the curtains but her towel kept slipping as she reached up. 'Were you asleep or something?'

'No.' I helped her draw the curtains. I was close enough to smell the perfume of clean, warm skin. Her shoulders were bare. Her arms and her chest were bare, and the towel didn't cover much of her legs. Her skin was brown and damp. There were drops of water on the nape of her neck.

'I bet you were,' she teased. 'Looking after those dogs, it must wear you out.'

It was only then that I realized she could have seen everything. One glance from any of the many rear windows. The window of this room, for instance. Had she? Had she seen me up on that wall, tormenting those dogs, turning them into time bombs primed with murderous hate?

'Those dogs,' she said. 'I heard them barking when I arrived. I guessed you were out there with them. I would have come round and said hello but I hate those creatures. I hate the sight of them. Still, at least you must be getting on with them. I don't know how you can. Ugh!' She gave a little shiver of horror and disgust.

We were standing quite close. It was sweltering in there – I didn't know what she'd done to the central heating. I should have taken my coat off, but I didn't. 'Welcome home,' I said. 'How was Madrid?'

'I was bored.' She turned away and walked over to the fireplace. 'And Madrid was cold. It was freezing. It reminded me of Warsaw. Ugh!' She gave another shiver of disgust. 'Cold and boring. So I came home.' She stared down into the fire, stroking the back of her neck with her left hand. The gold and diamonds on her wedding-ring finger caught the light. She sighed. 'I must get dressed. But what shall I wear?'

I didn't answer. I wasn't going to get caught up in that sort of discussion. She was talking to herself but it was the kind of comment husbands are supposed to pick up on. And I wasn't her husband.

She disappeared upstairs and I went into the kitchen and hung my coat up on the back of the door, made some coffee and started to cook. There was more than enough for two. Especially if I was going back to London the next day. No need for a house-sitter any more, with Greta here.

Greta reappeared. She'd put her hair up, painted her fingernails and toenails, but hadn't exactly dressed. She was wearing a big, thick towelling dressing-gown. A man's garment, striped red and blue. It came right down to her bare feet and she'd had to roll the sleeves back to her wrists.

'I could not decide what to wear.' She laughed. 'Pathetic, I know, but I have been travelling all day, and I am home now and I just want to be comfortable.'

'I've made coffee. Help yourself.'

'Marvellous.' She filled a mug and came over to see what I was doing. 'What is this, Nicky? A romantic dinner for two?'

I stopped stirring the sauce. 'Didn't you get enough of those in Madrid?'

That didn't amuse her. She turned away and began to lay the kitchen table. There was something defiant in the way she rattled around in a drawer for some candles, stood them in the middle of the table, lit them and turned off the lights. She opened a bottle of wine from the fridge and poured it into our glasses. I served up the salmon steaks and the vegetables and we sat down to eat.

'Tony tried to ignore me from the moment we left,' Greta said, almost pouting, as she stabbed at a segment of orange and angrily squeezed it over the salmon. 'He sulked because I had insisted on going with him. I thought it would be fun. A bit of a holiday. But it was no holiday. It was boring and cold. Tony moaned on about the cold even more than I did. But when I suggested we went to Marbella for a couple of days he wouldn't listen to me. I wanted to go to Marbella. I really wanted to go to Marbella.'

I didn't know whether to believe her. I couldn't afford to take anything at face value where Acton was concerned. If there was something odd about Tony and Greta going away together, if there was something odd about asking me to house-sit for the week, then there was certainly something odd about Greta coming home early. I watched her carefully but in the candlelight it was impossible to read any insincerity in her face.

She saw me looking at her. 'Have you been to Marbella, Nicky?'

'No. I've been to Spain but not the Mediterranean.' As I spoke I tried not to think about where I had been in Spain. Only last spring but already it seemed like a lifetime ago. I fought against memories of a whitewashed fisherman's cottage, green hills, a rocky inlet. The Atlantic cold and fresh. Seagulls and seaweed on the cleanest sand . . .

'You think it is common, don't you? Marbella. You think it is vulgar of me. That is what Tony said. But you see, Nicky, when I was growing up in Warsaw, a teenager, I read about Marbella. In some English magazine I think it was, I read about it and it seemed to me to be everything I wanted in life, everything that did not exist in Poland.' She laughed. 'You know, glamour and excitement, the sun, beaches, casinos, nightclubs. Rich men, fast cars, beautiful women. Arab sheikhs, film stars, bullfighters, flamenco dancers, fugitive gangsters. I used to dream about it, every night, as a teenager. And still I have never been there. Do you understand, Nicky?'

'It's a good reason for never going there. Reality can be very disappointing.'

'Tony doesn't understand. He doesn't understand anything about me. I *hate* him.' A familiar mood was settling over her. The bright and artificial girlishness was fading and something of her true self – something heavy and brooding and Slavic – was beginning to show through. 'I wish he was dead. I could kill him. I mean it. I want to kill him.' She looked me straight in the eye. There was nothing in her expression to suggest that she was joking or exaggerating or anything other than totally serious. She was waiting for some sort of response. No – she was waiting for a positive response. 'I mean it, Nicky.'

I forced myself to laugh. 'You shouldn't go around saying that sort of thing, Greta. Someone might believe you.'

'I am not saying it to anyone, Nicky. I am saying it to you. Don't you believe me? You, of all people? I know you hate him, Nicky. I see it every time you look at him. You wish he was dead, Nicky, just as I do. Why don't you admit it?'

I stood up and walked over to the other side of the kitchen and took a bowl of fruit from the top of the fridge. Neither of us had cleared our plates, but I needed the movement and the time to think. I needed to get away from the table so Greta couldn't see me deliberating.

Was she serious? Was she offering some sort of alliance? Was she trying to recruit me? Or was she Acton's *agent provocateur*, sent home early to flush me out, to manoeuvre me into revealing my hand? It was impossible to say. How much did she know? Was she really against Tony? Or was she secretly for him? And if so, how much did he know? How much did he suspect?

I carried the bowl of fruit across the room and put it on the table. I sat down again. She was still looking at me. I picked up my knife and fork and examined my plate. Pink salmon, green peas, white potato, orange carrot. Shadows flickering over them in the candlelight. Form, colour, light. I still thought like a painter, even if I could no longer paint like one.

'I think he has corrupted you, Nicky. I don't know how. You tell me. But I know him and I know you and I have a feeling for these things. I think he has got his hands on your soul. And he is eating it up. You have got to cut free, Nicky, and there is only one way to do it.'

I speared a scrap of pink flesh but I couldn't eat it. My hand was shaking. 'Perhaps your imagination's doing overtime.'

'No. I have seen it before. I know what can go rotten in the soul of an artist when he makes the wrong bargains.' She loaded a fork with salmon and potato, raised it to her mouth, chewed, swallowed. 'My father was an artist, a painter. In Poland. Did you know that?'

I shook my head. I didn't.

'Yes. A model socialist artist. He belonged to the Communist Party, he sat on committees of the artists' union, he said the right thing about the state and the system, both within the country and outside. Yes, they let him travel abroad with exhibitions and cultural exchanges. Paris, Rome, London. They knew he was a good boy, they knew he would behave himself. His work wasn't remotely subversive. He publicly condemned the dissidents, he laughed at samizdat art.'

She chewed and swallowed another mouthful, nodding to herself. 'Of course he was well rewarded for his good behaviour. The usual privileges – foreign travel, a dacha among the pinewoods in the mountains, no queuing for new cars, holidays at the artists' lakeside retreat. Parties with the country's so-called élite. And plenty of work – commemorative murals for conference centres and hotels, designs for the state theatre and film studios, private commissions from party officials. Exhibitions at the best galleries.'

Another thoughtful pause, another forkful chewed slowly and silently.

'Of course he never really believed in Marxism. He was simply playing by the rules. He knew the system he had sold himself to was corrupt and unjust, but its rewards made that easy to live with. At least, it did for some time. And then he began to change. When I was a teenager he began to crack up. I think he started to realize that the work he was doing for them was no good. The dishonesty and mediocrity of the world he had ingratiated his way into came out in what he created. That began to eat away at him like a disease. He realized that no one respected him, that he was despised both by the people he had sucked up to and by the people who had taken a stand against them. Times were changing – these were the early days of Solidarność, you see – the dissidents were beginning to make themselves heard. And their work had integrity and vitality and significance – everything that his did not. It was then that he realized what a disastrous bargain he had made.

'He tried to do something about it. As if it wasn't already too late. He tried to get a job with André Wajda, who was making *Man of Marble* at the time. You remember that film? Well, there was no place for establishment toadies on a project like that, was there? He didn't get the job. Nothing but an angry silence. Finally he realized that it was too late. The wind was changing – Lech Walesa was taking on the government singlehanded – and to change with it would simply look like another kind of opportunism. By this time he hated the system as much as the dissidents did, but for the wrong reasons – not because it was tyrannous, unjust and corrupt, but because it had paid him to misuse his talents and he had accepted its payment.'

She speared the last of her salmon.

'He killed himself. It was a lonely death. He got into his car, drove out to the dacha in the mountains, drank half a bottle of champagne and blew his brains out. It was days before his body was found – by his mistress, the very young wife of a very old military man, a general. My mother and I never knew where he was from one week to the next, but she always had a good idea where to find him. I suppose I should be grateful for that at least, or it might have been me or my mother who tripped over the body.'

She took a drink of wine.

'A sad story, don't you think? Yes, he was a coward and an opportunist, but he was the victim of more than just his own weakness. He should have struck out, he should have fought back, he should have done something before it was too late. Don't you think?'

She stopped talking and there was only silence. I didn't say anything. I didn't suppose she wanted me to. She had talked and I had listened, which meant she was in control. There was a moral to the story and she knew it hadn't escaped me. Now I listened to the silence. I could hear the wind in the darkness outside the house. The barking of dogs came and went, faintly and briefly, before the wind veered in another direction. Then Greta spoke again.

'That was a magnificent meal, Nicky. As good as anything I have eaten this week, in one of the best hotels in Madrid. *Better*. Thank you.' Her plate was clean. Greta was a woman who really ate food, she didn't just pretend or go through the guilty and pointless ritual of leaving half of everything on her plate at the end of the meal. She never dieted and was scornful of those who did.

Many people who didn't know Greta well often underestimated her. I'd never made that dangerous mistake but only now was I beginning to realize that her ponderous, rather absent-minded manner was in fact the caution of an extremely calculating personality. Far from being half a dozen steps behind everyone else and always trying to catch up, she was half a dozen steps ahead and already thinking ahead over the next dozen.

'I have some brandy which will do justice to the meal.' She had peeled an orange and was eating it segment by segment. 'Duty free Spanish cognac. Carlos V. The best. I think we should open it in front of the fire in the other room. Forget the washing up.'

I made coffee and carried it through. She was sitting on the floor with her back against the sofa. She hadn't turned the light on, but the fire cast a bright glow into the room which pushed the darkness into the corners and filled the space between with warm shadows. I put the coffee with the brandy bottle and the two glasses on the low table beside her. She turned from the fire to pour the cognac, then gazed thoughtfully into the flames as she warmed her glass between her hands.

I sat down on the sofa. 'How was the Spanish sculptor? The one who makes dinosaurs out of industrial scrap or whatever?'

'Oh!' she laughed quietly. 'That was a complete red herring. Someone had got their lines crossed. He has moved on from dinosaurs. All his work is abstract now, constructed from rural *objets trouvés*. It is supposed to be green but Anthony dismissed it as old hat. He was expecting post-modernist wit, he said, not revisionist whimsy. There was a terrible row about it. Angry Spanish passion and all that.'

'So it was all a waste of time?'

'Well.' She frowned, still staring into the flames. 'Not exactly. Tony found a video artist he became very enthusiastic about. He saw three of this character's installations and they signed a deal. Just like that. I don't know what he saw in them. A dozen screens. News footage announcing the death of Franco, more news footage showing people in Madrid casting their votes in the 1983 election and some original film of a nude transsexual revue in Barcelona.' She sighed. 'Socio-political commentary is not art, it is journalism. And this was a pretty poor example of it. I told him, but he wouldn't listen.'

'It isn't like Tony to fall for that sort of crap.'

'I don't think he fell for the art. I think he fell for the artist.' She raised her glass, taking a sip of the cognac without turning from the fire.

That didn't sound like Tony either. I tasted the

brandy. Greta had fallen silent. 'Carmen reincarnated, was she? All flashing eyes and raven hair?'

Greta turned to face me and there was a wry smile on her face. 'Not she. *He.* The video artist was a man. *Un hombre.* Very good looking, I must admit. Built like a bullfighter, thin but strong. Long dark hair.'

The fire hissed and crackled as some burning logs shifted and settled.

'Are you saying . . . ?'

'I don't know. Is my husband gay? You tell me.' She raised her glass and gazed intently at the firelight reflected in the brandy. 'Sometimes I think . . . Sometimes I'm certain . . . But I just don't know. He doesn't seem at all interested in me as a woman, in any way. From one week to the next he doesn't lay a finger on me. And when he does, it doesn't make anything better. There's nothing of himself in it, when we do it. He just isn't there. And it isn't because he's growing tired of me, because nothing has changed. It has been like this since the beginning. I thought it would change when we got married but it hasn't.' She sighed and drank some more brandy. 'And it isn't because there are other women. I'm sure there aren't. I know there aren't.' Then she turned suddenly to me. 'Has he ever made a pass at you?'

'Me?' I laughed. 'Ridiculous!' I got up and stabbed at the fire with the poker. A glowing log crumbled into embers and sent flames leaping up the log above. 'That's absolutely ridiculous.'

When I sat down again Greta edged along the floor so her back was against the sofa beside me and her shoulder was by my knee. Her crossed legs were stretched out along the carpet in front of her, her toes pointing towards the fire, and the edge of her dressing-gown had fallen away from her knees.

'Oh, who cares,' she said, helping herself to more brandy. 'To hell with him. To hell with Anthony Acton.' She knocked back her glass. 'He wouldn't take me to Marbella; he wanted to stay in Madrid with the macho video-man. To hell with him.' She shifted slightly and her head was resting on my knee. I couldn't see her face – she was staring into the fire. Her hair looked soft and golden. 'After the row I went out and bought myself some underwear – very expensive French underwear. I always do that after a row. It usually cheers me up. But it didn't this time. So I thought I'd come home.' She sighed. 'It's all such a shame. It's such nice underwear too. I'll show you.'

She stood in front of me, giggling, and opened her dressing-gown. I almost dropped my glass. Red silk. Golden skin, curves, deep shadows. Soft undulations as she laughed.

She knelt down in front of me, her elbows on my knees. She looked up, smiling, expectant. 'Why don't you kiss me?'

'I don't think that would be a good idea.'

Something flickered across her face, a minute tightening of the muscles, the shadow of a blink, but the smile remained in place. 'Oh, Nicky. We're both grown ups, aren't we? Why don't we enjoy ourselves while we can? No one need ever know. We can both forget about it tomorrow. Let's have some fun.' She pressed herself closer.

I didn't move. 'But will you still respect me in the morning?'

She stiffened and looked up. She saw the expression on my face and her smile disappeared. A quiver of anger passed through her. She stood up.

'All right,' she said, her brows frowning and her eyes narrowed. 'All right.' She spoke quietly but she was already trembling with an approaching rage. She looked down at me with something like hatred. 'You bastard.'

I held her gaze. Was it the hatred of a slighted woman or the hatred of someone whose carefully laid plans had gone off the rails, whose deception had failed? Was it *both*? She turned away and stormed from the room. That was that. No screaming, no violence, no tears. I was grateful for that at least.

I helped myself to more brandy. Greta had left her glass behind – there was a smear of scarlet lipstick around the rim. I shook my head. I could still see that red silk, that golden skin. I shook my head again. Think. Think hard. What was behind that little cabaret?

There were three possible explanations. One, she was seducing me for the hell of it, for the fun. Well, if I was arrogant enough I might just swallow that. But I wasn't and I didn't. Two, she was seducing me to get me on her side for whatever she might have planned against her husband. Three, Acton had instructed her to seduce me, to get a spy into his enemy's camp, and she had been lying to me all evening. Could a man do such a thing? Would Acton prostitute his own wife like that? Yes. He would. He would relish the perversion of it. And Greta, could she do such a thing? Would she enjoy doing such a thing? Yes, she would. They would both find the idea of it very exciting.

Well, to hell with them. My game was finished and I was no longer interested in theirs. Tomorrow I was going back to London and all bets were off.

I got up and went down the passage to the kitchen. The table was still littered with plates and glasses and used cutlery. Saucepans were piled in the sink. Leave it, I thought. She can do the washing up herself tomorrow, after I've gone. Leave the dishes; you've got to pack.

Before I turned in I filled the bucket to the brim with

frozen meat for the last time. Tomorrow the dogs would be fed and fed full rations. It made me mad but there was nothing I could do about it. There was nothing I could do about anything. The dogs will get what they don't deserve and Acton won't get what he does deserve. Nobody gets their just deserts in this world and I was a fool ever to think I could change that.

CHAPTER EIGHT

The next day was Thursday. There was no sign of Greta when I got up. I made coffee and toast and sat at the kitchen table still littered with the remains of dinner. I wondered whether to phone Stanley the journalist and cancel the next day's appointment. There was no point in it any more.

Greta still hadn't appeared by the time I'd finished so I made some more coffee – and more toast – and carried it upstairs on a tray. I knocked on the bedroom door. There was no answer. I knocked again and waited. Still no answer. I opened it and went in. The big double bed was piled high with blankets, duvets and clothing. The pile shifted and a fur coat slid to the floor. Greta struggled to sit up. She was wearing no make-up and her hair was a mess. She glared at me through tired eyes. 'What do you want?'

'Breakfast.'

She peered at the tray in my hands. 'Is that coffee hot?' she asked sharply. 'I'm freezing. I have been freezing all night.' She was wearing a man's cotton shirt, buttoned at wrist and throat. She cleared the bed in front of her and I put the tray down. 'This bloody ancient house. No one should be living here. We should leave it to fall into a ruin.' She poured herself some coffee and drank half a mugful, black. 'Have you come to apologize for last night?'

'Last night? What happened?'

She nodded slowly and refilled her mug. 'You might be a bastard, Nicky, but you make good coffee.' Then she sighed, shook her head and ran one hand back through her tangled hair. 'Oh, what am I saying? You are not a bastard. You are one of the few non-bastards I know. Perhaps *I* should apologize for last night. I should have known better.'

'Forget it.'

'Well, thank you for breakfast. You are a real gentleman. And I am an ungrateful bitch.'

I turned to leave as she reached for some toast but she said, 'No, don't go. I hate waking up on my own.' She spoke with some anxiety. 'Stay until I've finished. Please.'

I sat down on the bed, uncertain. I wondered what the time was. Now I just wanted to get clear of the place.

Greta spread butter and then marmalade on the toast, very thoroughly. 'Why aren't you married, Nicky?'

I shrugged.

'How old are you?'

'Thirty-one.'

'Thirty-one and not married. A man like you. Ridiculous.' She laughed, munching the toast. 'How have we let you get away with it for so long? You would make some lucky girl a marvellous husband. Why, no wonder Diana was so upset when you . . . Oh.' She stopped. She actually looked surprised. 'I am sorry. I didn't think that bothered you any more. I really didn't.'

I stood up. 'Listen, I have to get back to London. Now you're here. I have to pack and . . .'

'Ah.' She paused, toast in hand, suddenly serious again. 'Can't you stay?' The sharp note returned to her voice. 'You see, I shan't be here. I want to get back to Holland Park before Tony returns tomorrow. I couldn't stand another day here. The cold, the countryside, the quiet. Ugh. And anyway, I couldn't feed those dogs even if I was here. They terrify me. I never go anywhere near them.'

I sat down again on the bed, rather heavily. I didn't

say anything for some moments. 'So you still need a house-sitter?'

'Please, Nicky. Honestly, I would be bored stiff hanging around here until Tony gets back. No criticism of your company but Andrea is staying at Holland Park and it would be fun, just the two of us, without Tony or anyone. And I am sure she would appreciate the company. Poor Andrea.'

I laughed. 'Poor Andrea?'

'Oh, she's not so tough. She puts on a good act but she's only being brave. Mr Alvarez gave her a very bad time. I could tell you stories about their marriage which would make your hair stand on end. The way he treated her, you would not believe it. Even now she cries herself to sleep most nights. So don't be taken in by the tough ol' southern gal routine.' She sighed. 'So I don't like her being on her own. I think I should be keeping her company. So you will stay here?'

'I have to be back in London for lunch tomorrow . . .'

'That's fine. I have to pick up Tony from the airport, so I'll drive down to Gatwick with Andrea tomorrow, meet Tony at midday and then we'll be back here for the weekend. So that's fine.'

I nodded and stood up. 'You'll want to get moving then. I'll leave you to it.'

'Oh, would you open the curtains, Nicky? That might help me to wake up.'

I opened the curtains and looked out over the still-frosty lawn, the dog enclosure, the high wall, the wooded slope beyond. I could see the dogs moving around restlessly behind the wire fencing. All right, you monsters, play is resumed. The game continues. The meter is ticking once again, Tony Acton, and tomorrow you'll have to pay the full fare. Every last penny of it.

★

I had very little contact with Tony Acton during the first months of my relationship with his sister. It wasn't something I missed. My work was clearly going through some sort of transition, so I had no professional need for a dealer at that time. And socially, the less I saw of him the better. I was too wrapped up in Diana to give him much thought anyway. The only thought I did spare him was the bizarre one that we were soon to be brothers-in-law. All in all, I could hardly have seen less of him had we been deliberately avoiding each other.

Had I given it any consideration, I might have realized that it was only a matter of time before he tried to drag me into yet another piece of deception. But spring came and went without any such demand, as did most of the summer, and I was beginning to think that at last I might have seen the back of such projects.

I was wrong. One day in August he appeared in my studio. He was trying to be as cool as ever but he was clearly very excited.

'Listen, Nick,' he began as soon as I let him in. 'This could be the big one. The ultimate. You know the Buruki Institute – you know, the people who paid that ludicrous record sum for the Odilon Redon last autumn – I've heard they're on the prowl for European modernism. I've been checking up on Haramaka – Yukio Haramaka, their director. Went through his background with a fine-tooth comb. Know what I found? The dissertation he wrote for his first degree – History of Art – was all about the English avant garde. He had it printed, paid for by himself, while he was still at Tokyo University. Vain bastard. I got hold of a copy. Had it translated. Read it. Guess what? He's a huge fan of the Vorticists . . .'

I wasn't listening to him. I wasn't interested. I let him ramble on as he strode around the studio, stirring up all that hot air. It was like a greenhouse in there that summer. Acton's hyperactivity wasn't welcome – it was stifling in there without him. Don't we have other things to talk about? I thought. Why don't you ask about your sister? Why haven't we ever talked about Diana and her past and her future? You couldn't care less, could you? You aren't interested in anyone other than yourself. You selfish bastard.

'You see, I know what Haramaka dreams about,' he was saying. 'I can guess what he really wants. A big Wyndham Lewis. A huge picture. Oil on canvas. Unknown. Recently discovered. And I think we can find it for him. What do you think? I think we can do it. Don't you?'

I laughed and shook my head. 'No,' I said.

'Of course you can, Nick. Of course you can do it.' He came striding towards me, every gesture urging, encouraging. 'The pieces you've done in the past – they've been so convincing, utterly convincing, fooled everybody, no breath of doubt or suspicion about any of them. OK, this would be an altogether bigger job than anything you've done before, but you're ready for it. It's a challenge you're more than equal to. Of course you could do it.'

Then he was off again, striding round the studio, getting his thoughts together. 'Think about it. The whole deal could be absolutely huge. It's a perfect opportunity to "discover" a really major painting. Perfect.' He laughed. 'So perfect I can't believe it. Why? I'll tell you why. Three reasons.' He swung round, paused for breath, stood facing me. 'One, Lewis has been an ignored figure for half a century – no one will be surprised or suspicious if a large-scale work of his suddenly appeared on the market. Two, it's known he painted large-scale canvases before the war, but no one knows what happened to them – it's assumed they're out there somewhere, lost rather than destroyed. Three, the Buruki Institute would pay a high price for it – a rare canvas by a major modernist would give them exactly what they want. Alone among Japanese collectors, they would prove themselves as daring and discerning players. It would be a big deal. A very big deal. A deal we have to pull off.'

I shook my head again. 'You don't understand,' I said. 'I probably could do it. But I'm not going to. It's immoral and it's illegal.'

He spun on his heels, stared at me, froze. He could see that I was perfectly serious. He could see that at last I had the self-respect and the courage and the strength to stand firm. He could see that the weakness and the fear were no longer there. Even if he didn't know what or who had saved me. Diana . . .

He exploded with fury. 'Immoral? Illegal?' he shouted. The hot air inside the studio seemed to shake and quiver with the violence of his outburst. It bulged and quaked until I thought the glass ceiling was going to shatter. 'Where did you get your fucking high horse from all of a sudden? How dare you . . . ! After everything . . . ! You stupid shit! How dare you!' He was yelling, shaking with rage. Suddenly he was right in front of me. We were face to face. 'You bloody will do it! You'll bloody do it, or . . .' He made a grab for my shirt-front but I knocked his hands aside. I took a step back but kept one hand raised in warning.

He stood there glaring at me, wrestling for self-control. He was still shaking, and when he spoke again his voice was a hoarse whisper, barely audible. 'You've got to do this one for me, Nick. If it's the last one you ever do. You've got to do it. Just this one, then no more. That's it.'

I shook my head again.

'I'll drop you, Todd. I'll have you out of the gallery quicker than they chuck tramps out of the Savoy.'

I simply shrugged. I'll call your bluff on that one, I thought. The truth was that such threats no longer worried me. Self-respect and courage . . .

He raised a threatening finger and jabbed it at me. 'And I'll make sure no other decent dealer will represent you. Ever.'

I laughed. 'Is there such a thing as a decent dealer?'

'I'll blow the whistle on our previous collaborations. You'll be branded as a forger. You'll be ruined.'

'No you won't, Tony. For the simple reason that *you'd* be ruined as well.'

He glared at me for some time in silence until he was sure that he had control of himself once again. Then he nodded. 'You'll regret this, Todd.' His voice was quiet and cold. 'You will do this for me. I'll make you do it. You'll see. And you'll bitterly regret you ever tried to say no to me.'

Then he left.

Soon after that, in September, Diana and I went away for a fortnight to a cottage in Worcestershire in the shadow of the Malvern Hills. For Diana, it was a break from the traumas of divorce. For me, it was a break from the threats of her brother. By the time we returned to London, I was all the more determined to let Acton do his worst.

At the beginning of October I had a message from him to meet up one evening the following week in the gallery. I was tempted to ignore it, but didn't. We're going to be brothers-in-law, I thought. I have to give him the benefit of the doubt.

If only I hadn't. If only I had written him off as dangerous and untrustworthy and left it at that.

*

134

Greta was gone by eleven o'clock. I watched her car disappear round the long drive and then I carried the heavy tin bucket from the kitchen and across the lawn still bright with frost, and past the dogs' enclosure. I didn't stop at the wire fencing but walked straight on to the wooden door in the stone wall.

The dogs went mad. They saw me unbolt the door and step out into the woods and they went crazy. They knew they weren't going to be fed. The bucket had gone and there was nothing to eat. Not a thing. Not even the half-rations of the last three days.

I carried the bucket up the wooded slope to the clearing and emptied the lot on to the earth. Double rations for the fox today. Which was just as well, because there wasn't much more to come.

After lunch I collected the club from the woodshed. It was the last time I'd be needing it. I carried it across the lawn, scaled the water-butt and edged along the wall to the enclosure. The animals were waiting for me. I looked down at them.

All week I had been concerned by two possible flaws in my plan. First, that keeping them hungry – which was intended to put a lethal edge on their killer instinct – might leave them too weak for violence. Second, if I was too heavy with the club I might break their spirits and, far from tearing into anything which smelt of that now-tattered blue shirt with all the built-up anger and hatred of five days of frustration, they might run away whimpering and cowering.

Now I knew there was no cause for concern. No cause whatsoever. They were frothing at the mouth and rolling their eyes and snarling even before I climbed up on to the wall. They were circling round and jumping over each other and up at me even before I was standing over them. I lowered the club and they disappeared in a whirling mass of violence and fury without even waiting for a sniff of it.

I gave each one a smart blow on the snout and then withdrew. My job was done. A rolling storm of ear-splitting barks and angry howls followed me all the way back across the lawn.

I ducked back through the low door into the wood-shed. In the semi-darkness within I unbound the ragged shirt from the club and took a hatchet from a chopping block in the corner. I pulled off the balaclava helmet I'd been wearing and wiped the sweat from my face. I laid the club on the block and struck it with the hatchet.

An explosion burst from the low rafters above and behind me. I yelled in alarm and ducked and half-turned in time to glimpse the rapid beat-beat of big brown wings as a dark shape flew out of the door and away into the daylight. An owl. A barn owl. I gasped with relief. Perhaps it had been sitting up in the rafters for days and days, watching, still and silent, as I came and went. Peering through the shadows, I could now see that the rafters in one corner and the ground beneath were spat-tered with white birdshit. I knelt down and among the sawdust and wood shavings and pools of guano I found a furry pellet the size of my thumb. I picked it up and put it in my coat pocket. Then I returned to the block and chopped the club into four short pieces.

I carried them indoors and built up the fire in the sitting-room until it was roaring. I threw the pieces into the flames and watched them burn to cinders. Then I flung the remains of the shirt into the fire and waited until the flames had devoured it too.

It was getting dark. I shut myself in the kitchen and poured a glass of scotch. An owl hooted outside. The pellet . . . My coat was hanging on the back of the door.

I reached into the pocket, took out the furry pellet and looked at it. It felt light and dry and hard.

Owls eat their prey whole. Mice, voles, small birds – they all go down in one go. The indigestible bits – fur, feathers, bones – form a solid pellet which the owl coughs up and spits out.

I spread some paper on the kitchen table and put the pellet down on it. I opened a penknife and carefully crumbled the pellet into a small pile of dust. I sifted through it, separating out the tiny bones. There was a good collection of them, all fine and fragile little things – ribs, a spine, minute thigh bones. And a skull. A whole skull, tiny but complete. I picked it up between my thumb and forefinger and gently blew away the dust clinging to it. It was fantastically delicate. Beautiful and perfect. Little teeth, lower jaw intact, eye holes leading into the tiny, hollow cranium. I put it in the palm of my hand, held it up to the light and had a good look at it.

A mouse's skull. Not so very long ago it had been part of a mouse. A living part of a living creature. A mouse had lived in there. The collection of instincts, sensations and nervous impulses which was a mouse's being had known a world of fear, hunger, pain and lust in this piece of divine machinery no bigger than a fingernail. And now it was as clean and cold and functionless as a piece of abstract sculpture. Death had taken that world and moved on. Blown away those instincts and impulses like so much dust. And what a death. Flapping wings, striking talons, the snap of a beak. Darkness.

I sat there looking at it for a long time. Just looking at it. I was going to sketch it – that's what I'd planned from the moment I'd begun to search among the sawdust in the woodshed – but I didn't. I didn't even move from the table to get a pencil and paper. Even if they'd been to hand I wouldn't have bothered. I just sat there, looking at the skull and thinking. Thinking: This time tomorrow Tony Acton will be dead. This time tomorrow it'll be over. I don't know how long I sat there but it must have been hours and the one thought seemed to last all that time.

I came to, as if from a deep sleep, when the phone started ringing. I picked it up. 'Hello?' My own voice seemed to come from a long way away.

'Nick. Hello, mate.' It was Acton.

I was suddenly wide awake. 'How's Madrid?'

'Oh, not bad. OK, I suppose.' He sounded uncharacteristically hesitant. After he spoke there was a pause so deep that for one moment I thought we'd been cut off.

'And you?'

'Oh, I'm all right, Nick. Yes.' His voice was flat. He sounded tired, even sad. 'Just phoning to see how things are. How are the boys? Have you all had a good week together?'

'Everything's under control.'

'Any visitors?'

'Greta was here yesterday. But she went on to London this morning.'

'Greta. Yes.' I heard him sigh. His voice was quiet, as if he was talking to himself. 'I must make more effort. It's not her fault really.'

'And Eileen Ward called on Tuesday.'

Another long pause.

'Listen, Nick. I'm very grateful for your help this week. You're a good friend, a real friend.' His voice was slow and uncertain. He sounded low, dispirited, far from his usual fast-talking, hyperactive self. What was the matter? 'I know we've had our disagreements. I know I haven't always been straight with you. But all that's going to change.'

Another sigh, and a deep pause. I waited and he began to talk again.

'I've been going over a lot of things, stuff that's happened over the last year or so. I'm sorry, Nicky. I mean it. I am sorry.'

For a moment I didn't say anything. I didn't know what to say. 'Greta said she'd pick you up from the airport tomorrow. I've got to be back in London for midday.'

'So I won't be seeing you? That's a shame.' Another sigh. 'I was looking forward to seeing you. I can't wait to get back, Nicky. I'm really looking forward to it.'

I said nothing. I was waiting for him to say goodbye, to ring off.

'Well. So long, mate. See you soon.'

He rang off.

I drank some more whisky, got up, refilled the glass. I walked back across the room but didn't sit down. I wandered round the table, thinking: So he's feeling sorry for himself. So he's been left all alone. So he's had too much to drink or too little sleep or is having a bumpy landing after too much speed or whatever crap he's got hold of out there. Does it make any difference? No. It's too late for apologies, even if he meant it. Even if he remembers tomorrow, which he won't. He'll wake up in the morning with a headache and the novelty of remorse won't even be a memory come breakfast-time. It changes nothing.

I was tired. I felt as if I'd been working hard all week. But now everything was in place and I wanted a rest. I didn't know how late it was, but it was dark outside so it was late enough. I hadn't had anything to eat since lunchtime but last night's washing up was still piled in the sink and I wasn't hungry. I just wanted to go to bed.

I opened the freezer and filled the bucket for the last time.

I woke up later that night thinking I could hear the

sound of someone coughing in the next room. A woman's cough. It seemed to come from a long way away. But it was nothing. Just a dream. But I remembered being woken by the sound of a woman coughing one night four months ago.

It was soon after our return from the Malverns – the night before my appointment with Acton at the gallery. An appointment which Diana knew nothing about. I hadn't told her because I hadn't told her anything about my illicit dealings with her brother, hoping that they were all a thing of the past.

The sound of it had dragged me up from some vague nightmare full of undefined menace. Along with the unfamiliar sound, my senses latched on to the unfamiliar smell of cigarette smoke. I had sat up in bed. Diana was sitting in a chair against the wall on the far side of the room. She was smoking. She sat with her head back and her eyes closed. Every now and then a spasm of coughing shook her naked body. She looked very thin and white in the darkness. I had never seen her with a cigarette before.

'I didn't know you smoked.'

'I don't.' She opened her eyes but didn't lower her head. Staring at the ceiling. 'I used to. Many years ago.' She took another drag, and another spasm wracked her body. She looked different – older and ill. 'An old habit. Every now and then it comes back, like other old habits, like . . .'

She coughed again, and this time the violence of it threw her forwards in the chair. For a moment I thought she was going to be sick. She looked old and ill and ugly. I would never have believed, before that moment, that she could ever have looked ugly. I got out of bed and went round to her. I took the cigarette from her and

140

threw it away. I sat on the end of the bed and took her hands in mine. She pulled hers away.

'Other old habits? Like what?'

'Like . . .' She sat back again and closed her eyes. 'Like wishing I could die. Wishing I was dead.'

'Have you ever wished that?'

'Yes. Many times. Sometimes it was only the thought of Iphigenia which stopped me from doing anything about it.'

'And since we've been together?'

'No.' She shook her head, but she didn't open her eyes. 'But it's an old habit. It goes very deep.' She ran her hands through her hair, shook her head again. 'Just now, smoking that cigarette, thinking about how happy we've been, I thought – this can't possibly last. Something's bound to go horribly wrong. Why not end it all now, right now, before that can happen?'

I had the distinct feeling that she would rather have been on her own at that moment, that she wished I wasn't there. This was something I'd never sensed in her before. I wanted to shake her, shout at her for once, start an argument. But I didn't.

'That's nonsense. Nothing's going to happen.'

She shook her head slowly, as if she knew something I couldn't possibly understand. Now, looking back, I could see that was probably the case. At the time it filled me with intense irritation.

'If there's something you want to talk about, we'll talk about it.' The anger in my voice must have been evident, but she didn't react to it. 'If not, then I'll go back to bed.'

She didn't reply. She sat with her head back and her eyes closed, breathing slowly. I went back to bed. And as I began to drift off to sleep I heard her light up another cigarette and inhale. And cough, and cough again.

Whose fault was it? Should I have let rip, forced it out of her, let go of my anger? Should she have let go, instead of waiting for me to bully it out of her? I don't suppose it matters whose fault it was. It certainly doesn't matter now. All that matters is that it didn't happen. If it had, then everything might have been very different. But it didn't. So it wasn't.

CHAPTER NINE

Friday. I woke up early feeling drawn and tense. I got dressed as the light began to show through the curtains. Then I carried the bucket out on its last trip across the garden to the woods. The sky was dark with heavy clouds and a stillness in the air promised thunder.

The dogs were waiting. Stiff and quivering, necks stretching to aim their fury straight at me, throats firing hatred in volley after barking volley through gaping jaws. I walked straight past them but this time followed the line of the fencing as close as I could, to test their spirit. They flung themselves at the wire netting, the rattle and crash of fence against metal poles adding to their savage clamour.

I didn't even flinch. I realized with a shock that the last five days had cured my terror of dogs. Now I relished their anger and their hunger. I had created it after all.

I dumped the bucketful of charnel in the clearing in the woods, returned the empty bucket to the kitchen, and then went round to the garage and drove my car to the front of the house. My work here was done – all I wanted to do now was clear out. I packed quickly and locked up. I threw my bag into the back of the car and drove off with only one backward glance at the pale stone manor-house nestling in its southern fold in the wooded hills. Some Arcadia. The relentless din of barking dogs was still audible, a warning that the apparent tranquillity of the scene was a deadly sham. I wondered briefly what would happen to the place after today. I didn't care. I never wanted to see it again. I accelerated down the drive, round the curve between the sheep pasture and the wood, and out of the gate into the lane. The barking faded. I slid a tape into the car's cassette player and tried to relax.

About a mile away from the house, I suddenly remembered the balaclava helmet I'd left in the wood-shed the day before. I'd forgotten all about it. It meant a lot to me, that balaclava helmet. It had been a gift. Well, I wasn't going back for it now. It was too late. But what if someone found it? What if it was some sort of evidence? I shook my head. Ridiculous. I was on edge, imagining things. I must pull myself together. I drove on and thought no more about it.

I stopped at a service station on the M20 for breakfast. The motorway café was crowded and noisy. Everything about it – the clean plastic, the primary colours, the bright fluorescent lights, the dry warmth of the air-conditioning, the big plate-glass windows looking out on to a world of metal, machines and high speed – was a weird shock after a week of rural isolation in a house built over four hundred years ago. But I ate my bacon and eggs slowly. The place was a useful halfway-house between rural Kent and inner London. Like some sort of decompression chamber or acclimatization zone.

I bought a paper – Stanley's paper – and searched through it even before I'd had my first cup of coffee. Stanley had done his business. There it was, at the bottom of the third page. 'Doubts Cast On Authenticity Of Wyndham Lewis Masterpiece.' I read on.

'Research by our own correspondent has cast doubt on the authenticity of the Wyndham Lewis "masterpiece" recently sold by a London gallery for a record sum.

'The large canvas was sold by the Acton Gallery, Cork Street, as an early, outstanding and important work by Percy Wyndham Lewis, the pioneer of modernism in

British art. It is signed, and dated 1909. The documented provenance states that the piece was acquired by the gallery from the heirs of a London landlord who is known to have leased studio space to Augustus John and his circle between the wars. A number of pieces by other early twentieth-century British artists (including an Augustus John canvas of undoubted authenticity) from the same source have been sold by the gallery in recent years.

'Its date is important in terms of art history. It is apparently a superb example of modernism – and yet modernism at that time was only emergent in Europe and unknown in Britain. Or so it has been thought. This picture would suggest that British art was in fact at the leading edge of the international avant-garde, and that Wyndham Lewis was a pioneer modernist of international stature, rather than simply the man who tried to introduce modernism to Britain after it had been established on the continent. A radical re-writing of the text books. Thus it was its date which largely determined this picture's record-breaking sales figure.

'Ironically, it is also its date which has led to doubts about its authenticity.

'The British Library has a collection of correspondence between Augustus John and Wyndham Lewis dating from before the First World War. In June 1909 Wyndham Lewis returned to England after a number of years on the continent; he wrote to Augustus John, outlining his hopes and plans which included:

' "... A big canvas. Something huge and monstrous to hurl at England like a bomb. Shatter this little country's smug and complacent ignorance forever ... I can't remember the last time I painted with oils. I've been running about Spain like a gypsy since last summer, nothing but watercolours in my luggage. No canvas ..."

'Three months later, however, he still hadn't started. In September he wrote:

'"... still no bloody canvas. Can't afford the time or the material. All journalism and illustrations, just to stay alive. However, have started a longish short-story – the ideas come in such a rush they demand words, not shapes – and if I can sell it I will buy canvas and a week or two to get started ..."

'And at the end of December he wrote:

'"... how the innate mediocrity of this miserable country drags one down. Six months here and still no canvas. Six months of scraps, nothing more. The spirit of the place is working against me, consciously. It recognizes me as an enemy and does its best to deprive me of ammunition. Perhaps next year will be different. Next year I will strike out, fists, feet, teeth, nails and any weapon which comes to hand. Next year I will have canvas and oils, come what may ..."

'So, on the evidence of his letters, he painted no canvases in 1909.

'Yukio Haramaka was not available for comment when this contradiction was raised with the Buruki Institute. A spokesman, however, said that they had no intention of submitting the painting to chemical analysis ...'

Good old Stanley. I sighed with relief. I hadn't wanted anything published earlier because that would have brought Acton back from Spain earlier. But today – Acton might just get wind of it on his way home and feel it as the last twist of the knife before ...

I paid my bill and left. An aeroplane passed overhead as I turned on to the motorway. I imagined Tony Acton at Madrid airport. He would be boarding about now, waving goodbye to Spain and utterly unaware of the deadly welcome waiting for him at home.

★

I arrived at the Eagle a few minutes before twelve. Stanley the journalist was already there – a very tall, slightly crumpled figure standing at the bar with a gin and tonic in front of him. He raised his glass and grinned as soon as he saw me.

'Many thanks, old man, for the info. Absolutely delightful.' He laughed. 'Incredible, isn't it? Does this mean Tony put one over on the Japs?' He sniggered into his drink. 'It certainly means I put one over on Tony. The bastard. I've been waiting years . . .'

'I read your piece this morning, Stanley. Well done. Nice piece of investigation.'

'Oh, well, nothing really. I am a professional, you know. I'm the editor's blue-eyed boy at the moment, Nick, I can't tell you. I'm top of the class all of a sudden. The Japs have threatened to sue the rag, nothing like a bit of litigation in the wind to get an editor's blood thumping. Freedom of the press, and all that. Marvellous. They love it.'

'Glad to hear it, Stanley.'

'So tell me all. Is it a Sexton Blake? Who did paint it?'

'All in good time, Stanley. I don't like talking on an empty stomach. I haven't even had a drink yet.'

He waved to the barman, and when my drink arrived I downed it in one go. Stanley gave me a peculiar look, his horsey features losing their supercilious droop for one moment.

'Are you all right, old chap?' he asked, more curious than concerned. 'You look rather tense today, if I may say so. Rather stressed out, old boy.' He laughed and emptied his glass without waiting for a reply. 'You look like you need a holiday. Or another drink.' He put his empty glass down on the bar just to make sure I didn't mistake a piece of free advice for the offer of another round.

'I've just had a holiday. A week in rural Kent. Out at Acton's place.'

'Really?' His eyes sharpened.

'He needed a caretaker,' I said. 'He's out in Madrid, talent-spotting.' I tried to attract the barman's attention. 'What's yours? Another gin and tonic?'

'Capital,' he said. 'Tell me about it.'

We sat down at a table by the window. I looked out across Farringdon Road. The street was a river in flood. A tide of metal swept up and down it, cars bumper to bumper, red mail vans from Mount Pleasant, couriers on mountain bikes and motor bikes. I could hear the siren of a fire-engine screaming from the station around the corner in Rosebery Avenue.

'The North Downs,' I said. 'They could be a thousand miles away.'

'I'll drink to that,' drawled Stanley, drinking. 'Can't stand the bloody countryside. Cold, wet and tedious. A cousin of mine owns half of Somerset. Got me down there once, stag hunting. You know, horse, hounds, red coat, the lot. Rained all day, horse was a hundred years old, didn't see a single stag. Mud everywhere. Local pub full of sniggering yokels drinking lager and boasting about their exploits at Club 18–30 in Majorca. Dreadful. Never again.'

I looked at the clock on the wall above the bar. It was gone twelve o'clock. Acton would have landed by now. He'd be on his way through customs, Greta and Andrea would be waiting for him.

'So what's he after in Madrid?'

I shrugged. 'I heard something about a video installation.'

'Good grief.' Stanley leaned back and rolled his eyes towards the ceiling in weary disdain. 'He isn't falling for that emperor's-new-clothes sort of crap, is he?'

'I doubt it. But others are, so he'll want to be in there, getting his slice of it.' My glass was empty. More scotch. 'Another one?'

'Get them in, old son, get them in.'

I got them in. Stanley forced himself to buy the next round, and I got the one after that, and by that time it was one o'clock. He was halfway through a blow-by-blow account of lunch with the Heritage Minister but I couldn't concentrate. I watched the minute hand creep past the hour on the clock above the bar and thought: it must have happened by now. He must be home by now, it must have happened. It's all over.

He comes home, hears the dogs' racket. Puzzled, he goes to their enclosure. The dogs go insane. Alarmed, he tries to calm them. He opens the gate, steps inside . . .

A fire-engine went screaming past the window from the station round the corner. Flashing lights, ringing bells, roaring engine. I jumped, rattling the table and splashing the liquor in the glass I was gripping tight in my right hand.

'Steady on, old chap.' Stanley brushed irritably at his beaded tie. 'Only a fire-engine.' He gave me another look of odd curiosity. 'You're rather jumpy today, aren't you? Get a grip on yourself. You're looking more and more like one of Schiele's crazy neurotics by the second.'

We had lunch in a restaurant on the other side of Farringdon Road. We had a lot of wine. I drank too much too fast. I don't know what Stanley's excuse was, but he didn't lag behind. We both laughed at each other's incoherent jokes and it wasn't until we were halfway through the last course that Stanley snapped into a moment of clarity as he realized the end was nigh.

'So, Nicholas, tell me more. Tell me all.'

I sighed and sat back. The lunch had already served its purpose. I now had an alibi, should I ever need one.

But I reached into a pocket and pulled out a piece of paper and passed it across the table to Stanley.

'What's this?' Stanley squinted at it, began to read aloud. 'English Martyrs, pen and ink, William Holman Hunt. Burgh Castle, watercolour, James Stark . . .'

'It's a list of all the pictures you should investigate in the light of your suspicions about the Wyndham Lewis.'

He nodded gravely, folded up the piece of paper and put it away in a pocket. 'All this. It will finish Acton off good and proper. With a bit of luck.'

'I admire your fearlessness.'

'Oh, there's nothing to fear now. He's done for.'

I nodded. I looked at my watch. It was gone three o'clock. He's done for, all right.

It was cold outside and the sun was sinking. Stanley fell into a passing taxi and I staggered off down the road towards Farringdon underground. I was in no state to drive. Strange. I laughed. I'd spent the last week laying a trap which had just killed a man and I still had scruples about drink driving.

It was gone four when I got back to the crumbling Victorian mansion where I lived. Nothing had changed in the week I'd been away. No one had replaced the dead light-bulb in the hallway, the squatters on the first floor were still shouting at one another and the musician on the second floor was still learning how to play the double-bass. And it was still a long climb – four flights of worn and creaking stairs – up to the loft which was my home and my studio.

I let myself in, turned on the heating and drew the blinds across the dark and starry sky visible through the large portion of the ceiling which was all glass. In the darkness I could see the red light on the answerphone. There was a message waiting for me.

I fell on to the bed in the cubicle without turning on the light. I stared at the red glow in the darkness beyond the half-drawn curtains. The message had to be from today. I'd been phoning in and replaying the calls every day. I could guess who it was from and what it said. But I hesitated to replay it. There it was – final confirmation that at last it was all over – and I hesitated. What if I was wrong? What if it wasn't all over? What if Acton was still alive?

I told myself I was too drunk to listen to it. The room was spinning and the stars had slid unsteadily across the night sky before I'd shut them from view. Perhaps I wasn't drunk enough.

I lay back on the bed and tried to pretend the red light wasn't there. I tried to forget all about it.

Last October ... That appointment with Tony Acton ...

The gallery had closed for the day by the time we met. It was strange being there after hours, just the two of us, in the semi-darkness with the exhibits barely visible instead of bathed in the usual harsh and brilliant light, and the walls merely colourless instead of gleaming white.

I followed Acton into the lift and up to the inner sanctum. There was the leather sofa and the smoked-glass table and the bowl of tulips, and there was something new – a cine-film projector stood behind the sofa, aimed at the far wall. It was an ugly and ominous piece of machinery, out of place in that sleek, minimalist shrine.

'Sit down,' Acton said, smiling. 'I'd like you to watch something before we talk.'

I sat down, puzzled. Acton turned off the lights and set the film running. A wobbling square of grainy light fell on the far wall. It was cine film, super-8, the kind used to shoot home-movies before video took over. It was in black and white, and had that jumpy, grainy look about it. The camera didn't move – it had probably been propped up on a table or chair or something. One scene, one angle. A bedroom, a bed, and on the bed a young man and a young woman. Both naked. Head-on to the camera. My stomach turned and I began to shake. I felt self-control slipping away like water through the fingers of a man dying of thirst.

I held myself down. I closed my eyes and heard nothing but the whir of the projector, the thudding of my own heart, the gasping of my own breath. There was no sound to the film, but my imagination plugged that gap. I heard the girl groaning as her head stretched backwards over the edge of the bed, long hair falling away from her upside-down face, her neck taut, eyes closed, jaws clenched, lips open, gasping. The man grunting, his face invisible to the camera until the moment when he raises his head and looks straight into the camera, his eyes open but blank as if he didn't know who he was staring at from out of the blank screen, or who was out here staring back at it and at him . . .

I felt my stomach lurch and knew I was going to be sick. I leapt up and was sick all over the smoked glass, the white carpet, the immortal tulips.

The woman in the film was Diana Artemis. And the man? The man in the film was Tony Acton.

Acton stopped the film and turned the lights back on. He was laughing. He was glad I was sick. He couldn't care less about the table or the carpet or the flowers. He could replace those easily enough. He was laughing with joy and triumph.

'When?' I said after my stomach was empty. I sat slumped in the sofa. I still felt ill and dizzy. The light was too bright and the room was spinning.

'Oh,' he said, waving his hand as if the question wasn't important. 'A month ago? Two months? I don't remember exactly which moment of union I actually immortalized.'

'How long?' I managed. I tried to stand up but couldn't. Everything seemed to have lost its balance. The world had slipped its axis and I knew it would never recover.

'Years.' Acton was still laughing. 'Since . . . since we were both at school.' He turned back to the machine to rewind the film. 'Years and years.'

I said nothing. The whining of the film only emphasized the silence, like the wind blowing dust through a devastated city in the aftermath of some great catastrophe.

The whining stopped and Acton took the reel from the projector and put it back in its can. He waved the can at me. Suddenly he was no longer laughing.

'I'm going to send this to her husband's lawyer. It won't look good in the divorce court, will it Nicky? Adultery. Adulteress. No judge is going to let her keep her daughter, Nicky. A woman who sleeps with another man all through a marriage isn't a fit mother, is she, Nicky? Especially if that man is her own brother. Takis will keep Iphigenia, and it will break Diana's heart, won't it?'

I shook my head in a desperate attempt to clear it. 'They won't use that. They wouldn't use that as evidence. They couldn't.'

'Why not? Why ever not? Anyway, even if they didn't, they'd call me as a witness, as the other man, and I'd have to tell the truth, wouldn't I? I'd be under oath.'

'You wouldn't do it.' I shook my head again, still stupidly trying to work out what game he was playing. 'You wouldn't.'

'Only one thing would stop me. You know what I

want. Obviously you don't know how badly I want it. I want a Wyndham Lewis masterpiece. If you can give it to me within the next month, this film is yours. To do what you like with. Burn, sell, play on your wedding night. Because without it, Nicky, I don't think you'll have a wedding-night. Do you? If Diana had to choose between you and Iphigenia, I think you'd have to pack your bags, don't you?' He smiled. 'Now why don't you think about it while I put it back in the safe where it belongs, for the time being?'

Acton left the room and I tried to think about it. Acton was right – if Diana had to choose between Iphigenia and me, I wasn't sure that I wouldn't lose her. But that wasn't the point. Even if she did choose me, she would end up hating me for the loss of her daughter. But that wasn't the point either. The point was that if she lost her daughter, it would destroy her. And I didn't have to think very long to realize that I would do anything to protect her from that. It was my choice, not hers.

'All right,' I said when Acton returned. 'I'll do it.'

'Good man.' He grinned and slapped me on the back. 'I knew you'd see sense.'

We took the lift back to the ground floor in silence. I walked across the gallery to the street door without waiting for him. Without saying goodbye. I didn't want to talk to him ever again.

'Nick.' He called out as I was opening the door. I turned back to him, away from the cold gusts coming in from the street. The beginning of winter. 'Diana and I,' he said. He was turning off all the lights in the gallery, one by one. 'You couldn't possibly understand. Not you, not Takis.' His voice came hissing out of the darkness. 'You don't have the first idea.'

★

Tony and Diana Acton. More than brother and sister, less than brother and sister.

Their father was an academic. An eminent man, professor of history of art at the University of London. He married a young student of his – a rich and beautiful girl, daughter of a Viscount or something. They were a golden couple. She was glamorous, he was brilliant, they had money, a big house in Hampstead, and love. He was almost twenty years older than her, but they adored each other. However – they couldn't have children. Or so the doctors told them after they'd been married and trying for ten years. So they adopted. A little boy – two years old – called Anthony.

And then, two years later, as if by magic, she found herself pregnant. It sometimes happens like that, apparently. They had a daughter. Diana.

That's right. They weren't brother and sister. Not by blood. The strange thing is, they actually looked as if they were. There was an uncanny resemblance. Both dark, slight, pale skinned. If you saw them together in the same room, you'd assume that they were. The resemblance, however, went no deeper than that; when Diana had told me that he wasn't really her brother – yes, she had at least told me that – the revelation hadn't surprised me because I couldn't imagine two people being more unlike each other, in spite of the superficial resemblance.

Anyway, they grew up together as brother and sister, in that big house in Hampstead, surrounded by books and beautiful things and clever people and love. But all the time he knew that he wasn't really their child and she was, and as he grew up he couldn't help hating her for it.

He was a born egomaniac, you see. He couldn't stand the suspicion – the thought – that he wasn't the centre of everyone's world. For the first two years of his life he'd suffered who knows what hell, for the next two years he'd lived in an unimaginable heaven, and then suddenly his place was usurped – so he thought – by someone whose claim to it he couldn't hope to match. Of course, his mother and father loved him as if he was theirs by birth, loved him and his sister equally, spoiled them both, but he refused to see it. What he really blamed them for was having another child. He resented having to share their affection, especially with someone who, so he imagined, had more right to it than he did. He was a selfish, self-centred bastard from the word go. He was jealous, and as the years passed jealousy gave way to hatred. A hatred he kept well hidden, of course.

Deep down, very deep down, his sister sensed something of this, and did all she could to make it up to him. She couldn't do enough for him. She felt sorry for him, she felt guilty, and she adored him as a little sister always adores her big brother. He exploited all these feelings to the full, he took advantage of them, and little by little he had her completely under his control. For a while that was revenge enough.

He was a wild teenager. He gave his parents a very hard time. He was expelled from three very good schools. At eighteen, when his parents tried to talk to him about his future, he shrugged and said he wanted to go to art school. It sounded like fun and in those days you didn't need any talent for it. So they arranged for him to go to art school in Paris.

Before he left home he confirmed his domination of his sixteen-year-old sister by seducing her. He was not planning to relinquish his hold over her, and he knew instinctively that this would seal it forevermore.

He was her first lover, and they remained lovers. She would visit him in Paris, and later in Rome, as often as she could. For a long time he was her only lover, but he always took his pick of whatever caught his fancy.

He wasn't much of an art student. Eventually he got a job in a gallery in Rome. He lived a high life, the *dolce vita*, largely subsidized by his parents, who still adored him and spoiled him even though he had broken their hearts many years ago and had delighted in stamping on the pieces at every opportunity since. Of course, they never knew about the true relationship between him and Diana. His father died when he had been in Rome about eight years, and his mother died about six months later. She couldn't bear to live without her husband. Acton inherited a lot of money, came back to London, and opened his gallery in Notting Hill.

He really *found* himself in the Portobello Road, found his vocation. In Rome he'd been a mere dilettante, working for someone else without much enthusiasm. But now he was his own man, he took to the business like a duck to water. He'd failed as an art student – no creative talent – but he had a fine eye for creative talent in others. And an even finer eye for the market place. He was charming and sophisticated and, more importantly, he was greedy and unscrupulous. You could say that he was born to be an art dealer.

Diana had no illusions about him. She knew he was selfish, cruel and dishonest. But she couldn't break free. He was an addictive poison she just couldn't get out of her system. She tried; she forced herself to become involved with someone else, she allowed herself to get married (the shock of that sent Tony, in a rage of jealousy and spite, down the aisle with Greta). But in vain. Marriage to Takis was a drastic experiment which failed.

It explained so much. It explained everything. I remembered that encounter with Takis, the bizarre things he'd said about Diana. I remembered Greta, puzzled about her husband Tony just as Takis was about his wife Diana. They were looking at the same mystery but from opposite ends. And it explained why Tony and I hadn't seen anything of each other since the start of my affair with Diana, why we hadn't ever spoken of her or her relationship with me; awash with rage and jealousy, he'd been avoiding me. And Diana. . . ?

It was no good. There was no ignoring it. I looked up and there it was, still glowing red in the darkness. You'll have to listen to it sooner or later. It isn't going to go away.

Not yet. I'm not ready yet . . .

I decided to confront Diana as soon as I left the gallery. I drove as fast as I could, though I was hardly in a fit state to drive at all. I was half-insane with shock and anger and disgust. How could she do it? How could she ever have done it?

Her face turned white and her whole body trembled when I told her what I'd seen.

'He told me he'd destroyed it,' she whispered. 'He promised . . .'

'When?' I was shouting. 'When was it taken?'

'Years ago. More than ten years ago. It was in Rome. I didn't know he was taking it at the time. We were both high on drugs – cocaine, LSD, I don't remember. We were high all the time in those days. And I didn't care when I found out afterwards. Not then. I was young and unhappy and I was used to Tony doing what he liked, even if it was crazy and perverse. Especially if it was crazy or perverse.'

'Not last month? Not last week?'

'No. No!'

More than ten years ago. Could I believe that? The film was grainy and unclear. It had looked old. I flinched as I turned it over in my memory. Ten years old? It could be. But could I believe her? Could I believe anything she told me now?

'And since then? Was it some sort of sick one-night-stand, or . . . ?'

She turned away, wringing her hands. 'Nicky, I'm going to tell you the truth. I should have told you a long time ago. I wanted to, but . . .' She sighed. 'Tony and I, we were lovers when I was sixteen years old. He was my first lover, my only lover until I met Takis ten years later. And even then I can't really say that I loved Takis. He was just an attempt to break out of the hold Tony had over me. I thought if I got married, if I tried really hard, I could break free. Oh, I loved Tony but I knew what he was. That he was evil, that he took from me, that he took from everybody, just for the sake of taking. Well, I got married and I tried hard but it didn't really work. It didn't work between Takis and me because I found I couldn't break free that easily. In the end I found I couldn't break free at all.'

'So all the time you were married you were unfaithful with Tony?'

'Yes. And afterwards.'

I swallowed hard. My mouth was dry. I could hardly bring myself to ask the next question. 'And since . . . since we've been together?'

'It's over now, Nicky. I told him. Never again. It's finished.'

I grabbed her shoulders and shook her. 'Have you?' I shouted. 'Have you slept with him since you've been sleeping with me?'

She put her hands over her face. I could feel her shaking under my hands. 'Once. That's all. Just once.'

I let her go.

'I went to see him last spring, just before we all went away. I went to tell him it was all over. I . . . we spent the night together. For the last time . . . I'm sorry, Nicky. I'm sorry. But it is over. It is.' She looked up, frightened. She saw the expression on my face. 'Oh God, Nicky, please tell me this doesn't change anything. Please. It doesn't, does it? Please tell me it doesn't.'

This time she tried to grab me, but I pulled away. 'It changes everything.'

She was gasping, sobbing. 'But don't you see? What we have, it's made me free. You rescued me from Tony. I no longer love him, I don't need him, I don't even hate him. I didn't think it would ever happen, I didn't think anyone . . . But it has, Nicky. It has and it's a miracle. Don't you see? After all these years of darkness. I love you, Nicky. Please don't throw it away.'

I shook my head. Anger and disgust. I was more than half mad with them. There was so much of it there was no room for love anymore. Perhaps they planned it together, I was thinking. Perhaps it was all planned, from the very beginning, a trap to keep me eating out of her brother's hands for the rest of my life. 'It's over. You and me. Over.'

'But that's what he wants, Nicky.' She was crying now, tears of desperation. 'Don't you understand? That's why he showed you that film. He's insane with jealousy. He always was. Why do you think he married Greta, only months after I married Takis? When I went to see him, to tell him it was over, when I told him about you and me, he didn't believe me at first. And then when I proved it – when we went to bed together – that's why I did it, Nicky, to prove it to him and to me, to prove that I wasn't imagining what there was – what there is – between us. When he realized that I was telling the truth, he exploded with rage. He can't stand the idea of someone taking something from him. He can't stand it. I thought he was going to kill me. He threatened to kill you. And now he's trying to smash it all up. That's why he showed it to you. That's what he's trying to do. And you're letting him do it!'

I shook my head. I wasn't listening. I didn't want to listen. There was no point. It was all over. I simply turned and walked out.

So that was the end of that. Diana tried almost every day to see me or talk to me, but I refused to meet her or answer her calls or even read her letters. For weeks afterwards, that film replayed itself in my mind every time I closed my eyes, my imagination perversely supplying the sound and colour missing from the original. Eventually the initial shock of revelation faded, to be replaced by an overwhelming sense of desolation and loss.

I worked on the Wyndham Lewis pastiche for Acton. I could have told them all to go to hell, but even after everything I'd seen I couldn't stand the idea of Acton having that sort of hold over Diana. I did a good job, too. Acton was impressed and delighted. He didn't appreciate the significance of the date I'd painted in one corner. But I was sure someone would, sooner or later. I was sure it would screw up whatever dodgy deal Acton had lined up for it.

He handed over the film on the day I finished the picture. 'Look upon it as a wedding-present,' he laughed. The bastard knew there wasn't going to be any wedding but he wanted to make the most of his victory. 'Play it on your wedding-night. The two of you can watch it together. You, Nick, can learn some valuable lessons (Diana tells me you need a lot of help in that area). And it will remind Diana of what she's missing. Never mind.

It will help her to think of me when she's trying to do it with you.' The bastard. I sent it to Diana, to dispose of as she wished.

A month later my perfect Wyndham Lewis pastiche was sold to Mr Haramaka of the Buruki Institute as an original, complete with faultlessly documented provenance. I was wrong about the date – no one spotted that clue. I was appalled. The amount of money people are prepared to fork out without doing basic homework is amazing. Soon afterwards Acton sent me a cheque. My share, he said. No doubt he meant it as a peace offering. It was a lot of money, but I took great pleasure in burning it.

After that I tried to get back to work, my own work. But there was nothing there. No ideas, no images, nothing. My very ability to create seemed to have disappeared. I tried all kinds of things, tricks and exercises, doodling and still lifes, but nothing worked. I forced myself to draw and paint, but everything I put on paper or canvas refused to live. It was all dull, dead, lifeless. The well was empty – dried up or blocked up – and I didn't know how to get the waters flowing again.

Every day the gap left in my life by the end of my affair with Diana grew bigger and bigger, and my hatred for Acton grew stronger and stronger. It ate away at me, twisting every thought and feeling, until one day I decided I was going to kill him. I wanted to kill him, I had to kill him. He deserved to die. He was unfinished business. How could I put it all behind me unless I destroyed him? How could I hope to make a fresh start until I had erased him?

I forced myself up from the bed and across to the little red glow. I reached out and flicked the dial to replay. A mere second or two of high-pitched garble as the tape rewound itself (a very short message) and then Greta's voice rang out through the silent studio.

'Nicky? Oh, Nicky, where are you? Something terrible has happened . . . Tony's . . . the dogs . . . dead. Tony's . . . it is horrible, horrible . . .'

The voice – distressed, unsteady, barely under control – tailed off. Eventually there was the clunk of the receiver falling into place. The tape clicked and rewound itself, whirring.

Once more I flicked the dial to replay.

'Nicky? Oh, Nicky, where are you? Something terrible has happened . . . Tony's . . . the dogs . . . dead. Tony's . . . it is horrible, horrible . . .'

I stood up. I paced the floor, my heart thumping. I had done it. A surge of pure excitement swept through me. Yes. Yes! Then a surge of icy caution. I was suddenly very sober. I strode back to the telephone, picked up the receiver and dialled the Kent number.

A female voice, steady and official, asked who was calling. When I told her, there was a pause – 'one moment, sir' – then someone else was asking 'Mr Todd? Mr Nicholas Todd?' A young man's voice; calm, clear, intelligent.

'Yes?'

'I'm Detective Inspector Wilson. Canterbury CID. Can I ask why you're calling?'

'Yes. I'm returning a call from Greta Acton. She left a message on my answerphone. A confused message.'

'What was the message about?'

'Her husband . . . She sounded distraught . . . Look, what's happened?'

'Mr Todd, I have to tell you there's been a terrible accident. A death.'

I counted to five, slowly. 'What? Dead? What's happened?'

'Mr Todd, I believe you were looking after this house for Mr and Mrs Acton this week, while they were out of the country?'

'That's right. I came back to London this morning. So . . . So Tony's . . . ?'

'I can't talk about it right now, Mr Todd. I'm sure you understand. But I will need to talk to you, if I may. Tomorrow?'

'Yes. Yes, of course. Where's Greta? Can I talk to her?'

'She's asleep. The doctor had to give her a sedative. She'll be all right. What time can we talk tomorrow? Could you give me your address?'

I told him where I lived. Eleven o'clock tomorrow morning? Fine. He rang off.

So it was over. It was all over. It was like waking up from a nightmare and finding it had all been a dream after all; the evil warlock had disappeared, had never really existed in the first place. The relief, the euphoria . . . I went round and turned on all the lights.

It was over. The sense of release was overpowering. I could make a fresh start. Now everything could change, I could move forwards again. At last.

I paced around the studio, looking at the half-dozen abandoned canvases propped up beneath the big sky-light. They looked odd, unfamiliar, things from the distant past. They were stillborn, dead things from a previous existence. Tomorrow I'd gather them up and destroy them. I could make a fresh start now.

I found a bottle of scotch in the tiny kitchen and poured myself a glass. Perhaps I'll have a holiday, a real holiday, somewhere warm and out of the way. Travel light – pencils, watercolours only. I thought of the

Spanish meseta, the vast horizons of Old Castille. The Roman ruins of North Africa ... Start work again ... Yes. I'll drink to that. I raised my glass and drank.

CHAPTER TEN

I woke up late the next day with a cracking headache. I shelved the idea of trekking all the way to Farringdon to collect my car, took two aspirin and was about to go back to bed when I remembered the detective. He arrived on the dot of eleven. He was a clean and healthy looking individual. Clear, open face; pleasant smile. I wouldn't have taken him for a policeman. A young doctor, perhaps, but not a policeman.

'Mr Todd?' He let me have a good look at his warrant card. 'I'm Detective Inspector Wilson. Robert Wilson.'

'Call me Nick. Coffee?' I was desperate for caffeine. Yesterday's wine and whisky were still thumping around inside my skull like hyperactive trolls. I hadn't shaved and I hadn't had breakfast. I put the kettle on.

He was looking up at the sky through the glass ceiling when I returned from the kitchen. 'Has this place always been an artist's studio?'

'A Victorian painter had the whole house built. He worked up here and lived down below. I'm not so lucky.'

'Who was he? One of the Pre-Raphaelites?'

'I've never been able to find out. I've searched for records but there don't seem to be any. Some detective work needed there, Inspector. But I often imagine his ghost shuffling around up here. Some opium-addicted fin-de-siècle genius, broken by debauchery and self-destructive talent.' I laughed uneasily. I was talking too much. 'He was probably an upright Victorian family man. Faithful husband and loving father, keeping good accounts and churning out competent and flattering portraits of self-made industrial magnates.'

The thought of ghosts and dead men reduced us to silence for a moment, reminding us of the purpose of the detective's visit. He turned aside and peered blankly at the untidy row of unfinished canvases.

'How did it happen? You said . . . an accident?'

'Acton's dogs simply turned.' He sighed. 'It must have been terrible for his wife. She found the body when she arrived early in the afternoon. Already dead, of course. Torn to pieces. But the shock of it . . . horrifying.'

'The dogs?' I shook my head. 'Everyone told him they were monsters. He wouldn't listen. He treated them like kittens. Ridiculous.'

'I understand you were looking after the place this week?'

'That's right. Acton and his wife went to Madrid on Sunday. An old couple live in the lodge and work as housemaid and handyman, but they're on holiday. So I was roped in to watch the house and feed the dogs.' I stopped and looked at the inspector. 'But I kept as far away from them as possible. They stayed in the enclosure and I didn't go in there once. Threw all their food over the fence. Sounds like I had a lucky escape.'

'How did they seem? Any more aggressive or violent than usual?'

'I'd never seen them before the weekend, so I don't know. But they struck me as very violent, very aggressive by nature. Well, I'm no expert. I don't know anything about dogs. I hate them. They all scare me, even the small ones. Acton knew this. I told him but he wouldn't listen. I don't know why he wanted me to look after them. It was probably some sort of joke on *his* part.'

'You don't like dogs?' The inspector looked at me, curious and bewildered. 'I love them. Finest creatures on God's earth. I have two labradors. Lovely creatures. Wouldn't be without them.'

'Well, you've seen Acton's monsters. Could you love them? He did, and look what they did.'

'I saw them. I saw what they did. It was tragic. They had to be shot, and that was part of the tragedy.' He was indignant, almost angry. 'They should never have been kept as pets, but they were magnificent animals. They didn't deserve to die like that.'

'More coffee? Are you cold?'

He hadn't taken his coat off. The collar was turned up and his hands were clamped around the coffee mug. He looked at me and laughed. 'Freezing. I'm sorry, I don't mean to criticize your home, but it's so cold in here. How can you stand it?'

'It's always cold in the winter. You can't keep any heat in with a glass roof. That's the problem with artists' studios. And in the summer it's like a greenhouse.' I shrugged. 'You get used to it.'

He looked around. He was looking for somewhere to sit, but there was nowhere – every surface was crammed with junk. I tipped a mountain of rubbish from a dusty sofa beneath the skylight. He watched it cascade over the floor but didn't sit down. He really was a very clean, neat-looking individual. He was wearing a spotless raincoat, a light grey suit, a well-ironed shirt, polished shoes and a college tie. Medium height, slim, fair hair, brown eyes. He looked like every school's dream of a head boy – clean-cut, honest, responsible, conscientious. The head prefect of the sixth form.

'How's his wife taking it?' I asked.

The inspector sighed. 'She was hysterical by the time I arrived. Had to be sedated. I left a woman police constable with her. I understand a friend was coming down from London to be with her. Some American girl.'

'Andrea.'

'Imagine it! Wife drives down to the country to join

168

her husband for the weekend and finds . . . that.' He broke off, shaking his head.

'Didn't she pick him up from the airport? She and Andrea?'

'No. I suppose he got a cab.'

'I had to get back to London yesterday morning. If I'd stayed I might have been able to help. I could have prevented it . . .'

'Oh, don't blame yourself. You couldn't have done much once they got a hold.'

'His poor wife.'

He looked at me. 'You're not married, are you?'

'No.'

'You don't know what you're missing. How old are you, may I ask?'

'Thirty-one.'

'Well, well, so am I. How about that. I've been married two years now. Best years of my life. My wife's expecting our first – due in two weeks' time. Can't wait.'

'Congratulations.'

'It's strange coming up to London. I used to live here before I got married. Forest Hill. I was with Scotland Yard. Then I made inspector, moved out to the Kent force. Got married. I come back here and it's like another planet, I can't believe I lived here for so long. Can't get back to Canterbury quick enough. Wouldn't live anywhere else now.'

With that, he handed the mug back. Time to go. 'There'll be an inquest, of course. In Canterbury. Some time next week. You'll be needed – someone from the coroner's office will be in touch about it.' We shook hands. 'Thanks for your time.'

I lay down on the dusty sofa and looked up through the glass roof at the heavy winter sky overhead. Thinking about Detective Inspector Robert Wilson. The man who was sniffing around the corpse of Tony Acton. Would he find any tracks there? And if he did, would he be able to follow them back to me?

I'd been expecting a grizzled veteran, a real blood-hound. So I should have been reassured by the sight of Detective Inspector Robert Wilson, with his clear, bland face and his clean shirt. He seemed pleasant enough, after all; open, sincere, good-natured. Straightforward. Normal, in a word.

But I wasn't reassured at all. On the contrary, the encounter had left me feeling strangely uneasy. It was his very normality which scared me. Men like him had nothing to hide, nothing to fear; no inner secrets, no demons to torment or tempt or weaken them. They had all the strength and confidence of a clear conscience. And they would never be able to understand, forgive or sympathize with those who did not. They wouldn't have the imagination for it.

And an inspector at twenty-nine – that was young, wasn't it? That says something about him, doesn't it?

I closed my eyes and shook my head. Come on. He's just a normal, straightforward human being. He has a nice warm home in a nice town with two dogs and a nice wife who keeps the place tidy and makes sure he eats healthy meals and has a clean pair of shoes and an ironed shirt to wear every morning. You're not used to normal, straightforward human beings, that's all. In your world they're like creatures from another planet.

I got up and went to the fridge in the kitchen. I was going to get something to eat, but there was a four-pack of lager in there so I hooked it out and went back to the sofa.

I thought about Tony Acton, the state he must have been in when they found him. I tried not to but I couldn't help it. I wondered where his body was now. In a morgue somewhere, probably. Laid out for the autopsy, with clever scientists bending over him, opening him up in relentless pursuit of the secrets of his death. Of my secrets. Of me.

I thought about Greta. Perhaps she was upset by Acton's death, after all. Perhaps I should phone her. Maybe it's a bit too soon. Maybe later.

I didn't phone her. I just lay there, on the dusty sofa, watching the dark winter sky grow darker overhead.

The telephone rang but I ignored it. It rang and rang and then the answerphone clicked into life. Then I heard Stanley's voice speaking on to the tape and into the room.

'Nick. Have you heard the news? Acton's dogs . . . You must have heard. Incredible, isn't it? Incredible. Call me back.'

The tape caught the rattle of the replaced receiver, clicked and stopped. The room was silent again. I didn't phone him back.

That night I was woken by the sound of barking dogs. The barking stopped, but I couldn't get back to sleep. I got out of bed and checked the time. Three-thirty. It was very cold. I poured myself a scotch and pulled on my overcoat, thrusting my hands into the pockets. My left hand found something small and sharp and brittle. I pulled it out – the mouse's skull. I'd forgotten all about it. Sinister shadows filled its tiny cavities.

What have I done, I thought. What have I done?

Sunday morning. I got up, showered, shaved and dressed, feeling light-headed from lack of sleep. Then I went out to take the tube up west to collect my car.

I had to wait a long time for a train. I was alone on the platform. There was no one waiting for trains on the opposite platform either. There was no one on the train when it did arrive, and no one got into the carriage as the train carried me under and through the City. Aldgate East, Liverpool Street, Moorgate, Barbican. Any week-day morning the carriage would have been crowded, passengers hanging from straps and pushing and shoving to get on and off. It could have been the day after the end of the world. But it was only Sunday morning. I sat with my eyes shut as the train rattled westwards to Farringdon Road.

The world was still there when I came up and out of the station and back to the surface. But only just. A single car drove past as I walked up Farringdon Road and a black cab had stopped on the corner of Exmouth market to buy cockles or jellied eels from the seafood stall outside the pub. My car was still there, but a side window had been smashed in. Nothing had been stolen – there was nothing in there to steal – but I cursed the would-be thieves as criminals until it hit me that I was a criminal too. A worse criminal than any of them. The worst. A murderer.

I got in and drove home, back along the Clerkenwell Road. Surely Diana's heard the news by now, I found myself thinking. Perhaps she'll phone me as soon as she hears that Acton's dead.

I checked the answerphone as soon as I got back, but there were no new messages.

I knew I had to phone Greta. I didn't want to, but I knew I had to do all the obvious things – console the widow, enquire about the funeral. I was going to be very careful. The inspector wasn't going to get any clues from me.

I rang the Canterbury number and waited, listening

to the ringing tone. There was no answer, not even a recorded message. The house was empty and the machine switched off. I imagined the ringing echoing along the corridors and through the shuttered and dust-sheeted rooms, and hung up almost with relief.

Andrea must have taken her back to London. I rang the Holland Park number and there was an answer almost straight away.

'Hello?' Andrea's southern drawl, hard and deep.

'Andrea? It's Nicholas. Nicholas Todd.' I paused, but there was no response. Just a cold silence. 'Is Greta there?'

'Yes.'

'Can I speak to her?'

'No. Not right now.'

'How is she coping?'

'She's coping.'

'Can you tell her I called? Give her my condolences? If there's anything I can do . . .'

'There isn't.'

'What about the funeral? Has it been arranged yet?'

I heard her sigh and felt her manner beginning to thaw. 'We can't do anything until they've finished the post-mortem. There's a crematorium just outside Canterbury. We've spoken to them and made vague arrangements, but I don't think anything will happen before next Wednesday or Thursday.'

'I'd like to be there. Will you let me know as soon as you can?'

'Sure, Nick.' She paused awkwardly. 'Thanks for calling. I'll tell Greta . . . she'll appreciate it. It's just that she's . . . She's getting so many calls, I'm trying to protect her from all that. She doesn't need it. She needs peace and quiet. You know?'

'I understand. Thanks, Andrea. Call me as soon as you know about the funeral.'

It was cold and very quiet in the studio. As soon as I realized I was doing nothing except wondering whether the phone was going to ring I went out and crossed the road to the pub. I ordered a scotch. I drank it quickly and ordered another one straight away.

Diana. Was she going to phone? Why hadn't she phoned? I felt a sudden, desperate need to talk to her.

There was a telephone in the corridor outside the gents. I dialled her number and waited. The tone rang and rang. Come on, come on. I waited until there was no hope of a reply, and longer. Then I hung up.

There was a touch of sleet in the north-easterly wind when I crossed the road to go home. I climbed the stairs and let myself in. There was no message on the answerphone from Diana. No messages from anyone. I sat down on the dusty sofa. I was very tired. I closed my eyes and was suddenly fast asleep.

My dreams were very vivid. I was hiding in a big house where all the furniture was covered in white dust-sheets. The sound of . . . something, someone, pursued me from room to room. I couldn't shake it off. It was a terrible sound, not frightening but terrible. I couldn't face it. I was hiding from it. And then I was woken by the sound of dogs barking. It was still light. I was fully dressed and I felt completely disoriented. I grabbed my watch to check the time. I'd been asleep for barely ten minutes.

The same thing happened that night. I was so tired I fell asleep as soon as I went to bed. Again, I dreamt that I was hiding in a big house among dust-sheeted furniture. Again, I was woken by the barking of dogs. But this time I realized the dogs stopped barking as soon as I awoke. The noise wasn't waking me from the outside – it was coming from my dreams.

I staggered into the kitchen and ran some cold water, the echo of that final dream replaying itself as I came awake. Dogs, barking and snapping. Close-up flashes of teeth and eyes and frothing jaws. At first they were Himalayan mastiffs, Acton's dogs, and then Labradors, a pair of them. And then I forced myself to wake up. I drank some cold water, the last echoes of the dream drifting away. Those echoes were words. The words said: dead, murdered, murderer. Dead, murdered, murderer.

I went back to bed but I couldn't sleep. I lay awake until it got light again and Sunday became Monday.

CHAPTER ELEVEN

A letter arrived that morning from Canterbury, in an official-looking brown envelope. I didn't open it. I could guess what it was. Details of Acton's inquest, my presence required.

There was nothing in the kitchen for breakfast so I went out to the shop round the corner for coffee, milk and bread. I walked home through the cold streets, wondering if Diana had phoned while I'd been out, if she'd left a message for me.

There was a message on the answerphone, but it wasn't from Diana. It was from Stanley. He sounded excited. He wanted to talk to me. He wanted me to phone him back. I bet he does, I thought as I wound the tape back. I've given him the scoop of a lifetime for the price of a lunch. Who wouldn't come back for more of that?

I turned the answerphone off and the telephone started ringing almost straight away. Diana. Could this be it? I snatched the receiver.

'Hello?'

'Nicholas? Stanley here. I've been trying to contact you for days. What about those dogs, eh? What a way to go! And you were almost there! Almost witnessed the whole ghastly horror show. Missed it, bad luck. Still, you must tell me more about it. My editor's ravenous for it, any little detail, anything.'

'Stanley, I've given you enough already. *You*'re the journalist.'

'And you're the lead, old boy. And I'm following it. What else is a journalist supposed to do? What do you want, money? I'm sure I can squeeze the old editor for a bit of lubrication.'

'No. It's not that.' I paused to think. 'Would you be interested in the inquest?'

'Would I? You bet.'

'I'll let you know.'

'Great. I'll be there.'

'Ever been to a coroner's inquest before?'

'Me? Are you joking? I'm an art critic, not a crime reporter.'

'Shame. I was hoping you could tell me the form. Bye, Stanley.' I rang off.

I sat down and closed my eyes. But I couldn't sleep. I wondered about the inquest. What would I be asked? What would I answer? Would I lie, in court? On oath?

The court. Justice. The law. I wondered where I'd be now if I hadn't given it all in. If I had done my articles, qualified, become a solicitor. Earned a decent living, instead of . . . what? Ten dark years of struggle, of semi-success, of corruption, failure, desperation. A fragile, tenuous existence. A sordid descent to the very bottom line of murder.

It could all have been very different. I could have been a confident, successful, useful member of the human race. I could be like the head boy, good at my job, serving a practical purpose, returning to a wife, dogs and a family home after an honest day's wage-earning. A pregnant wife. Children. I could be normal.

For one wild moment I thought that it wasn't too late. I can go back, finish my articles, qualify, get a job. Work hard and live quietly. But of course it was too late. Acton was dead, and there was no bringing him back.

And what a death. No one deserved to die like that, no matter who they were or what they had done. Not even Acton. Did he deserve to die at all? I'd thought no one would miss him, but perhaps Andrea was telling the truth about Greta's grief. Perhaps he would have changed. No one is beyond reformation, given time. Perhaps he did have real regrets and a genuine wish to transform his life. Who can say what a man's life might hold? Might have held. I had destroyed a life, a whole world, wiped out all the infinite possibilities it contained, on the evidence of just a fraction of them. How could I have done that? How could I ever have justified it?

The unopened letter from the coroner's office lay on the dusty sofa where I'd dropped it that morning. An overwhelming sense of dread prevented me from going anywhere near it. All afternoon it screamed at me from the middle of the mess and the chaos in the studio. It was all still there, the tide of books and papers and magazines, the mass of dusty canvases, the abandoned work, the wall-to-wall layers of scattered brushes, crayons, crushed charcoal, squashed tubes of paint, dirty glasses, crumpled beer cans, unwashed plates, cups of coffee, empty and half-empty bottles of wine and spirits.

I had to get out. I still had the keys to the house in Kent, but I couldn't bring myself to return them to Greta at the flat. If I dropped them into the gallery, whoever was holding the fort there could pass them on to her. So I drove across to the West End, to Cork Street. The gallery.

A sign on the door said 'Closed' but I could see a dark-haired man and two assistants through the glass front so I pushed it open – it was unlocked – and stepped inside.

The place was being decorated. The walls were no longer a gleaming white, but a very light, very pale grey. Pots of paint, dust-sheets, trestles, planks and ladders were piled up in a far corner. The dark-haired man and the two assistants were already making experimental hangings with different-sized pictures.

'I don't care what the lighting used to be like,' the dark-haired man was saying. 'This is the way I'm having it now.' The assistants had a resentful, hangdog look about them. I could tell from their faces and the way they stood that he was throwing his weight around.

He turned as I came in. It was then, with a sudden shock like a blow on the back of the head, that I saw who he was.

'Hello, Nicky,' Anthony Acton said. 'How's it going, mate?'

Acton looked paler than ever, and very tired. He smiled, and the smile wasn't his usual boyish grin but something warm and sad and real.

'It's good to see you,' he said. 'I'm glad you came by. I've been meaning to call you. To say thanks, to talk about . . . the whole dreadful business. But what with the police, and the undertakers, and . . . and now this crap about the Wyndham Lewis, what a bombshell, all bullshit – the time just, you know, where does it go? But it's good to see you again, Nick. Let's go up to the office.'

I didn't know what to say. I couldn't say anything. Stunned, I followed him into the lift. And up and out, into the inner sanctum of the gallery.

I sat down on the white leather sofa. Collapsed into it. My numb brain snagged on the nightmare of the last time I was here. Less than six months ago, but it seemed like an eternal moment, without end, playing and replaying itself continuously in some corner of my mind. The room gleamed as white as I remembered it, as white as a psychiatric cell or operating theatre. I tried to move away from that memory by imagining the moment when Yukio Haramaka confronted the Wyndham Lewis in this very room. The hush in which the picture was unveiled, the awe which couldn't fail to draw a gasp from Acton's prey, the seductive whispers of Acton himself as he steered the man towards his trap.

Acton was speaking again. I couldn't hear him. Was he real? Was any of this real? I shook my head, listened. What was he saying?

'What was it Hamlet said – "When sorrows come, they come not single spies, but whole battalions"? The last week, it's been one blow after another. That ungrateful bastard Stanley, how could he write such poisonous rubbish? Talk about kicking a man when he's down . . .' He rubbed his face in his hands. 'At least there's no sign that the Buruki Institute intend to sue the gallery. And there can be no criminal investigation if they don't. And to be quite honest, I'd be very surprised indeed if they did. They'd have to admit that the thing was a fake first, and that would be an intolerable loss of face for them. So they'll stay silent and they'll convince themselves the whole thing never happened.' He sighed. 'Drink?' He disappeared through one of the sliding doors at the far end of the room. 'I'll get another glass.'

I stared at the smoked-glass table in front of me. There were no white tulips this time – the glass bowl was empty. Was any of it real?

Acton returned with a bottle of vodka and two glasses. 'I don't know whether the gallery's going to survive all this, to be quite honest. But I'll tell you something, Nick, we're going to put up a bloody good fight.' He sat down and filled the two glasses. 'I've been on the phone to Madrid all week. Did you hear I signed up Martin Iruni?'

I found my voice. 'Greta said something about video installations . . .'

'Oh, sod video installations. That's just a bit of light relief for Iruni. No, he's the leader of Luskadi Matuzcoa. That's his real business.'

Luskadi Matuzcoa. Swine Chaos. I'd heard of them. They were a group of performance artists from the Basque region, anarchists and guerillas of the avant-garde. I vaguely remembered reports of one of their recent stunts – an immaculately-staged car crash in the middle of Madrid – blood, victims, all faked – which had paralysed the rush-hour traffic and fooled the emergency services. The 'victims' had fled their hospital beds only one step ahead of the police. I remembered other reports of a whole season of Mozart ruined at the opera house in Barcelona – Swine Chaos had taken an irrational objection to a particular production of The Magic Flute and ruined every performance of it by infiltrating the audience and staging a massive punch-up halfway through the second act. Daring artists or irresponsible criminals? It was simply a matter of opinion, and by all accounts they were equally pleased with either verdict.

'You've signed up Luskadi Matuzcoa? Is that wise? Playing with fire . . .'

'They're just what we need right now. Something extreme, outrageous. We're going to fight fire with fire. I'm going to throw the party to end all parties, Nick. It's all arranged – a week tomorrow. My place in Kent. I'm going to invite everyone, all the critics, collectors, dealers, everyone who might be afraid or delighted that the gallery's going down the pan. We'll show them that it isn't. Iruni and his gang will be doing their stuff, seamlessly integrated with the rest of the party. They'll be powerful, violent, outrageous. No one will know what is performance and what isn't. It'll blow their minds.

They'll be talking about it for months, years, afterwards. We'll come out of it right back on top of the whole heap again. You just see.' He emptied his glass, refilled it. 'I've had to put off the New York adventure, though. Just for a month or two. I'll pick it up again once all this trouble has blown over.'

He was pacing up and down the white room, but suddenly he stopped. 'But why am I talking business? The gallery, it's pretty insignificant when you think about ... that terrible accident ... dreadful ... dreadful ...' He sighed and sat down again, slumping back into the sofa with his head in his hands. 'And you, Nick, for you ... it must be even worse ... I can barely sleep at night, thinking about it, but you ... how are you coping? Are you all right?'

I found I couldn't speak. The shock of finding Acton alive was, if anything, becoming more and more intense. And there were so many questions, and the answers were all hidden, and somehow I knew even before I could begin to uncover them that they would be too terrible to confront.

'You mustn't blame yourself. It was an accident. A terrible accident. Those dogs, I'm sure the same thing would have happened if anyone else had been looking after them. Don't blame yourself.'

I still couldn't speak.

'I do understand that the loss must be as great for you as it is for me. You must believe me. Greater, perhaps. Such a blow, the wounds never recover, the dead can never be brought back to life, but we must nevertheless try to salvage what we can from the tragedy, it's the only way. We must try to keep moving forwards or we'll be destroyed by it. You and I – perhaps the common loss, the shared grief, can bring us closer, clear the ground between us. Whatever has happened, we must seize this opportunity to bury all the differences, all the grudges, the hostility. Perhaps it can help us go forwards together. We must try to rescue something positive from the disaster or it will destroy us as well.'

I had to get out of there. I emptied my glass and felt the vodka burn its way down my throat. Another glass and I'd be able to move, to speak.

'And the dogs as well . . . dead. So much death. I miss them, too. And you, perhaps you miss them as well. You spent a week with them, you must have got to know them, to like them. I miss them so much, almost as much as . . . as . . . but it isn't the same thing, of course . . . But sometimes I think I can still hear them, barking, at night . . .'

I stood up. I licked my lips, wiped a hand over my eyes. 'I must go,' I managed to say.

'Of course. If there's anything I can do to help, anything, you must let me know. You and I, Nick, we can help each other through this. Let me know what I can do . . .'

I left him in his office and took the lift down to the ground floor where the assistants were arguing amongst themselves over the hangings, the light, the colour of the walls. The future of the gallery.

If the dogs hadn't killed Acton, who had they killed?

I could guess the answer to that one, of course. But it was horrible, impossible. It would take more than guesswork and deduction to make me confront it. Until I saw it in black and white I wouldn't believe it.

I drove home as fast as I could through the early darkness, my heart thumping and my mind racing. I tore open the letter from Canterbury, horror squeezing the breath from my lungs as I read the coroner's words. The inquest on the death of Ms Diana Artemis was to open at three p.m. on Wednesday 25 February. My presence was required.

Diana. Diana was dead. I had killed Diana.

That was Monday. The inquest was on Wednesday. The Tuesday was just a blur, little more than a complete void. I remember a total and overwhelming numbness. I remember lying on my bed, shaking uncontrollably from the cold and the shock. I remember getting up every hour or so in a blind panic to search the room for a big overcoat and a balaclava helmet I had once owned but knew I no longer possessed. I'd lost them, but it was of the utmost importance that I found them again. If I could find them and put them on again, then everything would be alright. But if I couldn't find them . . .

They were presents from people I had loved, people who had loved me, and I had lost them. The guilt of it was unbearable. I kept getting up and searching for them, in the bedroom, in the studio, everywhere, but they weren't there. I couldn't find them anywhere.

It was my birthday, my first with Diana. It was a Saturday. Diana arrived at midday. She had just seen Iphigenia off to spend the weekend with her father. Diana was usually intensely depressed at such times, but that day she was making an effort to be cheerful because it was my birthday.

'I have a present for you,' she said. 'Wait here. I'll go and get it.'

The present was no surprise. All winter she'd been looking for a good warm overcoat for me. She was determined to find one I really liked. I wasn't much help. There's an early self-portrait of Picasso (I had a postcard of it pinned to a cupboard in the kitchen) where he stares out of the canvas with all the aggression of young genius, black-bearded, white-faced, wild-eyed, wrapped in a big dark overcoat with the collar turned up, 'looking for all the world' as one critic put it, 'like a terrorist about to throw a bomb into the middle of the twentieth century.' All I could do was point to the postcard and say 'I want a coat like that'.

But the way Diana gave the present was a surprise. When she came back into the room she was wearing it. And nothing else.

'I always think unwrapping a present is the best bit, don't you?' I said, taking the coat off her and looking at the finest present anyone had ever given to me.

She was laughing. 'Diana in her birthday suit,' she said. 'And it isn't even my birthday.'

We were in the studio. 'Bed, or life-class?' I said.

She shivered, still laughing. 'It's too cold for life-class. So I suppose it will have to be bed.'

When it was dark I got up and made some coffee and some toast – with honey for me, with marmalade for her. She got up and put my coat back on and followed me into the kitchen. She gave me a parcel awkwardly wrapped in brightly coloured paper.

'This is from Iphigenia,' she said. 'She made it herself.'

It was a balaclava helmet. 'She knitted this all by herself?' I was immensely impressed.

'Well, nearly. Mummy finished it off for her.'

I shook my head. 'She's such a bright child. So clever.'

'It was her idea. She worries about you. She knows how cold it is up here. She wants you to promise to wear it when you're working up here. She's afraid you'll get the flu. She's . . .'

Diana stopped talking. She was looking down at the floor. She was biting her lower lip. I could see her shoulders trembling inside the big overcoat. 'I'm not going to cry,' she said angrily. Her hands were clenched together tightly under her chin with the effort of self-control. 'I am not going to cry.'

'You won't,' I said. 'It's my party. I can cry if I want to, but you're not allowed to.'

She managed to laugh, but her shoulders were still trembling. 'She didn't want to go to her father's this weekend. She never does, but with your birthday . . .' She unclenched her hands and threw her dark hair back from her face. 'She wanted to come here with me, to give you her present herself, to say happy birthday . . .'

'Diana, we both wish she was here. If we could have our own way, she would be here. But we can't.' I put my arms round her. 'It's her father's turn this weekend, and I can't come between a father and his daughter. I wouldn't want to. I'd hate to turn Iphigenia against her own father.'

Diana shook her head. 'She hates her father for reasons which have nothing to do with you. And she loves you for reasons which have nothing to do with her father.'

'She'll be back tomorrow night. And the three of us will spend next weekend together.'

'Next weekend isn't your birthday.' Diana pushed herself away from me. 'There's a cake as well. But I didn't make it. You know I'm no good at that sort of thing.'

We sat in the middle of the studio and turned out all the lights and lit all the candles on the cake. We opened a bottle of wine and drank a toast to next year's birthday when Diana and Takis would be divorced, Diana and I would be married, and Diana, Iphigenia and I would be a family.

I wore the overcoat all that winter. When spring came I meant to take it to the dry-cleaners but never got round to it. Time enough before I'd need it again. All summer it lay in the bottom of the wardrobe in Diana's bedroom in Diana's flat, forgotten. And then, that autumn, when the end came, the coat stayed there, not only forgotten but abandoned. And the balaclava helmet – that was still in Acton's woodshed where I'd left it the day before Diana's death.

But that Wednesday my brain was too numb to register anything more than the fact that I no longer had that beloved overcoat or balaclava helmet. There was a block which let through nothing other than the loss of those two garments, and out of the chink through which they had forced themselves up into my consciousness seeped all the guilt in the world, like blood pouring from the hiding place where a terrible secret had been concealed in haste and horror.

CHAPTER TWELVE

The Crown Courts at Canterbury are outside the old city walls. They stand just to the east of the foundations of Saint Augustine's abbey, on a site where the Romans buried their dead.

The drive up from London was quicker than I'd expected. Too quick, for an appointment I was dreading. For half an hour I wandered around the remains of the abbey. Trying to ignore the cold, damp Kentish air. Trying to think about the ordeal ahead. But I couldn't. I was still numb with shock. I couldn't think of anything but the terrible truth that Diana was dead and I had killed her. Diana dead? I couldn't believe it. I didn't want to believe it.

At two forty-five I climbed the steps outside the courts and went in through the big double doors. It was very hot inside the building. There was a reception desk in the large entrance hall, and an old man in uniform sitting behind it. He directed me to the coroner's court.

The courtroom was full but silent. Heads turned as I opened the door and walked in. I saw Acton, Greta and Andrea sitting at the front, and Stanley a few rows behind them. The bench was unoccupied. I slid into a seat at the back. It was almost five minutes to three. Everyone was waiting.

Stanley turned and waved at me, grinning. Stanley. I suddenly remembered the list I'd given to him. Had he done anything with it yet? I'd given it to him because I wanted to clear my conscience, shed a guilty secret – but I'd assumed that Acton would be out of the way by then. If it got out now, Acton would know immediately who had blown the whistle on him. I thought about that while we waited. Should I try to stop Stanley using it? Was it too late?

We were still waiting at five past three. By ten past three the court room was no longer silent but rustled with the murmur of low voices, the voices of people who had been waiting long enough to grow tired of respectful silence. At a quarter past three the door at the back opened and all heads turned to see the inspector – the head boy – come in. He slid into a seat at the other end of the row in which I was sitting. It seemed to me that he was aware of my presence but unwilling to catch my eye. A clerk stood up and disappeared through a door at the far end of the room.

A moment later the coroner appeared and took his place. He shot a glance at the inspector and at a clock on the wall. He wasn't impressed. Then he cleared his throat.

'Ladies and gentlemen, may I begin by apologizing for the delay? We've all had to wait, due to circumstances beyond my control, so let's make a start straight away.

'Perhaps I should explain why we're all here today – what a coroner's inquest is.' He cleared his throat again. 'If the manner or circumstances of a death are unusual or not straightforward, it is often necessary for the opinions of various experts and the statements of various witnesses to be put together, in a public place, in order for the cause of death to be made known and officially recorded. That is why we are here. To enquire about a death, to reach a conclusion about its causes, and to record that conclusion. That is all. This is not a trial.'

I was the first witness called to the stand. The coroner asked me questions with the bored voice of an old man who had been doing the same job for too long, and I tried to keep him bored. Yes, Acton had asked me to look after the house while he and his wife were out of the country. Yes, that did include looking after the dogs. No, I hadn't looked after the dogs before. Yes, looking after the dogs did mean feeding them. Yes, that was all, except Acton had suggested I might like to play with them from time to time. No, I hadn't. Because they frightened me. Because they looked dangerous and behaved aggressively. All the time – it seemed to be in their nature, their character. Yes, it did seem to get worse as the week progressed. I don't know why. Perhaps because I ignored them, kept them locked up. Perhaps they wanted exercise, attention. I don't know. I don't know what 'usual' behaviour is for such dogs. It didn't strike me as unusual because I hadn't seen them any other way . . . Acton had an old tin bucket, and I filled it to the brim every day. From the freezer. First thing in the morning. No. I don't know. I didn't notice. I didn't pay them any attention at all. As little as possible. I didn't like them and I don't think they liked me . . . No, I've never owned a dog myself. In fact I dislike dogs of any sort. I don't know why he asked me. Perhaps he couldn't find anyone else to put up with them. Midday on Friday. No, I had a lunch appointment in London. About ten o'clock that morning. There was a message from Greta – Acton's wife – on my answerphone when I got back from lunch. No. I had no idea what Diana was doing there. Thank you.'

I walked back to my seat. My shirt stuck to the sweat on my ribs as I moved. I felt light-headed with the euphoria which comes when an unpleasant task has passed.

It was Greta's turn next. She was wearing black and white. No make-up. She looked terrible, as if she was dreading the ordeal even more than I had. The coroner silently noted her condition and softened his voice when he spoke to her. She answered quietly, glancing at him only occasionally. Yes, she had gone to Madrid with her husband, but had returned alone on Wednesday. She'd gone back to London on Thursday. She'd driven back down to Kent on Friday afternoon, arriving at about three o'clock. Acton hadn't returned from Spain. Soon after her return, and before her husband's, she'd glanced out of a window and seen the dogs' enclosure . . .

At this point she stopped. She took a deep breath, pressing a handkerchief to her eyes. The coroner didn't press her, and eventually she carried on unprompted.

The dogs were quite calm. They weren't barking or running around. They were just lying there. Perfectly calm. She hadn't seen the body at first, but as soon as she did, she'd thought it was her husband. She remembered running out into the garden, but she didn't remember calling the police or the ambulance. She didn't really remember anything after that until they arrived, when her husband returned. No, she had no idea what Diana was doing there. It must simply have been a terrible accident.

Then they called Acton to the stand. He was wearing a dark suit, and looked thinner and paler than ever. He stood upright, but his voice was quiet as he answered the coroner's questions. He'd had the dogs for four years. No, he'd never known them to show any aggression or any real violence. Only in play, in natural high spirits. Yes, he had left them before. They'd been fed by Mr Kennedy, the caretaker. No, he'd never had any trouble with them. He was in Florida, on holiday. Nicholas Todd. No, he hadn't had anything to do with the dogs before. No, he didn't know what his sister was doing in the enclosure that day, or indeed at the house. He assumed she had simply called by to see him, seen that the dogs were agitated and on their own, thought they were hungry or in need of reassurance or company, and ... well, it was just a terrible accident, a dreadful case of being in the wrong place at the wrong time ... He hadn't returned to the house until after four o'clock, after the police.

The next person called to the stand was an academic, an expert on canine behaviour. He was a young, fit looking vet. He confirmed that the Himalayan mastiff is a powerful and aggressive dog. Yes, dangerous would be a fair description. No, in his view they shouldn't be kept as pets. They were bred to guard herds grazing in the foothills of the Himalayas, bred to kill wolves and see off bears. No, the conditions in which Acton was keeping them were relatively good, but they weren't what the breed was naturally accustomed to, or intended for. No, there was no one reason why they might have turned violent. Perhaps they were angry and resentful because their owner had abandoned them for a week. That would explain their hostility to ... er ... to the man who was looking after them, and their growing discontent throughout Acton's absence. Perhaps their discontent had been misinterpreted as hunger by their victim, and she had gone into the enclosure to feed them. Perhaps she had gone into the enclosure to calm them down, to reassure them. Their resentment and anger would have boiled over and their natural aggression and violence burst to the surface.

Then it was the inspector's turn. He took the stand looking serious and determined. The coroner questioned him impatiently – he still hadn't forgiven him for holding up his inquest. He began by asking him precisely when he arrived at Acton's that afternoon. At three twenty-five, your honour. And where did you find the deceased? In the dog pen – a big area enclosed by wire fencing against a garden wall, at the far end of the lawn behind the house. And where were the dogs? Also in the pen, your honour. The door or gate into the pen wasn't open? No, your honour. It was fastened shut. Could it be fastened from the inside? It could, your honour. And what sort of mood were the dogs in at this time? They were calm to start with – but as soon as we approached the enclosure they began to bark, and the closer we came to the wire the more frenzied and aggressive their behaviour became. So they were still dangerous? They were. Within five minutes of our arrival they were completely out of control. And the deceased – what could you see of her? Well, she was lying motionless some yards inside the enclosure; we could see that she had been badly mauled – very badly indeed – we could only assume that she was in fact dead. And you couldn't get to her because of the dogs? That's right. We concluded that the dogs were still capable of violence, so we had no alternative but to put them down. A marksman was called and the dogs were shot. We then entered the enclosure – with a doctor, who confirmed that the victim was indeed dead. Her body was removed for examination, as were those of the dogs. And is there any suspicion of foul play? There is, your honour.

An absolute silence and stillness fell on the court. For an immeasurable instant time seemed to stand still. Then a murmur of surprise kick-started it once more as the seated crowd leaned forwards, suddenly alert. The coroner was taken completely by surprise. Blinking and swallowing, his mouth opened, shut, opened again, and he looked down, pushed his glasses up his nose and poked at the papers in front of him. 'But . . . but . . .' He looked up at the inspector, irritated and accusing. 'But there's nothing here . . . I know of nothing . . . what . . . ?'

'I'm sorry, your honour. It's new evidence. It's come to light only very recently. This afternoon, in fact.'

'Well . . . are you going to tell us what it is?'

'I'm afraid I can't, your honour. Not in an open court. That might prejudice our enquiries.'

'Well . . . what about the pathologist? Can we hear his report?'

'I would rather it wasn't made public at this stage, your honour.'

'So you're asking me to suspend the inquest?'

'Yes, your honour. I'm sorry. I can confirm that Diana Artemis's death is now the subject of a murder enquiry.'

Another murmur swept through the court room. The inspector looked straight at me. By this time I was shaking openly and uncontrollably.

'Well. I see. Well, that leaves me with no alternative.' The coroner had collected himself by now, but he was indignant, almost angry, at this development. No doubt he saw it as chaotic, melodramatic and unprofessional. The looks he gave the inspector made it plain that he regarded it as a typical police cock-up. 'Ladies and gentlemen. This inquest is suspended as the death under enquiry is now the subject of a murder investigation. Thank you and good day.' With that he gathered his papers together, nodded at a clerk, and stalked out of the court.

I couldn't get out of there fast enough. A knot of journalists trying to question Acton and Greta were blocking the exit. I tried to squeeze by, hearing Stanley shouting above the uproar. 'Is the Wyndham Lewis a forgery, Mr Acton? Mr Acton! Who really painted the picture you sold as genuine, Mr Acton?' There was relish in his booming questions – at last he was getting his own back after years of humiliation. He was making the most of it. 'Mr Acton!'

The other journalists, emboldened by Stanley's front and having to shout to make themselves heard, joined in the fray. 'Mr Acton! Mr Acton! Do you have any idea who killed your sister? Mr Acton . . . !'

Someone grabbed my elbow as I pushed for the door. For an instant I was about to pull free and make a run for it.

'Nicky.' It was Andrea. 'Nick Todd.'

I stopped and turned.

'Diana's funeral. It's tomorrow . . .'

I looked at her, speechless, my thoughts refusing to come together.

'You said you wanted to know. Remember?'

I shook my head. 'Yes. Yes, of course.'

She mentioned a time, and the name of a village, just south of Canterbury, and then I was out of the court-room and out of the building, hurrying down the steps and across the street. I didn't dare to look back in case the inspector might come running after me. Fifty yards down the road I turned, but there was no one in pursuit. The steps and the doorway were clear. The building looked as deserted as Saint Augustine's abbey.

The crematorium was on a chalk hill some miles south of Canterbury, surrounded by bare orchards and hop-fields and grey ash-woods as far as the eye could see. It was very cold. The landscape was frozen and silent. There were no birds, no wind. Nothing moved. Nature's pendulum had come to rest at its lowest point and it was difficult to believe it would ever start moving again.

I sat in the car for some time after I arrived, staring blankly out at the still and empty view, grief pulling me in one direction, guilt in the other. Eventually I got myself out of the car and stumbled up the gravel drive to the chapel.

The service had already started. From the back row I

could see Acton and Greta and Andrea at the front on one side, and a big dark man with two dark women at the front on the other. The big man sat slumped forwards with his face in one hand. It was Takis. The older woman could have been his mother, the younger woman his sister. I saw with a strange mixture of intense relief and yet disappointment that Iphigenia wasn't with them.

Acton gave a short address and then the coffin rolled out of sight to the sound of Verdi's requiem mass, and into the flames which reduced that torn and battered body into something even less than the mouse's skull I had held in the palm of my hand six days and a whole lifetime ago. Takis sat motionless throughout, his face in his hands.

A crowd of journalists were waiting outside. Stanley and a few fellow critics were outnumbered by a whole gang of hard-looking men and women who I could only assume were crime reporters. The revelation at the inquest had made every national paper that morning. I was one of the first to leave the chapel, intending to slip away quietly, but the sight of the press pulled me up short.

'Nick. I'm glad you could make it.' Acton came up behind me from within the chapel and put a hand on my shoulder.

I said nothing. How was I going to get away from all this?

'You should talk about it,' Acton said. 'It helps to talk, Nick. Really. Come and see me, any time.'

And then the reporters closed in and Acton stepped forwards, his hands raised, to clear a path through them for the people behind us.

There was a car parked next to mine which hadn't been there when I'd gone inside. My heart lurched when I saw who was sitting in it. The head boy. He was watching me. He didn't get out, just watched as I unlocked the door, sat down behind the wheel, started the engine.

I caught a glimpse of myself in the rear view mirror. My face was thin and white. I looked like I hadn't slept for years. My suit was crumpled and my shirt needed changing. It was the suit I'd worn to the inquest the day before. The same shirt, the same underwear. If it looked like I'd slept in the outfit, that was because I had. Well, I hadn't slept. I had simply lain on the bed in a hotel room in Canterbury and waited for the night to pass. There's little point in getting undressed for the night if you aren't going to sleep, let alone change into clean clothes in the morning.

I drove off. The head boy made no move to follow. He simply picked up a newspaper from the passenger seat and disappeared behind it.

I don't know how I got back to London. I don't remember because I drank myself into a stupor as soon as I arrived home. I couldn't think of any other way to get through the night. I wasn't going to sleep and I didn't want to spend those long empty hours alone with my own thoughts.

I came to just before dawn. I was lying on the kitchen floor. It was very cold and I felt as if I'd been dragged back from the dead. I got up and had a bath, shaved, put on fresh clothes. They were going to arrest me that morning, I was sure, and I wanted to be clean and sober when they came to get me.

By the time it was light I was dressed and ready for them. I sat down to wait, my head clear, thinking of nothing, simply waiting. The winter sky looked thick and heavy beyond the glass ceiling. There was a greyish-yellow tint to it which promised snow.

Ten o'clock came and went. Eleven o'clock . . . I sat

there, listening hard for footsteps on the stairs, the knock at the door. It was very quiet. It was still very quiet at midday. Something inside me, stretched almost to breaking point, began to quiver with an almost unbearable tension. Come on, you bastard, I thought, don't make me suffer. Let's get it over with. Don't make me sit here and sweat.

They came at one o'clock. The head boy, his sergeant and a uniformed constable. The sergeant was balding and ageless, tall and thin, with spectacles and watchful eyes. All three looked very serious, their faces expressionless masks.

'Mr Todd? Mr Nicholas Todd?' the head boy asked as I let them in, as if we'd never met before.

'Yes.'

He licked his lips. 'Mr Nicholas Todd, you're under arrest for the murder of Diana Artemis.' He gave the constable a nod. The constable reached into the breast pocket of his uniform shirt and took out a piece of card. For one bizarre moment, numbed and bewildered as I was, I thought we were about to exchange business cards.

He read me my rights. I didn't catch more than two or three consecutive words out of the whole lot. I tried to concentrate but they just swept right over me.

'You can make two telephone calls,' the sergeant said, 'as long as you tell us who you're calling.'

I shook my head. I could have made all the calls I wanted that morning. But I didn't then as I didn't now. There was no point. Who was I going to call, anyway? I shook my head again. I just wanted to get on with it.

They put handcuffs on me and led me down the stairs and out into the street. A police car was waiting for us at the kerb, with another uniformed man behind the wheel. It was colder than ever. The constable glanced up at the thickening dirty-whiteness of the sky. 'Snow on the way,' he muttered.

They sat me in the back between the head boy and the constable. The head boy nodded to the driver and away we went.

The police station at Canterbury stands just outside the old town, facing the best preserved stretch of the medieval city wall on the other side of the inner ring-road. But the historic town wall was not visible from the yard behind the station where we came to a halt. We got out of the car. The air was very cold and very still. The clouds were thick and dark overhead. And then, as we were crossing the yard, it began to snow. A few flakes at first, and then thicker and faster. There was no wind. It just came straight down, white and thick.

Inside the station they took the handcuffs off me and handed me over to the duty sergeant. In a windowless office I surrendered my belt, shoelaces, watch and the contents of my pockets. I signed a form telling them who I was, where I lived, when and where I was born, whether I had been arrested before, and all the other questions I answered without protest. I signed an inventory of the personal effects I'd surrendered. I was photographed (stand against the wall, look straight ahead, turn to the side, the right side, now the left) and finger-printed.

Along a corridor and down a flight of stairs. The sergeant punched a number into a touch pad beside the closed door at the bottom. The door buzzed open. There was another door two yards further on. Another touch pad. Buzz. Another uniformed man was waiting for us beyond that. A bunch of keys jingled in his hand.

The three of us set off along another echoing corridor, this one lined with cell doors. The man stopped, inserted a key into a lock in the nearest door, turned it, swung the door open. I stepped inside. When the door closed behind me I could hear the echo of its metallic clang bouncing along the corridor.

The sound of the key turning in the lock filled the cell. Then there was silence.

CHAPTER THIRTEEN

The cell measured about twelve feet by eight. It contained a bed, a washbasin and tap, and a toilet. There were no windows. It was brightly lit by an electric light-bulb recessed into the ceiling. The floor was tiled and sloped down towards a drain in one corner. The walls were white. It was clean, warm and very quiet.

I felt strangely at home in there. It was where I belonged. I had killed Diana and I had been arrested, and now here I was awaiting trial and punishment. It was what I deserved.

The sense of relief as the door closed behind me was overwhelming. I sat down on the edge of the bed. I felt utterly drained. Numb and exhausted. I swung my legs up on to the bed, lay down, and fell fast asleep.

A soft click and rattle woke me up. I looked around in some confusion. The light was still on. Nothing had changed. I had no idea how long I'd been asleep or what time of day it was. I looked at my watch but of course my wrist was bare. I lay awake for some time in the silence, and then I heard the click again. It came from the door. There was a spy-hole in the door and as I looked at it, it seemed to blink and I heard the rattle again. So that's what it was. Someone was checking that the prisoner was behaving himself.

It felt a bit colder. There was a blanket folded up on the bed at my feet. I shook it open, wrapped myself in it, and went straight back to sleep. I didn't wake up again until much later, when I heard the key turning in the lock. The door swung open and in came a policeman with a mug of tea in one hand and a plate of toast in the other. 'Breakfast,' he said.

'What time is it?'

'Breakfast-time.' He went out. The door swung to and the keys turned in the lock.

I sat on the edge of the bed, eating the toast and drinking the tea, and then I went back to sleep again.

There was no clock in the interview room, but I caught a glimpse of the head boy's watch as he sat down at the table opposite me. It said eight forty-five. In the morning, presumably.

'Well,' he said. 'Are you going to tell us all about it?'

I didn't reply. How could I ever begin to explain myself to them? I didn't have the will or the energy. Just get on with it, I thought. Do your job and then let me get some rest.

The head boy sat back and sighed. He seemed deep in thought. His clear face looked as untroubled as ever but his eyes were unfocused. Eventually he leaned forwards and slid something from a file lying on the desk in front of him. A handful of photographs. Large ten by eights. Colour.

'I'd like you to have a look at these.' He passed them over. 'They were taken between three-thirty and four o'clock last Friday afternoon. I don't need to tell you where.'

The first photograph was an overhead shot of a misshapen bundle lying on the ground. The bundle looked like a mighty wind had twisted it into an impossible shape and almost smashed it to pieces. It was wrapped up in old rags which the wind had torn to shreds but which were still holding it together.

'That was how we found her.'

With a shock I realized the bundle was a human body.

The background was green grass, muddy and trampled, with a wide, dark stain spread out across it. The same muddy stain spread out across the body and the few rags holding it together.

'Go on. There are more.'

I didn't want to look at them, but I forced myself. Diana (I had to take his word for it – there was no way the body could be identified from the photos, and I felt a coward's gratitude for that) looked like a toy doll which had been dropped from a great height and kicked from one end of the playground to the other. The posture was so unreal, but the deathly pallor of the skin and the dirtiness of the dried blood were all too convincingly organic.

'Of course, the close-ups are more rewarding. The throat area. You have to look at that one twice to work it out. Go on, look at it twice. No throat there. They practically chewed her whole neck off. That's why her head's at such an odd angle. What's left of it.'

My hands were shaking. I turned the photos quickly, escaping from horror to even greater horror.

'Now, that shot won't mean much to you if you're not familiar with the anatomy of the inner gut.'

I threw the photos on to the table. They skidded across the surface. 'Why show them to me?' I asked.

The head boy didn't reply. He watched me closely as I struggled with faintness and nausea. The images repeated themselves in front of my eyes. For a moment I seemed to hear the baying of hounds. For a moment it was deafening. Barking, snarling. Then it passed.

He picked up the photos, tapped them together, and put them back in the folder. Then he took out another photo. I flinched from it, but he held it out, insistent. The shot was of another area of trampled, muddy grass. By the fence of the dog enclosure. The dogs were lying in a heap against the wire, as if they'd all suddenly fallen asleep on top of each other while trying to attack something on the other side of it.

'We had to shoot them. An easy job, technically speaking, but pulling the trigger is something else altogether. I didn't envy our marksman. A dog lover, like me.'

The photo must have been taken about half an hour later than the others. Four o'clock. The sun beginning to go down. The edges of the picture were dark, the dogs in the centre lay in a pool of harsh artificial lighting. The wire fencing, the floodlights, the carcasses, the half-darkness, all combined to make the picture even more chilling than the others.

'It was sickening, but it had to be done. Three reasons. One, to prevent further deaths. Two, to recover the body. Three, so the pathologist could examine the contents of their stomachs.' He took the photo, looked at it, then put it down on the table in front of him. 'Very interesting, the contents of their stomachs.' He looked up at me. 'What was Diana doing there? Why did she suddenly show up at Acton's at that particular time on that particular day?'

'I don't know. Unlucky coincidence . . .'

'Why did she take it upon herself to go in and feed those dogs?'

'I don't know. Perhaps she didn't. Perhaps she went in just to quieten them down, to reassure them.'

'No. The empty bucket was found in the enclosure with her. With what was left of her.'

'Perhaps she thought they were hungry. There was no one there – perhaps she thought they hadn't been fed.'

'Why was she wearing Acton's sweater?'

'What?'

'She went into that enclosure wearing a sweater of her brother's. There wasn't much left of it, but forensics identified it and Acton confirmed it.'

Dear God. She wouldn't have stood a chance in there . . . 'Perhaps she thought the scent of their beloved master would reassure them,' I said, thinking aloud. 'Calm them down . . .' The irony of it all. The terrible, unbearable irony . . .

'Could you tell us where you were and what you were doing at one o'clock in the afternoon last Friday?'

'I was having lunch with a journalist called Stanley Farquar. We were in a pub called the Eagle on Farringdon Road from midday. Then we went to a restaurant across the road for lunch. The QC. We didn't leave until mid-afternoon.'

'Stanley Farquar.' The inspector sighed and nodded. 'Ah yes.' He reached down into a briefcase standing beside his chair, pulled out a newspaper and threw it down on the table between us. 'What about this?' Friday's newspaper folded so Stanley's article was face-up.

'What about it?'

'Have you read it?'

'Yes.'

'Tell me about it.'

'Well, I'm surprised Stanley has shown so much initiative.'

'Stanley. Yes. The journalist you had lunch with last Friday. An hour or so before Diana died and a day or two after Stanley just happened to be poking around in the British Library and just happened to come across those letters.'

'Even journalists deserve a bit of luck now and then.'

'Is the picture a forgery, then?'

I shrugged. 'The world of commercial art is a very dishonest one. I hear half the Rembrandts in the Queen's own collection are questionable. It's a natural and accepted hazard of collecting, so I'm told.'

'So who did paint it?'

'Surely you're not in charge of that investigation as well, inspector?'

He looked down at the photo of the dead dogs, studying it, scrutinizing it. Then he reached into the briefcase again and, like a conjuror, produced some sort of glossy brochure. 'Dead animals seem to appear quite a lot in your paintings,' he said, quite casually. He held up the brochure so I could see what it was. The catalogue of my one-man show.

'Not really my kind of thing.' He flicked through the glossy pages. 'No criticism intended. I just don't understand art. That's all. But my sergeant, he's right on the ball. Explained a few things to me.'

He took a loose piece of paper from between the pages and unfolded it. It was a press cutting. He began to read aloud.

'"Todd's Field Sport series could not be hung in the trophy hall or above the gun-cabinet or in the club-room. These pictures do not celebrate the kill, but condemn it. They are a cry of compassion for the prey and a shout of rage against the killers. Nor do they exploit a potentially sensational subject matter (indeed, it is difficult to say exactly which of his dark tones is intended to represent blood), and by ignoring such easy effects he has successfully transcended his subject matter. These aren't anti blood-sport statements, nor are they meant to be; here hunting is merely a myth or vehicle to carry his universal vision of the stupidity and evil of predatory destruction. By focusing on the quarry – the victim – he succeeds in communicating this vision with a truly Aristotelian charge of pity and terror."'

He sighed, folded the cutting again, and put it back

among the pages of the catalogue. 'Now, I didn't have the faintest what all that meant, so I read it to my sergeant, and he said it simply meant that you'd sympathize with the dogs and wouldn't have liked to shoot them either.'

'The dogs were an even better example of the stupidity and evil of predatory destruction than anything I could have painted.'

'And you're an expert on predatory destruction, are you?' He stared at me for some moments. Then he stood up, nodded to the constable standing by the door, and walked out.

Back in the cell I thought about Diana wearing Acton's sweater when she went in to feed the dogs. My thoughts circled round and round the horror of it, unable to fully confront it, unable to fully escape it, unable to settle elsewhere.

I lay down on the bed and stared at the ceiling, forcing myself to think about other things. About the rest of the interview. What sort of game was the inspector playing? A patient one. He wanted a confession but he was taking his time. Softening me up before he really got down to business. And what would that involve? The evidence. And what could that be?

I heard keys turn in the lock and saw the door swing open. A policeman came in with a mug of tea in one hand and a packet of sandwiches in the other. 'Lunch,' he said.

'What's the time?'

'Lunchtime.' The door clanged to, the keys rattled in the lock.

That afternoon the head boy himself came and collected me from the cell. 'We made a thorough search of Diana's flat earlier this week,' he said as he and a uniformed constable escorted me along corridors and up stairs. 'We found something we thought might be of interest to you.'

He held a door open and I walked into darkness. Into a room where heavy blinds were drawn across windows and the lights were off. I knew immediately what it was they had found and were going to show me. I didn't want to see it. I had seen it already and I didn't want to see it again.

There were seats in that room, arranged in rows facing a screen pulled down over one wall. A group of figures were already sitting in the front row, laughing and restless with boredom and impatience. We sat in the back row, the projector behind us. Just as my eyes began to adjust to the darkness, someone switched the projector on and a wobbling square of grainy light fell on the screen. Some bored cheers and impatient clapping came from the front rows, and then the film began to roll.

It was the film Tony Acton had shown me the previous October. Tony and Diana Acton. Brother and sister. More than brother and sister, less than brother and sister.

I felt my stomach lurch and knew I was going to be sick. I stood up and pushed my way out through the darkness towards the door. Scattering chairs, ignoring cries of protest from the front rows as my shadow cut across the screen and a shaft of light cut into the room from the open door. I staggered out into the corridor. I could see a door to the gents a few yards further down. I rushed through it and made it to the first basin as my stomach erupted.

Then I turned the taps full on and drank some cold water. I stood up and looked at myself in the mirror. The night's sleep in the cell had made no difference to my appearance. My face was thinner and whiter than ever. I still looked like I hadn't slept for years. And now there was vomit down the front of my jacket. I stood there looking at myself until my stomach turned again, with disgust, and bent down to be sick once more into the basin with the taps full on and the water pounding round and down the plug hole.

When I looked up again, the inspector was standing behind me, just inside the door. I hadn't heard him come into the gents but now I could see him in the mirror. His face was expressionless. I drank some more cold water and he watched me, silently.

The door opened and some policemen came in. From their voices I recognized them as the front-row audience. They stood at the urinals, their loud voices echoing around the gents as they pissed.

'Didn't rate that as a show, did you Jimmy?'

'Nah. No colour, no dialogue. Didn't even see her tits. What sort of a mucky movie was that, eh?'

'Not like that Brazilian video they ran last month, John. You missed a classic there, mate. Broke at least six laws, Jimmy reckons. A classic.'

One of them rinsed his hands in the next basin. He looked up, about to speak, then caught sight of me and fell silent. He turned away to dry his hands and a moment later they were gone, their voices and laughter disappearing down the corridor.

The inspector came closer. I saw him in the mirror, standing at my shoulder. 'The man and the woman in the film. Tell me who they were.'

In the mirror I could see my own face, hollow and white, looking up at his. The stink of vomit filled my nostrils. 'You know. You saw it.'

'I want you to tell me. Who were they?'

'You saw it, you bastard!'

'The man was Tony Acton. Wasn't it? I want you to tell me who the woman was.'

'Diana. Diana Artemis. Diana Acton. You bastard!'

He stood there, nodding. 'And it wasn't the first time you'd seen the film, was it?'

I shook my head. No. It wasn't.

The door opened and a policeman came into the cell carrying a tray. The tray held a plate of something with chips, a dish of something with custard, and a glass.

'Supper,' he said. He stood in the doorway, waiting.

I didn't speak. I lay on the bed, staring at the ceiling.

'Supper time?' he said. Then he shrugged, put the tray down and went out, shaking his head.

I didn't feel like playing the game that evening.

Why fight them, I was thinking. If they want a confession, why not confess? Tell them all. Why not? With Diana's death, all I could hope for was punishment. And even punishment was little to hope for. It wouldn't bring Diana back, nor could it ever atone for her death. The grief and the guilt would remain. At the most, it might make them bearable. So punishment was all that mattered. I had no fear of conviction, of imprisonment, of punishment. On the contrary, if they could ease this terrible burden of guilt, the dreadful responsibility for her death.

I ate my supper and spent most of the night tossing and turning. In the morning, I decided, I would confess. I went through it in my mind, the whole account, preparing myself word for word. I would tell them everything, about Acton and me, about Diana and me, about Acton and Diana. I knew exactly what I would say. I could hear myself telling them how I laid the trap for Acton, how I beat and half-starved those dogs, how one sniff of Acton's scent was enough to send them into a killing fury by the time I'd finished with them on Friday morning and went back to London. Word for word.

'. . . You know what followed. Now you know that it wasn't what was supposed to happen. It all went horribly wrong. It should have been Acton, not Diana.

'And if it hadn't gone wrong? If Acton had died? Do you know, for some days I actually believed that was what had happened. And those few days were enough to convince me that there would have been no fresh start, no release. Murder would have been even harder to put behind me than everything else I'm trying to escape. Obvious, really. I should have known. But I haven't been able to think straight or see clearly for a long time.

'And what has happened is worse than anything I could have imagined. Diana's dead, and it's all my fault. I can't believe it, but it's true. I'm responsible for her death. I killed her.'

In the morning, it was the detective sergeant who took the lead in the interview room. The head boy sat at his side, listening and watching, but silent.

'We know you murdered Diana Artemis,' the sergeant began as soon as I sat down. 'We know why you murdered her. And we have proof.'

'It wasn't murder. Diana . . .'

He cut in on me. 'Nonsense. You murdered her. It was what you'd planned all along. You set up those dogs to kill her. You invited her down, told her to feed the dogs, knowing they'd tear her to pieces.'

'No! You're so wrong. That doesn't make sense.' I looked at the sergeant, taking in his thinness, dryness, hardness. His thin face, his thin body, the lines of disapproval around his thin mouth, his baldness, the thin metal frames of his spectacles, they all seemed deliberate extensions of his hard, thin, dry manner. How old was he? It was impossible to say. He could be an old twenty-five, or a man of seventy, well-preserved through desiccation. And he seemed so certain of his facts. Why? 'Diana . . . I . . .'

'You couldn't stand the thought of her cheating on you, could you. Cheating on you, Mr Nicholas Todd, with Tony Acton, of all people. You couldn't stand it. It tore you apart. You hated her for it. You wanted to kill her and that's precisely what you did. Isn't it?'

'Diana . . .' I paused, swallowed. Began again. 'Diana was the last person in the world I wanted dead.'

'All right.' He opened a file and took out a sheet of paper. 'I have here the text of a note found in Diana's handbag. The handbag was found in Acton's house. Let me read it to you.' He cleared his throat.

'Dear Nick. Here I am. Where are you? It's midday, and there's still no sign of you. I can't wait much longer, but before I go I will feed the dogs as you requested. I think you're right – they're not going to wait until you get back from your walk. I think I'll wear that sweater, too – a good suggestion. You say the smell of it calms them down; well, let's hope it does, because they're so hungry they're all in a bit of a state. Well, if it's worked for you all week . . . The bucket's a bit heavy, but I'm sure I'll manage. Nick, I'm glad you've decided we do have things to talk about after all – I just hope your absence this morning doesn't mean that you've changed your mind. It does mean that I've come all this way for nothing this morning, but I would do the same again even if there was only the slightest chance of talking things over with you. Well, the ball is in your court, as ever. With all my love, Diana.'

There was silence. For some moments I couldn't speak. 'That's not . . . It's ridiculous . . . A fabrication . . .'

The sergeant shook his head. 'Genuine enough.' His thin smile returned. Suddenly he looked very pleased with himself again. 'Now, isn't it about time you made a full statement?'

'That note . . . let me see it . . .'

He held out the sheet of paper.

'No – not just the text. The actual note . . .'

The sergeant turned to the head boy, eyebrows raised in questioning silence.

'Show him the photocopy,' the inspector said.

The sergeant opened the file again and took out another piece of paper. This one was held in some sort of clear plastic wallet. He passed it across the table.

I looked at it. Dear Nick. Here I am. Where are you? It looked like her hand, all right. And it was certainly her notepaper . . . My hands were shaking. I felt dizzy with the unreality of it. I tried to read the rest of the note, but the words swam in front of my eyes, too blurred to read.

I closed my eyes and shook my head. Concentrate, I told myself grimly. Handwriting can be faked, notepaper stolen. It had to be a fake. A good one, but a fake nevertheless. I looked at it again. The handwriting really was a very convincing reproduction. And the language, the turns of phrase . . . Dear Nick. Here I am. Where are you . . . ? I nodded. Yes. It sounded like her. The whole thing, the rhythm, the phrases. I could almost hear her voice as I read it.

So who could have done it? The police, fabricating evidence? No. It had to be someone who knew Diana well, very well, knew the way she wrote and thought and spoke. My head was beginning to spin. Whoever wrote it was setting me up. Whoever wrote it might even be guilty of Diana's death . . .

I could feel a cold sweat breaking out under my shirt.

I stared at the letter again. The paper was shaking in my hands. I saw that my knuckles were white.

Who could do it? Who knew her well enough to write the letter? Who might have wanted to kill her? Who would want me to go down for it? It was as if someone had opened a door in my brain which I hadn't known was there before. It was as if I had just discovered I had a sixth sense.

There's only one candidate, I thought. But it can't be. He's changed. He's been so . . . kind . . . helpful. I nodded. The bastard. So that's what it's all about. The kind words, the offers of help . . . and I took it all in. The smile on the face of the tiger.

'Who found the note?'

'We found the note in the handbag. But Acton found the handbag and handed it in.'

I nodded again. The bastard. All those kind words. He was just stringing me along, playing with me. It was just a smoke-screen.

'You set up those dogs to kill her. Didn't you?'

'No. Not Diana. I . . .'

'We know how you did it. You half-starved those beasts, didn't you? Half-rations all week. Well, we found the surplus, hidden in the woods where you dumped it. A big black bin-liner full of rotting meat. We've got it, Todd. Back in the deep freeze, ready for judge and jury.'

No! No, I got rid of it all, I made sure of that! It all went. Eaten. Scavengers. Black bin-liner? What were they talking about?

'Forensics know exactly when it was dumped. And Acton's confirmed that it's his dog food.'

Acton . . .

'But you didn't just starve them, did you? You wanted them mean as well as hungry. How do we know? Well, look what we found hidden in the woodshed.'

He reached down behind his chair, then straightened up to put something on the table where I could see it. Something long and heavy and wrapped in clear plastic. A length of well-seasoned timber about four feet long and about as thick as my wrist. Scraps of a blue silk garment, stained with blood and saliva, lashed to one end. The club.

But . . . but . . . I'd destroyed it . . . chopped it up . . . burnt it . . . Hadn't I? Perhaps I hadn't. Perhaps I'd left it in the shed, imagined its destruction only, dreamt it . . . My head was reeling. Perhaps I'd lost my grip on reality. The stress, after all, the pressure, the last six months . . . Perhaps I had just dumped the surplus dog-meat in the woods, in a black bin-liner. Simply imagined the fox . . . Perhaps I had invited Diana down there . . . No! No, not that. Never.

'You thrashed them into a killing fury. Didn't you?'

I shook my head. Concentrate, think. I stared at the club. No, it wasn't my club. It was a copy. Different wood . . . The blue of the silk – a different shade of blue . . .

More deception, more forgery . . . Acton. Yes, of course. He had me trapped. He had me exactly where he wanted me.

'You made sure those beasts were hungry enough and angry enough to kill. Then you invited Diana Artemis down there and got her to go in with them, knowing they'd tear her apart. That's murder.' The sergeant leaned forwards, licking his lips. 'Now, about that statement . . .'

'No.' I shook my head. Acton, you bastard. I'm going to get you. One way or another I'm going to get you and this time I won't muck about. I had to get out of there. And I had to tell them nothing. If they knew, there was no way I'd be able to get at him. They would have him, I wouldn't. I shook my head again. 'No way.'

The sergeant glared at me. 'You're not being very clever, Mr Todd. I thought you were supposed to be a clever one.' He took his glasses off and polished them on the end of his tie. He put them back on and squinted at me, frowning. 'We know all about you, Mr Todd. We know just how smart you are. You qualified as a lawyer, didn't you? Never practised. Became a bohemian instead. A wise move if I may say so. Policemen don't like lawyers. We don't like them at all.'

I stared back at him, saying nothing.

The head boy sighed. 'We're having you charged and committed for trial, the day after tomorrow, whether we have a statement or not. You'll be sent to prison, on remand. So you've got a day and a half to be sensible.' He leaned across and took the plastic wallet from my hands. 'We're going to use all this, you know. Whether you make that statement or not. We're going to use it, and it will get you sent down for murder. A jury would need less than half an hour to reach a decision. Your only hope for any sort of mitigation is to plead guilty in the first place. Make a full statement and stop wasting our time.' He stood up to go. 'We'll see you again tomorrow.'

I thought about that mountain of fabricated evidence all afternoon. The forged note in particular. The image of it swam in front of my eyes as I lay on my bed in the cell, trying to make sense of the day's bombshells. The more I thought about the note, the more I realized how much it stank of Tony Acton. His passion for fakes and forgeries. I could imagine his malicious delight in it. In the irony of dispatching a forger with a forgery. In the hurt and outrage he must have known that the sacrilege of putting false words in Diana's mouth would cause me. In the sheer pleasure of deception. Who else but Acton was capable of that sort of relish?

And the purpose of it all? Was it simply a malicious attempt to frame me for an accidental death? Or was it part of a bigger and more deeply planned stratagem? A ploy to deflect blame for a death which was not accidental? The latter, surely. Acton wasn't a mere pragmatist. He was a master of complex and cunningly-woven manipulations. A prime mover, not a mere reactor.

Besides, the club, the bin-liner full of meat – they proved that Acton had known what I was up to with those dogs. And knowing that, he had invited Diana down, I was sure, had invited her down and got her in with those killers, had set me up for her death. But how had he known? How had he invited her? Hadn't he been in Spain all that time?

Well, such questions were almost irrelevant. Acton was responsible for Diana's death, I was sure of it, and all that mattered was making sure he didn't get away with it. There was only one way of doing that, and I was going to do it.

This time I was going to do the job properly.

The despondency and numbness of the last four days had suddenly evaporated. I was reanimated with a hatred and anger which I'd thought had died with Diana. But they were back, and like old friends they were going to see me through this, to the very end.

I had to get out of there. Bail . . . If I was going to be charged the day after tomorrow, I had just over a day to sort it out or I'd be sent to jail on remand. How much would I need for bail? More than I had, for sure. How many very wealthy people did I know? One. Tony Acton. More irony. No – there was someone else . . .

'Am I allowed visitors?' I asked when my supper arrived.

'Depends on who you want to see. Depends on the inspector.'

Inevitably there was a form for it. I filled it out and gave it to my guard who promised to take it straight to the inspector.

The next day, an hour or two after breakfast, I heard the key turn in the lock. The door opened and a policeman entered the cell. Both his hands were empty. 'Visitor,' he said.

'What time is it?'

'Time to get moving. Come on, you don't want to keep him waiting.'

Takis Artemis stood up when I entered the room. He nodded but he didn't shake my hand. 'Well, well, well,' he said, sitting down. 'It's the boyfriend. The ex-boyfriend. The man who wanted to marry my wife. The man who killed my wife.'

I shook my head. 'I didn't do it, Takis. I'm not innocent, but –'

'I didn't come to hear your snivelling denials, your pathetic excuses.' Anger flashed from him. 'I came to see what sort of man you were again, to see who could have done that to that bloody bitch of my wife.'

'Thanks for coming.'

'I don't want your gratitude,' he growled. 'I didn't come as a favour, I came because I was curious.' He pulled out a packet of cigarettes and lit up. He inhaled deeply, exhaled. 'What the hell,' he said, leaning back. 'Listen, my friend. I can't find it in myself to blame you for it. I can tell you there were times when I wanted to kill her myself. Yes. Many times when I thought, quite seriously, about doing it. I understand, my friend. What did I tell you? You'll end up hating her, I said. You'll hate her so much you'll want her dead. Remember? I know what it's like.'

The door opened and someone brought in a cup of tea for the policeman who was sitting in with us. Takis raised a hand to order the same for himself.

'No, my friend, I don't blame you. I feel sorry for you.' He looked at me, perfectly calm and steady. 'You and me, we should understand each other very well. We've both been through it, haven't we?' He nodded slowly, drawing on his cigarette. 'But I'm sorry it happened to you. I'm sorry you ended up in here.'

'How's Iphigenia?' Yes. How was she? Iphigenia. I had been trying not to think about her, how much I missed her, how she must miss her mother.

'Beautiful.' He smiled. 'But difficult. She isn't used to living with her father. But – give it time. It's what I've always wanted; I should thank you for that, at least. I owe you for it. So perhaps I can help.' He looked around the room. 'Is there anything I can do for you?'

I took a deep breath. 'I want bail. Would you stand bail for me? Please?'

He looked at me, frowning. 'How much do they want?'

'I don't know.'

He looked at me uncertainly. He was considering it. From this angle, from that angle. The world stood still. The blood was thumping in my ears.

Then he nodded. 'OK. I'll stand bail for you. But on one condition.' He leaned forwards. 'As long as you promise to stay away from Iphigenia.'

I had never really thought myself to be Takis's rival as a potential father. As a potential husband, yes, but not as a father. But of course I was, or had been. Takis's condition was proof that she was missing me and that he knew it.

I thought about the condition. It was hard, unfair and

impossible. My first reaction was that I would be free to break any such promise because Takis had no right to enforce it. If Iphigenia wanted to see me, that was her business. My second thought was that what I was planning to do would put me out of bounds for Iphigenia for ever, anyway, so it didn't matter. It was a thought which filled me with an immense sadness.

'I never tried to come between you and Iphigenia, Takis. I would never try to come between a father and his daughter. I promise.'

'Very well.' He nodded again, satisfied. 'You have a lawyer? No? It doesn't matter. I'll get my lawyer on to it. Simpler that way.' He suddenly smiled. 'Don't worry, Nick. You'll soon be free.'

My possessions were returned to me the next day after breakfast. I put on my belt, my shoes, my watch (eight forty-three) and was taken from the cell for the last time, handcuffed to a uniformed policeman, and led out to the yard behind the station and into a waiting police van.

It was my first breath of fresh air for three days. It seemed colder than ever. The snow had been cleared from the yard but the streets beyond were thick with it.

We were on the road for about twenty minutes and then the van stopped, the doors swung open and I was bundled out and across another yard – this one deep with snow – and into another big, stone-built, unwelcoming civic building. Along corridors, down stairs and through swing doors to another cell – even smaller and more oppressive than the last – where I was uncuffed and left on my own.

At ten o'clock, a very tall man in a blue suit was shown into the cell. He looked very uncomfortable, physically and mentally, in the cramped space. He gave me his card and introduced himself as Takis's solicitor – my solicitor.

'I've read the police papers,' he said. 'How are you pleading?'

'Not guilty.'

He didn't look impressed but didn't try to argue with me. 'If bail is granted, you'll be out of here early this afternoon. It takes a bit of sorting.'

'If?'

'That's right. It's at the discretion of the magistrate. The police could oppose it.' He ducked his tall frame out of the cell. 'See you in court in half an hour's time.'

The proceedings took only slightly longer than that conference with the solicitor. I was brought up to the courtroom at ten-thirty, and I was back in the holding cell by ten forty-five. The inspector stood up and read out the charges against me, the magistrate asked the lawyer how I was intending to plead (not guilty, your honour) and whether I was applying for bail (yes, your honour). Was the accused posting bail himself? No, your honour, a colleague – Mr Takis Artemis, a respected businessman and valued member of his community – was standing bail for him. Any opposition? The inspector was silent. Jolly good. Bail granted, pending the trial, the date to be set before the end of the month. Thank you, inspector, next please.

At one-thirty they released me from the cell. I signed a couple of forms, shook hands with the solicitor, and then stepped out into the snow-covered streets. I was free.

The head boy was waiting outside for me. He was leaning against his car and he didn't look entirely happy. He opened the passenger door. 'I've got business in London this afternoon. Want a lift?'

'Aren't you going to congratulate me?' I asked as we drove off.

He grunted. 'I could have had your bail dismissed, you know. I nearly did. Perhaps I should have done.'

Neither of us spoke as we drove out of Canterbury. I peered out at the world passing by. It looked big and wide after four days in my cell. The countryside of Kent. The fields were icy and patched with snow. Wreaths of mist hung around the turreted roofs of oast-houses and among the hop-poles which marched like giant skeletal armies across the frozen landscape.

'That note,' the inspector eventually said. 'If Diana didn't write it, who did?'

Had my protestations of innocence convinced him? Was that what this journey was about? It occurred to me that perhaps the inspector had no business in London after all. I looked at him but his eyes were fixed on the road ahead. Well, I wasn't going to give them anything. Acton was mine, not theirs.

'OK,' he said. 'I'll tell you something. Perhaps I shouldn't. But if I scratch your back . . .' He turned and grinned at me. 'I checked the passenger lists for all flights from Madrid to Heathrow, and Gatwick, on the Friday Diana died. Tony Acton isn't on any of them. He returned on the Wednesday, two days before. Iberian Airways, three forty-five from Madrid.'

Two days? What did he do with those two days? Where was he? Well, at least it confirmed my suspicions. So he wasn't just using an accident as an opportunity to put me away for murder. He was indeed playing a bigger game than that, which meant it wasn't an accident in the first place.

'If you didn't invite Diana down to Kent that Friday, and if her presence wasn't a mere coincidence, then who did?' the head boy asked.

I looked at him again. I was beginning to suspect that he knew what my answers would be to all his questions without me telling him. He had a hunch about Acton and he was hoping my reactions to his questions would tell him whether that hunch was right or wrong. That's what this journey was all about. I knew I couldn't afford to underestimate him. But I was curious; exactly how much did he know? 'Have you tried her office? A and B Securities? There's a colleague of hers – Tim Reels – he would know if she took any personal phone calls that week. She'd have had to take a day off, she'd have discussed it with him, I'm sure.'

The inspector glanced sideways at me as he drove. His expression was curious. 'Diana wasn't working there. Hadn't, for weeks.'

'What?'

He paused. 'She was given the sack.'

'Why?'

He sighed. 'She hadn't done a decent day's work for months, apparently. Days off at a moment's notice. When she was there she didn't concentrate. Turned up late, left early.'

'For months?' A sick, empty feeling was growing in my stomach. 'Since when, exactly?'

The inspector didn't answer immediately. When he did, he kept his eyes on the road. 'Since the time the two of you split up, Nick.' He nodded gravely. 'Some days she just sat at her desk and cried, apparently. She couldn't work, she couldn't think, she could hardly speak.'

I turned away and watched the frozen landscape pass by outside. I felt a pain in my hands. Looking down, I saw they were twisted together so tightly it took an effort of will to separate them.

We drove the rest of the way in silence. When we reached London I got out at the first underground station.

'Listen,' the head boy said before he drove off. 'You might be free for the time being, but you'd better behave yourself until the trial or the completion of our enquiries. Do you understand? I don't want any loose cannons or muddy water in this case.' He put the car into gear and eased the brake off. 'I don't want to hear anything about you or from you for a long time. Go home and hibernate. It's too cold to do anything else.'

I turned up my coat collar as I walked into the underground. A mountain of fabricated evidence which had me on trial for murder, and two secret days. Pieces of a bigger picture. What were the other pieces, Acton? What was the bigger picture? Did it matter? Not really. I knew what the result had been, and I knew who was responsible. That was enough for me. It might not be enough for the police, but that was why I would reach Acton before they did, even if the head boy was now on the same trail as I was, which was what he had seemed to be hinting. I would get to Acton first because I didn't have to worry about the details. Because I didn't need evidence or proof. And because I had anger and hatred on my side.

Anger and hatred. I was half-mad with them. If the head boy thought I was going to keep my head down and hibernate, he had a big surprise coming.

CHAPTER FOURTEEN

I arrived home to find the studio flooded with the brightness of snow-reflected light. Blue sky showed through the skylight, where patches of icy slush glittered like a sackful of diamonds scattered across the glass.

A mountain of mail was waiting for me. Most of it was rubbish, but two items caught my eye. The first was from the Acton Gallery. An invitation to the party to end all parties. I checked dates – the day after tomorrow. Saturday night. I laughed sourly, looking at the computer-printed address label. The bastard takes the trouble to get me locked up in jail, but my name and address remains on his mailing-list database.

The second item was a letter from Spain. The postmark was Pontevedra, and it was three weeks old. It was from Diana. I could tell from the address – that handwriting. I slumped on to the dusty sofa. She'd said she'd been away. She'd said something about a letter. It must have been delayed in the post. I tore it open.

Dear Nicky,

Perhaps I shouldn't have come here. But I was so happy when we were here last spring – happier than I can remember – so it was the natural place to run to when I had to get away from everything.

We're staying at the inn in the village, Iphigenia and me. Do you remember the village? Those little white houses, the fishermen's boats pulled up on to the beach, the pine trees around the bay, the oakwoods on the hills behind? Our cottage is still there, beyond the headland, nestling in its little creek, but it's all shuttered up, unoccupied at this time of year. I still think of it as 'our' cottage, and Iphigenia still calls it 'our' cottage when we pass it on our walks. And I don't think she just means hers and mine, Nicky, but yours as well. There's something of all three of us in that pretty house.

It's cold here at this time of year, and it rains a lot of the time, but there's a huge fire in our room where we burn driftwood and coal, and the countryside is greener than ever, a brilliant emerald green, and when the sun shines – sometimes even while it's raining – the gleam of it on the water out at sea is breathtaking.

We've been here five days now, so it's almost a week since I ran away. I know running away isn't a very brave thing to do, but I had to get away from it all, away from London. I just couldn't cope there any more. I had to get away from you, from Tony, from Takis, from everyone. But mostly from you. I had to go somewhere far away where I could curl up and forget about everything that's happened for a while. I haven't told anyone where we are, I didn't even say goodbye to anyone. With everyone else, I simply didn't bother. With you, Nicky, it was different. I wanted to see you and wanted to say goodbye to you, but I didn't let myself even consider it.

No, I don't regret running away and I don't regret coming here. It's only with distance that you begin to see clearly, that you can hope to see the whole picture (remember the view from Midsummer Hill?). And this place is full of memories, but they aren't unpleasant ones. It is familiar but apart, it connects me with what has happened without drowning me in it. Nowhere else would I be able to come to terms with what has happened without burying it or distorting it.

Yesterday a storm blew in from the Atlantic. It came rampaging through the village like the end of the world, crashing against doors and windows, rattling chimneys, sweeping chairs and tables and plant-pots from balconies, throwing them along the street. It brought down a number of those tall pines along the shore and shook branches from the oaks in the hills. The sight of the waves crashing on to the beach was terrifying; we didn't go out, but we could see them through the window. We stayed in our room, huddled in front of the fire, listening to the wind and the rain, the thunder and the crashing waves, waiting for it to pass. It blew itself out last night, or rather in the early hours of this morning, while it was still dark.

Today everything is quiet and calm. We went out after breakfast for a walk along the shore, as we do every morning, collecting driftwood for the fire. But this morning was different. The world looked as if it had only just escaped complete destruction. The village streets, usually so clean and tidy, were full of all kinds of broken rubbish. The beach was strewn with all kinds of fantastic flotsam and jetsam – smashed furniture, scraps of clothing, plastic bottles and buckets, old shoes and boots. Where did the storm find them all? Some of the fishing boats have been tossed all around the place, one or two smashed beyond all repair. And yet the world was smiling. The sun was shining, the sky was a brilliant clear blue, the sea sparkled and the breeze was not cold. Iphigenia ran ahead, singing and skipping over the sand, the terror of the day before forgotten, and a cloud of gulls wheeled around above us, very clean and white against the sky. Noisy and alive. Perhaps the world was celebrating its survival. Perhaps it was all relief that the worst was over and everything that mattered had come through alive. The storm had refreshed the world.

And today I too feel the euphoria of survival. Because today I realize that the storm for us is over, and I have come through alive, and what matters has come through alive also. Because I still love you, Nicky. I loved you before the storm broke and I still love you. I believe I always will. And although the storm tore us apart, I can admit that I will always hope that somehow we will come back together again. Perhaps I shouldn't write to you like this. I know I have no right to. But there's no point in writing to you if I'm not going to be honest. Because that's all I'm doing, Nicky. Trying to be honest. I'm not trying to persuade you, plead with you, beg anything from you. All I ask is that you are honest too. Honest with yourself if not with me. Can you honestly tell yourself that the storm has carried everything away with it, destroyed everything? Can you honestly tell yourself that you don't miss me? Or Iphigenia?

Because we both miss you. Terribly. Last night when Iphigenia was frightened, it was you she called for. You, Nicky.

It's late afternoon now, but the sun is still shining outside. The sea is agleam with it. I do believe that the winter is over. Iphigenia has left the door open and the breeze coming through is not last week's cutting wind. It carries a freshness with it. The fire is burning low and I'm reluctant to put more wood on it. I'm sure, soon, that there will be new birdsong in the oakwoods and green shoots on the branches. Flowers. And, who knows, perhaps even a word from you?

All my love,
Diana.

Diana and Iphigenia had lived in the bottom half of a big end-of-terrace house in north London. The shutters were closed and the blinds pulled down across the windows at the front. The snow covering the path to her door at the side of the building was smooth and undisturbed – mine were the first footprints to mark it.

I rang the doorbell without expecting a reply. There was none. I took the keys from the pocket of my coat – the spare keys she'd given me what seemed like a lifetime ago, and which for some reason I'd never returned – and opened the door.

I could tell the place was deserted as soon as I stepped inside. It was cold and very quiet. I went through to the sitting-room overlooking the garden at the back. The curtains there weren't closed, and the afternoon sun filled the room with pale winter light. It was exactly as I remembered it: books and papers scattered over the table, magazines on the floor, postcards and invitations and theatre tickets propped up behind the clock and vases on the mantelpiece. Parties and plays which Diana would never go to.

It was months since I'd been here, but I knew where everything was. There on the bookshelf was a row of photo albums – I knew I had only to reach out and open them to see again images of the three of us in Spain, out in that garden, here in this very room. But I held myself back. There were books which we had shared, there music which we had listened to together. Above the mantelpiece was a picture I had painted soon after Diana and I had met. I was amazed it was still hanging there. A still-life of two pairs of shoes; a woman's elegant high-heels and a little girl's scuffed sandals. Diana and Iphigenia.

I missed them so much. I didn't know how I'd survived the last few months without them. And I didn't know how I was going to survive the rest of my life without them.

I turned away to the French windows and looked out on to the snow-covered garden. I thought the cold, white neutral view would help, but it didn't. I looked back at the picture and something inside me broke. I sat down and put my head in my hands until the panic waves had passed.

I went upstairs to Diana's bedroom. I opened a cupboard and gazed at the dresses hanging inside. There was the one in dark green silk which she'd worn to Acton's last party. The last time I'd seen her. Now it was hanging there, empty, fresh from the cleaners in a clear plastic wrapper. I took it from the cupboard, tore the wrapping from it and pressed it to my face, hoping wildly for a breath of her scent. But not a trace of it had survived the rigours of dry-cleaning. I threw myself on to her bed, pressing my face against her pillows, but not a trace of her hair-spray nor a hint of her perfume remained. I closed my eyes and was suddenly fast asleep.

Sunlight. A beach. An early morning walk along the seashore. I could see Iphigenia running ahead across the sand, dancing in bare feet, gulls wheeling overhead. I could hear Diana laughing, see her bending down to pick up a piece of driftwood. Holding it out for me to examine, to share her delight in it – in the way the sea had transformed it into something intricate and fascinating and strangely beautiful. I could see it in her hand, feel it, feel how I could recreate its shape and texture, its colours and shadows. Create something new out of it. Something for Diana. Yes.

I woke up as suddenly as I had fallen asleep. It was dark. I stood up and found I still had the green dress in my arms. I hung it back up in the cupboard and left the room without putting on the light. I didn't go into Iphigenia's bedroom. That would have been too great a trespass and I couldn't have coped with finding the Christmas card I'd drawn for her still stuck to the wall above her bed. I left the door closed and went downstairs. I let myself out, leaving another set of footprints in the snow on the pathway behind me as I left.

It began to snow again as I drove home to the studio. Big flakes blew thick and fast through the darkness, like a vast cloud of frantic moths swept by car headlights.

I knew now what I had to do, and I was looking forward to it with a savage relish.

CHAPTER FIFTEEN

The long driveway to Acton's house was lined with flaming torches. They were a weird and frightening sight, in the middle of the vast darkness of the North Downs. Snaking their flickering way between the unseen emptinesses of the beechwoods and the sloping fields, they looked threatening and tribal, as if they were lighting a processional avenue leading to some sort of occult and primitive ritual centre.

And then I turned the corner past the wood and there was the house, bursting with light and activity at the foot of the dark hill. Lights shone from open windows and doorways, from bonfires on the lawns, and from cars parking in the field just beyond the house. It was a very cold night but there were guests everywhere. I could see them through open windows. They were spilling out of doors and across the lawns, and passing to and fro between the house and the car park.

A crowd of them were watching some sort of altercation in the car park as I pulled up. The drivers of two cars, head to head, were shouting at each other. Neither was giving way. Eventually one driver got out and went round to the other's window. Drawing back his arm, he smashed his elbow through the window. The crowd gasped.

The other driver cowered beneath a shower of fragmented glass. The first driver drew back his arm again and smashed his fist into the cowering face. Then he opened the door, dragged his opponent from the vehicle, threw him to the ground and started kicking him.

The victim's girlfriend got out of the car and started

screaming, whereupon the first driver's girlfriend got out of their car and started slapping her. The first driver left his opponent on the ground, returned to his car, opened the boot, took out a baseball bat and started to smash in all the windows and lights of his opponent's vehicle.

The crowd was shouting now. Some of the women in it were screaming.

'What's happening? What's happening?' someone wailed.

'It's all right. It's only a performance. A sort of play . . .' A voice of reassurance, breathless with excitement.

'But I can see blood . . . ! That's blood! Isn't anyone going to stop him?'

The man with the baseball bat returned to his car. He dropped the weapon into the boot, reached further inside, and produced a chainsaw. A communal sigh of amazement swept through the crowd. They moved back in fear as the man jerked the saw into life and began to hack the doors off his opponent's car.

It was a weird scene, lit by the headlights of surrounding cars: one man sitting on the ground weeping as his car was being reduced to scrap, one woman screaming as another swung her round and round by the hair. A scene ringed by a bank of silent faces, aghast but fascinated, watching. And beyond that, the darkness.

I made my way through the crowds and down towards the house. Everyone I passed was gripped by an air of intense, even neurotic, excitement and anticipation, as if they knew that anything might happen, at any time, right in front of them. A luxurious sense of release ran through them as well, as if reality had suddenly become a spectacle laid on exclusively for their own entertainment, to be enjoyed with the complete absence of responsibility granted only to gods.

A uniformed doorman stood at the top of the steps leading into the house, just inside the front porch. The open door behind him spilt brilliant light and loud laughter, screams and music out into the night.

I didn't go in but carried on down the side of the house towards the crumbling outbuildings. It was darker and quieter there. I went into the woodshed and pulled an electric torch from my pocket. Where was the axe I'd used to chop up the club? There it was, on the floor, covered in sawdust and bird droppings. I remembered something else. There was the balaclava helmet, still lying where I'd left it on the woodpile. The birthday present from Iphigenia. I picked it up. Surprisingly, its wool was still dry. I tugged it on over my head. Not only would it keep me warm; no one would recognize me now. I put the torch away and picked up the axe. I dusted it down and walked out of the shed.

The garage doors were shut and locked. No matter. I'd go in through the front door.

'Good evening, sir.' The doorman didn't raise an eyebrow as I walked up the steps and past him into the big hallway. 'I hope you enjoy yourself, sir.'

It was very hot indoors. The hall was full of guests elegant in dinner-jackets and long dresses. Silk, diamonds, pearls. They were laughing nervously as they watched a spectacle at the foot of the stairs.

Another uniformed doorman was arguing with a policeman.

'I want to see whoever is in charge,' the policeman was demanding. 'These premises are not licensed for this sort of entertainment.'

'You're not seeing anyone, sir.' The doorman was firm

but polite. 'And unless you can show me your invitation, I shall have to ask you to leave.'

'I'm a policeman, for heaven's sake! I'm on official duty!'

'I don't care, sir. Will you leave now, please? You clearly haven't been invited. If you don't leave the premises I shall have to remove you myself.'

'This is ridiculous! I insist –'

The doorman, grinning, knocked the policeman's peaked cap off his head. The crowd burst into laughter. As the policeman lunged forward, fumbling to catch it, the doorman kneed him in the stomach. The policeman went down on all fours, coughing and retching. An ugly, painful sound. The crowd's laughter changed to gasps of horror, disgust and embarrassment. The doorman leaned down, grabbed the policeman by the collar and dragged him back across the hall to the doorway.

'Give us a hand, Bob.'

The other doorman leaned down and grabbed an ankle. Between them they carried the retching policeman into the porch and threw him down the steps and out into the darkness.

The guests turned away from the door, chuckling uneasily among themselves, raising eyebrows and sipping from champagne glasses in nervous anticipation of what might happen next. I pushed past them, catching eyes wide with the thrill of fearful expectation, and turned right into a long corridor.

A handful of people followed me. What's he doing? Where's he going? Why has he got an axe? Why is he wearing a mask?

I went up a short flight of stairs which ended in a door which was closed and locked. It was the door to the gun room. I stepped back and swung the axe. It buried its edge in the door above the lock. I pulled it out and swung it again and again. Crash, crash, crash. The wood around the lock splintered, disintegrated. I kicked the door open and stepped inside.

The room was dark. I groped for a light switch and flicked it on. A long, narrow room with a sloping ceiling. Walls lined with glass cases crowded with racks of rifles and shotguns. I tried the nearest case. It was locked so I simply smashed the glass. I dropped the axe and reached inside. I grasped a shotgun in both hands, feeling polished wood and tooled metal.

This time I wasn't going to mess around. I was beyond that. I was just going to do it.

I opened a drawer and took out a box of cartridges. I opened the gun and fed a cartridge into each barrel. I snapped the gun shut and dropped the box into my coat pocket.

Right. Let's go and find him.

A small crowd had gathered in the doorway to watch. They scattered as I approached them, pressing themselves against the walls of the staircase and corridor to let me pass.

I looked into each room I passed. The dust-sheets had gone, carpets were back on floors, pictures back on walls. I looked into room after room of laughing, drinking, dancing, elegant people, but I couldn't see Acton. Waiters scurried past along the corridors, carrying magnums dripping with icy condensation, or trays loaded with bubbling glasses or succulent dishes of roast and sliced meats, pastries, fruit desserts. Where was Acton?

In the big sitting-room off the main hallway, two bearded and laughing men were play-fighting, emptying tins of baking powder over each other's heads. Laughing, one man put a cigarette in his mouth and lit a match. The moment he raised it to the cigarette, the cloud of powder drifting around his head ignited, and the powder in his hair and beard went up in flames. He ran across the room, a human figure with a huge ball of fire where his head should be, through screaming onlookers parting before him like panicked zebras before a lion's charge. Acton was not among them.

He wasn't in the big dining room next door, either. As I was looking there, momentarily spellbound by the mountains of exquisite fare loaded on to tables all along one wall beneath the chandeliers, a door burst open and a squealing pig ran into the room, closely followed by a man in a chef's hat and bloodstained apron, wielding a meat cleaver. He chased the pig around the room, under the tables, between the diners, waving the cleaver about with a dangerous abandon. The pig disappeared out into the terraced garden through one of the open French windows, followed by the shouting cook.

The diners laughed. Seconds later the cook reappeared, yelling triumphantly, the cleaver in one hand and a pig's carcass in the other, both dripping blood. He swung the carcass with the same mad abandon as he'd swung the cleaver, spraying the walls, the diners, the tables and the food with a heavy pink rain. More screams. The cook left the room, singing drunkenly.

One of the dinner-jacketed diners dabbed at a pink puddle on a table and licked his fingers. 'Yum yum,' he said. 'Strawberry juice. That pig's probably still running around outside somewhere.'

The women's screams of alarm gave way to angry concern about whether the stains would ever wash out of the dresses.

I went upstairs, trailing an ever-growing group of curious onlookers. It was very hot in there. I was stifling in my heavy coat and balaclava. I could feel the perspiration soaking through the woollen mask.

The first room I went into was quiet. Nothing seemed

to be happening in there. A few groups of people were simply standing and chatting. The atmosphere was relaxed, a long way from the super-charged ambience downstairs.

I saw Acton and heard his voice at the same time. On the other side of the room, by the fireplace. He was talking to a man and two women I hadn't seen before.

I came to a halt. The sight of him struck me with a strange fear. He looked towards me, smiled with delighted anticipation as he took in my appearance, then looked away. He hadn't recognized me. At that moment the fear evaporated, and hatred and anger made the blood thump in my head and my breath choke in my throat. I strode forwards again and pushed the man and two women to one side. I saw a frown of irritation on Acton's brow give way to an indulgent smile. Then I raised the shotgun and smashed its butt right into the middle of that lean and handsome face with its blue eyes and pale skin, its noble brow, its dark gypsy curls.

He staggered back against the fireplace, hands up to his face, blood already scarlet down the front of his starched white dress shirt.

I slammed the butt into his stomach and he went down, choking and gagging, at my feet.

I turned to our audience. Shocked faces, some nervous laughter, a few cheers, a few hesitant protests, excitement and uncertainty. 'All right,' I shouted. 'Over on the other side of the room. All of you. Move!' Back they shuffled, against the wall, leaning forwards, peering over each other's shoulders, anxious not to miss anything. Hypnotized, intoxicated. Nobody left the room.

I leaned over Acton, tucking the point of the barrel under his chin. He looked up at me with fear and shock in his eyes. 'Hello, Tony,' I said quietly, so only he would hear. 'It's me, Nick. Remember?' Surprise widened his gaze. I laughed. 'Well, I've got you now, haven't I? I can do what the hell I like to you. Our audience won't interfere. They think it's all simply a performance. Show time, folks.'

One side of his face was already swollen and bruised. There was blood around his mouth. His eyes flickered and he turned his head to the crowd on the other side of the room. His mouth opened as if he was about to appeal to them.

I reached down with my free hand, grabbed him by the lapels and shook him. 'I wouldn't bother, Tony. Whatever you say, they won't take it seriously. They won't believe you. They're anaesthetized to reality. You did that to them, Tony, and look where it's got you.'

He closed his mouth and his eyes flickered back to meet mine.

'I'm going to kill you now, Tony. I'm going to blow your head off. There'll be a great deal of confusion. I'll slip off, and I'll be far away by the time anyone realizes that this is reality and not performance.' I shook him again, and pressed the barrel tighter under his chin. 'You can delay your death by the odd minute or two by telling me all about that note you wrote for Diana, and why you sneaked back from Madrid two days early. At this point I imagine a minute of your life is the equivalent of a decade of anyone else's. So start talking.'

He shook his head and laughed. 'Just do it, Todd. Just pull the trigger.' He coughed violently. 'I'm not going to tell you anything.'

I shook him again. He closed his eyes and winced. 'Tell me what you were doing with those two days. You were arranging Diana's death, weren't you? Weren't you!'

Again he laughed. 'I'm not going to tell you anything. And you're not going to pull the trigger. Are you?'

I looked down at his battered face, at my left hand gripping him round the throat by a fistful of lapel and bloodied shirt-front, at the shotgun barrel tucked under his chin. I could feel my finger on the trigger. I knew exactly which one it was. The index finger of my right hand.

I was vaguely aware of cheers and shouting in the distance, growing louder, downstairs then upstairs. And of a strange thundering coming closer and closer along the corridor. I can do it, I thought. I can pull the trigger. Can't I? It's what I want. Isn't it?

The door burst open. The room was suddenly full of chaos and animal. Huge, rearing, screaming, kicking animal. The crowd against the wall scattered, shouting, screaming, laughing. A horse. Someone had ridden a horse into the room.

I looked up. A huge black horse, rearing and kicking, eyes rolling in fear and fury. The animal was out of control, the rider tugging at the reins, swearing, biting at his lip. The beast towered above me on its hind legs, hooves lashing out. I cowered beneath it, one arm raised.

Acton was on his feet and the shotgun was in his hands. I saw it there before I realized I wasn't holding it any more. I saw the grin on his battered face, the barrel coming up, and then hurled myself across the room under the rearing mass of crazed animal and out of the door.

I ran along the corridor. The top of the stairs . . . There was a roar of thunder, a spattering as of rain, and a blow from behind like the kick of a giant horse (that horse?) which knocked the breath from me and threw me across the landing and over the top step. Suddenly I was tumbling down the stairs, head over heels, over and over and over. Crash, crash, crash, crash.

I lay at the bottom, stunned and winded. I couldn't

move. How many bones were broken? There was an intense, throbbing pain down the left side of my back, and a sensation of dampness which was more than perspiration. I managed to twist over, gasping with the pain, and slip my right hand under my coat. It came out wet and red. Blood. I was soaking in it.

I heard screams dying away, cheers and applause. A large group of people in the hall were watching me. They were mostly drunk. 'Amazing. Truly dangerous art,' I heard someone exclaiming. 'Incredible. You'd think it was real blood . . .'

Someone was coming down the stairs towards me. It was Tony Acton. He carried the shotgun in both hands and he was still smiling. I twisted back to the crowd, searching for faces I knew, someone who would recognize me. I tried to call out, but the balaclava was gagging me. I reached up, groaning, and tried to tug it back from my face and off my head.

Acton was standing over me. 'I wouldn't bother, Todd. Whatever you say, they won't take it seriously. Remember? They won't believe you.' He laughed. 'Well, the boot is on the other foot now, isn't it? Or should I say, in the other face?' He drew back his foot and kicked me, hard, in the face. Once, twice. I tried to roll away, groaning, consciousness spinning away in a shower of sparks and a burst of darkness.

He reached down and grabbed my coat and shook me until the world came back into painful focus. 'You and me, Nick, we're going to have a little chat somewhere quiet and peaceful.' He began to drag me across the hall floor and to the front door.

'Would you like a hand there, sir?' one of the uniformed doormen asked.

'Much obliged,' Acton replied. 'And perhaps your colleague would care to join in the fun?'

The two doormen took an ankle each and dragged me out over the threshold, following Acton down the steps and into the cold and dark of the night. Each step smashed against the back of my head as we descended.

Acton led the way along the gravel drive to the side of the house and down the path to the back garden. I could see him ahead of us, a flaming torch in one hand, the shotgun in the other. 'This way gentlemen, please.' A score of curious onlookers trailed along behind us from the house. The two doormen dragged me across gravel, brick paving, bare earth and grass as carelessly as if I was a sack of rubbish. The agony was indescribable.

We were crossing the lawn now. I could feel myself skidding over patches of ice, ploughing through drifts of snow. A bonfire blazed away on one side. Then we came to a halt. I could see the high wire fencing of the dog enclosure towering over me in the darkness.

'OK gentlemen, I'll take it from here. Thank you very much.'

The doormen dropped me in the snow and turned back to the house, eager to return to the warmth of indoors. I could hear Acton unlocking and unbolting the door into the enclosure. The crowd of onlookers kept their distance, peering at us through the darkness. I tried to move, to stand, to sit up at least, but couldn't. The pain was too great. I could feel unconsciousness waiting to drown me.

I felt Acton grab me roughly by the collar of my coat. He began to haul me the few yards into the enclosure. I could hear his breathing, heavy and ragged from the exertion, and then we were through the gateway and inside, and he dropped me again. I heard him closing the metal gate, bolting and locking it. Then he seized my collar again and hauled me across grass, snow, ice, mud and slush to the far side of the enclosure, by the wall.

'Here we are, Nick,' he said. He was standing over me, the flaming torch in his left hand shedding a flickering light over both of us. He leaned down, pulled my coat open and peered inside. 'It's a bad one, Nick. Deep wounds, very extensive. Lots of blood. You're dying, mate.' He straightened up. 'I thought you'd want a bit of privacy for it. It's the least I could do. That, and keep you company while you go under. No need to thank me, it's my pleasure, really, as I'm sure you'll understand. And there's no rush. We've got all night, haven't we? Although, to be brutally honest, I don't think it'll take that long. Loss of blood, damage to internal organs, trauma, hypothermia, it's a race any one of them could win.'

He stuck the torch in the ground and took up the shotgun again. He broke it open, checked the barrels, and then leaned down and groped around in my pockets until he found the box of cartridges. He took them out and reloaded the spent barrel. He snapped the gun shut, shivered, hunched his shoulders and stamped his feet. 'It's a cold night,' he muttered.

The crowd outside the enclosure had come up to the wire and were peering through the darkness at us as if we were animals in a cage at the zoo. I groaned. 'Help. Please . . .' But either they couldn't hear or they thought my appeals were all part of the show. Even as I watched, desperate, I could see the crowd thinning out as people wandered back to the house. They were almost sated with extraordinary spectacle, and there didn't seem to be much going on out here any more. They couldn't really see or hear anything, anyway. They were bored and cold.

'Listen, Nick.' Acton was peering down at me. 'I'm going back inside for a few minutes, to sort a few things out. Don't go away. OK? I'll be straight back.'

He disappeared. I heard the metal gate clang open, then shut, bolted, locked. I could see no one out there now. I was on my own and I was going to die, here in the dog enclosure where Diana had died. The pain was duller now, but spread throughout all of my body. It was very cold, and my clothes were soaked from the inside with blood and from the outside with snow and ice and wet grass. The ground was hard beneath me, and seemed to be sucking the last of the heat from my body. The torch stuck in the ground beside me was guttering – any moment now it would go out altogether.

Then Acton was back. He had put on a thick overcoat, wellington boots and gloves. He was carrying the shotgun, a bundle of fresh torches, and a light kitchen chair. He put the chair down beside me. 'I might as well be comfortable while I'm waiting, don't you think?' He lit a new torch from the old one and stuck it in the ground. Then he sat down. 'Take a look up there, Nick. The car park in the field.'

I looked. It was dark – only the headlights of a few cars coming or going marked out the place. Then, to one side, obviously in the next field, came the blaze of something on fire.

'That's your car, Nick. I told Iruni's boys to use it in their show, to get rid of it. Evidence. Nobody knows you're here, thanks to this.' He leaned forwards and tugged off the balaclava helmet. 'And now no one will ever know. In the morning, when you're dead, I'll carefully dispose of your body and that will be that.'

He pulled a bottle of brandy from his coat pocket, uncorked it, tipped it back. 'I loathe you, Nick. I hate you almost as much as I came to hate Diana. You took Diana from me. You persuaded her . . . you persuaded her that she preferred you to me. How could she? How? How could she prefer *you*?' He shook his head, angry and bemused. Then he laughed. 'And the Wyndham Lewis – I know who spilled the story to that fool Stanley. Yes, Stanley told me all about it, once I got hold of him. I knew he couldn't have done all that research himself. And he told me about that little list of yours as well. But don't worry – I made sure Stanley isn't going to do anything with it. I told him something he didn't know I knew – something about him and a certain titled person and some Hellenic bronzes illegally imported from Turkey. And he agreed that my silence was worth his silence.'

He got up and stood over me. 'Did you think you could ruin me that easily?' He kicked me in the stomach, hard. 'That little trick of yours – the date on the Wyndham Lewis. Oh, so clever. You stupid bastard. Did you think you could get me like that?' He kicked me again. Then he walked away, gazing into the darkness beyond the house.

'Diana . . . Strange, I came to hate her so much . . . She thought she could live without me. The stupid bitch. We belonged to each other. We . . . we were two halves of the same whole, until she . . . until you . . .' He was speaking very quietly. I could barely hear him. 'The two of us, it wasn't an accident, we came together in the bosom of one family. It was fate, destiny. We could have spent all of our lives looking for each other, lost, wandering . . . But we didn't. We were so lucky. And she thought she could turn her back on all that. It hurt me so much. The stupid bitch. I couldn't stand it.'

He came and sat down. He took another swig of brandy.

'I despise you, Nick. I've always despised you. You're so bloody stupid. I set you up right from the start, you stupid bastard. I wound you up like a clockwork toy and away you went, doing exactly what I wanted you to do.'

He laughed. 'Yes. I planned it all. I wanted Diana dead. The idea of her with someone else . . . I couldn't stand it. If I couldn't have her, no one else would. And if I could set you up for it, well, two for the price of one. Yes, Nick, you were very stupid and I was very clever. That's why you're dying now and I'm laughing.'

The light from the flaming torch threw manic shadows across his face as he chuckled.

'I had it all worked out when I asked you down to look after the dogs while we were away. I knew you wanted to kill me. People like you, you're an open book to me, Nick. I can see right through you. I can read your thoughts. You were groping for a murder plan, a method. Well, you found one. But whose idea was it, to use the dogs? Yours? No, Nick. It was mine. I planted that idea in your mind, Nick, and I knew it would grow. I knew it would become a beautiful plant which you would love and cherish. That story about the Mongol Khans. The Chinese kings, Nick, remember the Chinese kings! All bullshit. I made it up for the purpose. The Mongols' favourite method of execution, actually, was to roll the victim up in an oriental carpet and kick them to death.'

He stood up and kicked me three times – in the head, the stomach, the chest. Then he sat down again.

'I came back early to keep a watch on you, to make sure everything was going according to plan. I must admit, I'd been a bit worried when you told me about your phobia. I hadn't anticipated that. But in the end, no problem. Well done! Brave man. Of course, I had to make sure Greta was having such a bad time that she came back even earlier. I wanted her out of the way. That wasn't difficult. It was me who persuaded her to come to Spain, to leave the ground clear for you; I suggested a holiday might bring us closer together, a last-ditch attempt to save the marriage. What a thought!' He laughed. 'Yes, Nick, you weren't on your own on Wednesday and Thursday. I was watching you. I moved into the Kennedy's lodge, secretly, and had a pair of binoculars trained on you as soon as I arrived.'

The bastard. I felt consciousness beginning to slip away from me. Hold on, I told myself. I must listen. Hold tight. I fought oblivion with anger and hatred. But oblivion was warm and soft and painless. No! Don't let go until you've heard everything . . .

'What's the matter, Nick? Are you going under?' He leaned forwards. 'Don't go yet, mate. I want you to hear this. You hang on.'

He picked up a handful of snow and rubbed it in my face. Everything snapped back into focus. The pain returned, as sharp as ever, but I could see and hear again.

'That phone call, on Thursday. It wasn't from Spain. It was from the box down the road. And it wasn't the only call I made, either. The other one was to Diana. She thought I was phoning from Spain, as well. I told her that you'd been here, looking after the place for the week, but were having to go away on the Thursday night. I told her you were coming back on Friday lunchtime for the weekend. I told her that the two of us, you and me, had decided that the three of us had to get together to sort everything out between us. The Friday afternoon. We both wanted her to be there. Sort everything out, once and for all. She agreed, of course. She sounded desperately relieved. Yes, she'd be there. Oh, Diana, as Nick won't be around to feed the dogs on Friday morning, perhaps you could get there early and sort them out? Don't be alarmed if they're in a bit of a state, they just don't like to be kept waiting. There's an old sweater of mine, wear that when you go in to feed them, their master's scent will calm them down . . . She was only too grateful, poor bitch, she couldn't wait.'

He stood up and walked up and down, stamping his feet with the cold. He lit a fresh torch and stuck it in the ground.

'It all worked perfectly, didn't it? Like clockwork. Amazing.' He shook his head and laughed. 'I found her handbag in the house and wrote that note. I filled a bin-liner full of dog food and dumped it in the woods. I made a copy of your club and hid it in the woodshed. I hung on for a few days – you see, Nick, it occurred to me that you might do away with yourself, once you heard how Diana had died. Guilt, grief, all that. I'd have thought it would all have been too much to bear. Perhaps you're a bit tougher than I'd thought. I didn't mind, though. You'd go to prison for her murder instead. That was the original idea, after all. I got my copy of the film – yes, Nick, of course I took a copy of it – and hid it in her flat, somewhere I knew the police would find it. Your motive for hating her, you see, for murdering her. Sexual jealousy. What other motive is there? And then I gave the police the handbag and left them to it. Again, clockwork. Wind them up, the boys in blue, and away they go. And all the time I was being so nice to you, and you were completely fooled. You'd walked right into my trap and knew nothing about it.'

He stood up, shotgun in hand, and walked over to me. I felt the point of the barrel scrape my cheek, my chin. The metal was colder than ice. 'Something did take me by surprise, though. The dogs. I knew I'd have to sacrifice them, but I didn't know what a blow it would be, losing them. I miss them. They're dead, and it's your fault. Another reason for hating you, Todd. I saw you thrashing them. Through the binoculars. It's all your fault. If you hadn't come between Diana and me in the first place, none of this would have happened. The dogs would still be alive, Diana would still be alive, Diana and I would still . . .'

I felt the barrel of the shotgun pressing against my temple.

'I could shoot you now, I suppose. Get it over with. Finish you off. But I saw you baiting those dogs. Making them suffer. Thrashing them for five days. Half-rations for three days. No food for two days. So why should I show you any mercy? I'm going to let you die in your own good time, Nick. I'm going to sit here and watch it happen.'

He sat down again.

He wouldn't have long to wait. Death wasn't far off, I was sure of it. I could feel my whole system closing down. The pain was fading, the coldness was fading, even the darkness seemed to be lifting. I was losing awareness of the ground pressing up against me, of the clothes wet and cold against me, of breathing . . . I was spinning off somewhere else, into sleep . . . then back again. Everything sharp and focused once more.

'. . . You're out on bail, I assume?' Acton was talking again. 'Well, they'll simply presume you've jumped bail and disappeared. A sure sign of guilt. No one will find you. You'll be tried and sentenced in absentia . . .' He laughed and tipped the brandy back.

You bastard! I tried to struggle up, to get to my feet. But there was nothing there except agony and the threat of unconsciousness. I fell back again. So this was how it was all going to end. The cold was unbearable. I was shaking with it. And then it was fading, and I was spinning off again, into some sort of hallucination. A beach, bright sunlight, gulls, a little girl, her mother. I laughed. Yes. Here I am. Over here . . .

Then back again. The darkness. The intense cold.

The agony. The hard ground. The light from the house and the dying bonfire. The flickering torch illuminating Acton as he sat forwards, the shotgun across his knees, waiting. The shadows across his face hid his expression, masked his eyes. It was very quiet now. Perhaps the party was over. There were no raised voices from the house, no lights in the distant car park.

I closed my eyes. Perhaps I should sleep. That might help. Get some strength back. I felt exhausted. Oblivion came billowing towards me, maroon clouds of the stuff, huge and gentle. I tried to fight it, but it was warm and soft and soothing. Rest now. I let go . . .

'Nick? Nick, mate? You still there?' A rough shaking jerked me cruelly back to the surface. With a sudden sick lurch the agony was all there again. I opened my eyes. Acton was leaning over me, his face close to mine, his hands grasping my lapels. 'Don't go, mate. I've had an idea.'

For one pathetic moment I thought he'd changed his mind. He was going to let me go, call an ambulance, get me to hospital. No. I shook my head. Impossible. I closed my eyes again.

Another rough shaking. 'I said don't go, you stupid bastard!' Something splashed on to my face. 'Wake up! Wake up!' Acton was pouring brandy over me. He shoved the bottle into my mouth. I tasted the sharp spirit, drank, choked, coughed. Suddenly I was wide awake. The brandy burned its way down my throat and seemed to scorch its way to the far end of every limb.

'That's better! Drink, you bastard. That'll keep you awake.'

He poured more brandy over my face. It stung where the skin was cut and broken. I shook my head, gasping and groaning.

'That's the stuff.'

He opened my coat and poured more brandy on to my shirt over the wound. The dull agony of it suddenly burst into flames. I screamed and sat bolt upright.

'OK. Now we can start.'

He lit another torch and stuck it in the ground beside us. Then he walked away towards the far side of the enclosure. I watched him disappear into the darkness. The bonfire on the lawn had almost burnt itself out, and the light from the torch didn't reach that far. I strained my eyes to see what he was up to, but to no avail. I heard a few indistinct words, the click of a bolt drawn back, the rattle of a chain. What was he doing? Who was he talking to?

It was then that I realized the dog kennels were over there. At the same time I heard a snorting cough, a growl, two sharp barks. And back out of the darkness came Anthony Acton. A huge canine shape was loping along at his side. Lean, muscular, glowing a silvery-yellow in the light of the dying bonfire and the flaming torch.

Acton stopped some yards away. He was laughing. The dog sat down at his feet. It raised its head, sniffed the air, realized they weren't alone and started to growl. Its eyes followed its nose and it began to bark as soon as it saw me.

Acton pulled at the dog's chain and the barking ceased. 'Nick, meet my new friend.' He reached down and patted the beast on the shoulder. 'I can't live without dogs, Nick. I had to get a new one straight away, or I'd be in mourning over the others for the rest of my life. Not another Himalayan mastiff, though. That would have been too upsetting. Besides, I decided I wanted something even bigger and meaner, especially if I was having only one of them.'

The dog was on its feet again, padding around Acton, tongue hanging out. It looked fitter and rangier than the mastiffs. Its haunches were leaner and its legs were longer, but its neck and shoulders were more muscular. It looked as powerful and streamlined as a shark.

'This one comes from even further east. China. At least, that's where the breed comes from.' Acton wrapped the chain around the metal trough where the dogs ate. He then took up a dead torch and pulled something from the pocket of his coat. It was my balaclava helmet. 'Twice as deadly as the Himalayan mastiff. Just as powerful, but more athletic. The turn of speed on him, you wouldn't believe it. Needs more exercise than the mastiffs, of course. And more food.' Acton was binding the balaclava helmet tightly around one end of the dead torch. 'I've just promised him a midnight feast, Nicky, and guess what's on the menu? Or rather, who's on the menu?'

I watched with overwhelming horror as he took the dead torch in his right hand, holding it by the opposite end to the balaclava. He swung it at his side like a swordsman testing his foil. He held it out for the dog to sniff at. My scent.

'An appropriate end for you, Nick, wouldn't you agree? It's what you deserve. And what you're fit for. You look like a well-tenderized steak. Very rare. Just how he likes them.'

He swung the club and caught the dog on the jaw. The dog leapt in the air, snapping and barking. The chain pulled tight, the links grating against the metal trough. Acton waited, then let the dog have another sniff of the balaclava helmet. The dog snarled. Row upon row of huge teeth shone in the torch-light. The club swung again. Smashed into the animal's snout. The dog exploded with fury.

I thought I was going to pass out with sheer terror. Acton saw me and quickly pulled out the brandy bottle.

He splashed the stuff over my face, poured it down my throat. 'You're staying wide awake for this, Nick. Till the very end. There's no way out.'

He went back to the dog. The beast was straining at the end of the chain, only yards away, barking madly. Its jaws were gaping wide. Huge teeth dripped froth and saliva. Acton waited until some of the madness had subsided and then he leaned in and thrust the balaclava against the beast's nose. The dog snarled and growled and snapped at the club but it was just out of reach. Acton swung the club hard. A heavy blow on the side of the head. The dog went mad, leaping up in the air, out against the length of the chain, rolling on the ground and kicking itself. The noise was deafening. And all the time Acton danced in and out, thrashing the beast into a killing rage. Then he unwrapped the remains of the balaclava helmet and threw it to the animal. The dog tore it to shreds.

Acton peered at the flames on the guttering torch. He was checking the direction of the wind. He grabbed my collar and dragged me across the grass and through the snow until I was up-wind of the dog. The dog was still barking and leaping, taking the chain to full stretch in an attempt to get at something, anything, on which it could vent its rage. With one last blow of the club, Acton nipped round behind the dog and untied the chain from around the metal trough.

The dog lurched forwards as the chain came free. It almost stumbled, and then checked itself. The barking stopped. For one moment there was silence and the dog stood still, looking around. It was almost as if it knew it could take its time now it was free.

I could hear Acton's excited breathing. 'Come on, boy, come on!' he hissed. 'Yes! Yes!'

The dog closed its eyes and raised its snout, sniffing

the air. It turned its head this way and that. It began to growl. Suddenly it turned round, its eyes rolling madly, and with a snarl of triumph and rage launched itself straight at Acton.

I saw an arm half-raised, eyes wide with horror and surprise, a mouth open for a cry of alarm which never came. And then the dog hit him. It smashed into him like a freight train into a stalled bus. He went down, but the dog's forward rush didn't stop. It carried him screaming across the turf and crashed him up against the feeding trough. Even then the dog didn't stop but ploughed into and through him until there was no more room for forward movement.

All the time Acton was screaming. The dog spread its legs and shook itself, its head buried somewhere deep inside its prey. Acton shook with it. I heard the dog's snarls and growls, muffled now but terrifyingly guttural. I heard chomping, tearing sounds. The dog's head came up for breath – Acton was groaning horribly – then chopped downwards with the speed of a guillotine blade to seize him by the throat.

Again the dog shook itself. Again its horrific strength threw Acton around like a straw doll. He was no longer screaming. There was a limpness to him which suggested he might already be dead. The dog dropped him and he lay still. The creature backed up a few paces, then charged forwards once more, smashing Acton's still form against the trough yet again. Its paws scrabbled for purchase in the turf and mud and slush. It growled through jaws and teeth burrowing themselves deep into its prey. There was no sound from Acton. Eventually the dog's snarls subsided and the only sounds were the terrible chomping and tearing of its teeth and jaws.

I saw the creature's huge silvery-yellow shape hunched

head-down over Acton's still, dark form and knew it was all over for him. Every now and then the dog raised its head and looked around. Coughed, snorted, shook itself and changed its position slightly. And then the head went down again . . . There was no way Acton could still be alive.

I had watched it all in spite of myself. It was the most terrible thing I had ever seen, but I hadn't been able to tear my eyes away from it. Now I thought I was going to be sick. I struggled against the waves of nausea and brought them under control. I had to lie very still and very quiet – it was my only chance. I closed my eyes and tried to control my breathing, harsh and ragged with agony and terror. If I didn't draw attention to myself then the dog might be content with the one death, the one body.

The chomping and tearing sounds stopped. They didn't resume. Instead, I heard the dog's heavy panting coming closer and closer. It came so close I could feel the creature's breath on my face, smell the stench of it. I wanted to scream. Instead I held myself very still and opened my eyes. The animal was standing over me, its snout inches from my face. The fur around its muzzle was dark and matted and dripping. It was sniffing my face. With a huge effort of will I stopped myself from flinching. Its eyes were tiny and blank, and when they met mine – for a split second before I looked away in terror – there was no connection, only confusion. The beast was somehow confused. The snout moved away from my face, passed down my body, sniffing. Then the dog recoiled, coughed, snorted, sneezed and turned away. It slunk back towards Acton's corpse and I began to breathe again, realizing I'd been holding my breath all that time.

I saw the dog lie down across Acton's body. I closed

my eyes, and saw and heard nothing more. I was spinning off again. Floating away from the pain and the terror. Utterly drained and exhausted. There it was, coming closer. The sunlight, the gulls, a little girl's laughter.

Chapter Sixteen

I was in hospital for ten days, unconscious for two. On the third day the police came to interview me, and they were there each day for almost a week. Sometimes the sergeant, sometimes someone else, but never the head boy, although I was told it was still his case.

Greta came to see me on the fifth day. Most of the drips and tubes had been taken out by then, but her opening comment still wasn't at all complimentary.

'You look awful, Nicky. Dreadful. You look a hundred years old.' She sat down beside the bed, shaking her head and laughing. 'To think that I once tried to sleep with you. That's what marriage to Tony reduced me to – a lonely, confused, poor cow desperate for sexual reassurance from someone, anyone. Even you.'

'Thanks, Greta. I'm surprised you bothered to save me.'

That night, Greta had realized something was amiss when the party was drawing to a close and there was no sign of Acton. She had missed the confrontation which had led all the way from the upstairs sitting-room, through the house and across the garden to the dog enclosure, but had been told about it on asking the last guests if they knew what had happened to her husband. She guessed something of what was going on, and had left the house and crossed the lawn to the enclosure.

Even in the darkness she had been able to see enough to make her call the police and ambulance. I had vague memories of the gate opening. I'd been delirious. I'd thought it was Diana. We had been waiting for her. Acton had told her to come, the three of us were going to sort it all out. We'd been waiting all night for her. And now Acton was going to shoot her. I tried to warn her, but I was so cold all I could do was ask her if she'd brought my coat back.

'I didn't know it was you, Nicky,' Greta said, 'but I wasn't surprised. I knew it was something to do with Diana's death, and all along I couldn't believe you did it, and I was convinced that Tony was somehow responsible. What I don't understand is why? What did Tony have against Diana?'

Should I tell her? I shifted uneasily in the hospital bed. Was this the time and the place for it?

'She was a strange one, Nicky – even you have to admit that,' Greta continued. 'Do you know, for years after Tony and I were married, she didn't speak to me? Not one word? It was almost as if she was jealous. I know some little sisters are very jealous of their big brothers, but . . . I sometimes felt Diana hated me for marrying her brother. She was very strange then.'

She looked at me, genuinely puzzled. I had to tell her. It was the least I could do for her. She'd find out sooner or later. There'd be an inquest, official enquiries, even my trial . . . Better here and now, just the two of us, in private.

So I told her all about Tony Acton and Diana. And me. She listened in silence from beginning to end. No interruptions. And when it was over she got up and walked over to the window and looked out across the hospital grounds for a long time.

'Thank you, Nicky,' she said eventually. 'It explains so much, looking back over our marriage, everything that was wrong. I thought it was *me*, but no. It is a great reassurance.' She turned, shook her head – and smiled.

'A huge relief. I thought it was all my fault . . . But the shock of it. Well, you of all people must understand that.' She sat down again. 'I'd decided I was going to divorce him anyway, on the plane back from Madrid. But what I really wanted to do was to kill him. Yes, I meant it. So I should thank you for the way things turned out.'

'Thank you, Greta. You probably saved my life.'

'What a bastard. He deserved what he got.' She looked across at me, suddenly very anxious. 'I'm sure the police think I had something to do with it, just because I'm not helpless with grief.'

'I can assure them that you didn't.'

She gave a huge sigh and smile of relief. 'The police, I hate them. Their uniforms, their power. They're all the same. If you had been brought up in a totalitarian state, you would understand.' She looked around and leaned closer, laughing. 'That detective sergeant, he reminds me of one of the secret policemen who used to escort my father about the place. Do you think he has this room bugged? Do you think he is listening to us right now?'

When I left the hospital I'd been back on my feet for three days, but I was still a bit unsteady. The head boy came to see me just before I was discharged. I was hobbling around, packing.

I hardly recognized him. He wasn't the healthy, clean-cut, smartly dressed young man I remembered. He looked like he hadn't slept since I'd last seen him. He hadn't shaved for two days at least. His face was pale and thin, there were hollows under his eyes and his clothes were crumpled. But he was clearly a very happy man. 'I'm sorry I didn't come to see you earlier. Other things . . .'

I remembered. He had told me, that time he came to the studio: his wife was expecting their first child. 'Boy or girl?'

'A little girl.' He smiled. 'We're going to call her Emma.'

'Congratulations.' A daughter. A family. I could have had both. An unexpected jealousy and bitterness surprised me. 'You're a lucky man.' I meant it. A daughter. Iphigenia . . . 'Mother well?'

'Very well, thanks. Tired. We both are, of course.' He laughed. 'Haven't had more than two hours' uninterrupted sleep since she was born.' He sat down beside the bed. A black bin-liner he had been clutching bulged out when he put it down on the floor. He stroked his chin. 'In fact, I could do with putting my feet up in hospital for a week or two myself.'

'Prison cell and hospital bed,' I said. 'I feel pretty institutionalized. How am I going to survive in the outside world?'

'Well, you're going to have to, because the charges against you will be dropped. You won't go to trial, let alone back to prison.'

I laughed with relief. 'Thanks.'

'You're very lucky. Greta has saved you in all sorts of ways. She can corroborate your story. She found Diana's handbag in the house before Acton did, and being suspicious about the whole business had a good look through it. She swears there was no letter in it at that point. And being suspicious and scared of the police, she didn't hand it in but left it where she found it.' He scratched his head. 'What is it about her and the police?'

'She was brought up in communist Poland, remember, where your lot had powers you could only dream about. And which they didn't think twice about abusing. I don't suppose anyone co-operated with men in uniform unless they really had to. But she isn't under suspicion – about any of this, is she?'

'Of course not. You missed the inquest. She came out of it pretty well. Some sort of heroine. We used your statements, of course, in your absence.' He paused. 'I guessed we'd got the wrong man within two days of your arrest. You were so genuinely bewildered when we threw that letter at you. After all, you're an artist not an actor. Hence my hunch about Acton.' He sighed. 'That letter. One of our forensic people reckons he can prove it was written by Acton. He's been comparing it with samples of Diana's writing and samples of Acton's writing. The funny thing is, he reckons Diana's writing and Acton's writing are pretty close to start with, amazingly close. So perhaps Acton was right. Perhaps they did belong together. Perhaps Diana knew that. It seems to me that she knew she was doomed from the start, whichever way she turned. It seems you were simply caught in the crossfire. I'm sure that wasn't what she intended, but there you are.'

I didn't say anything. It wasn't something I wanted to think about just yet.

The head boy leaned forwards. 'Why do you think the dog went for Acton? And left you alone?'

'I don't know. I've asked myself the same question a hundred times.'

'What was Acton wearing?'

I thought hard, trying to remember. 'Dinner jacket. Coat. Wellington boots . . .'

He reached down into the black bag and pulled out a coat on a hanger inside a clear polythene wrapper. It looked like it had just come back from the dry-cleaners. But this coat was anything but clean; it was tattered and filthy. He spread it across the bed without removing its wrapper.

'Take a good look at it.'

It was something even a scarecrow wouldn't have worn. The remains of a black coat, hanging together in shreds. Stained and stiffened, caked with mud, striped with white tide marks, splashed with rusty gore. There was only one sleeve. Its buttons and collar and much else was missing.

'It's the coat Acton was wearing,' the head boy said. 'Well, what's left of it.'

Seeing it there on the bed, and knowing what it was, I felt something of the horror of that night beginning to return. The cold and the darkness. The agony. The fear . . . My hands began to tremble.

'Do you recognize it?'

'No, I . . .' I didn't want to look at it. 'It was dark. There was –'

'No, I mean, do you recognize it as anything other than the coat Acton was wearing that night?'

What did he mean? I shook my head. I just wanted him to take it away. To destroy it or something.

'There are two initials embroidered on the label just below the collar. An N and a T. Mean anything to you?'

N. T. Nicholas Todd. So that's . . . I didn't believe it. I reached out to grab it from the bed.

The head boy leaned forwards. 'Don't touch. Evidence.'

'That's my coat!' I could see it now. The colour, the material, the pattern on the lining. It was the birthday present from Diana. 'But . . . why was Acton wearing it? How did he get hold of it?'

The head boy nodded slowly. 'When did you first see him in this coat?'

'When he left the house. No. He was just in his suit then. He went back into the house soon after we got to

the enclosure. When he came out again he was wearing the coat. And wellington boots and gloves.'

'What did he go back for?'

'Well, it was cold. Freezing. He needed the coat and
stuff to keep warm. And the brandy. And the kitchen
chair to sit on. Extra torches. And he organized the dis-
appearance of my car . . .'

'Was he gone long?'

'No, he was very quick, considering.'

'Obviously he'd be in a hurry to get back.' The head
boy nodded again. 'I asked Greta about the coat. She
remembers seeing it hanging up on the back of the
kitchen door. It appeared there after your week at the
house. She presumed you'd left it there, forgotten to
take it with you when you went back to London. So it
hangs there until that night. Acton dashes back to the
house, arranges the disposal of your car, grabs what he
needs as he rushes back out through the kitchen. Including the big, thick, warm overcoat to hand on the back
of the door.'

'I didn't leave it there. I haven't seen it for months. It
got left behind at Diana's flat when . . . when we split
up.'

'So . . .' The head boy looked at me. The answer hit
us both at the same time. 'So Diana took it to the house
with her, that Friday. The day you left the house, the
day she was killed. It was she who left it in the kitchen.
She went out to feed the dogs and she never came back.
But what was she doing with the coat? She could have
been wearing it, I suppose. Took it off to feed the dogs
because she had Acton's sweater on.'

I shook my head. I could see exactly what had happened. She had gone to the house that Friday expecting
the three of us to sort the whole mess out once and for
all. She was expecting, well, if not a reconciliation then

at least a resolution. And she wanted to make a gesture – she wanted to show that she still cared, that she could still make an effort on my behalf. She knew how much the coat meant to me because it meant a great deal to her. She wanted me to have it back. It was important to her that I should continue to wear that coat, whatever happened, however things were sorted out, as a sign that her feelings for me hadn't changed since she had given it to me on that birthday.

But I didn't try to explain any of it to the head boy. I wasn't sure that I could.

'And it sends him to his death,' he was saying. 'The irony of it. He winds up that dog to kill anything carrying your scent, unaware that he's wearing your coat, that he's reeking of you himself. No wonder the dog went straight for him.'

So that was it. I felt an enormous relief now that the question had been answered. The mystery of it had lodged itself in my subconscious and, more than once during the last week, had dragged me awake at night, sweating and mumbling. Now that I knew the thing wasn't completely arbitrary . . . But there was something else. 'Why didn't the dog attack me? Was it because I'd been rolling around in the snow and the mud and everything? Had my scent washed off or something?'

He shook his head. 'You stank of brandy when they dragged you out of that enclosure. You were drenched in it. It's a pretty powerful scent. I guess it simply masked everything else.'

Of course. No wonder the dog was confused. It was obvious. I could see it now. I had been too afraid of the memory of that night to think too closely about it.

I stared at the remains of that coat and thought about Diana. In a sense she had been there that night. She had reached out from beyond the grave and taken her revenge on Acton. He had lured her to the house that Friday to kill her and he had succeeded; but she had left behind a time bomb which was to kill him in turn. It was almost as if she had known what was going to happen. As if she had planned it all one step ahead of her brother. She had died, but she had saved my life.

I sat down on the bed, my face in my hands. I couldn't speak, I could hardly breathe. Diana.

The head boy put a hand on my shoulder. 'Come on,' he said. 'It's time you were out of here.' He put the remains of the coat back into the bin-liner.

The sun was shining outside. It was warmer than a winter sun. There was no wind, and the snow in the street had almost disappeared.

'When's Easter?' the head boy asked as he pulled on his coat. 'Is it early or late this year?'

I had missed Acton's funeral while I was in hospital, as well as his inquest. It had taken place at the same crematorium as Diana's. I drove out there on my way back to London. I asked in the chapel, and was told that their remains had come to rest side by side in the garden of remembrance. A woman in black took me out to see their memorial stone. It was a simple marble slab set into the verge surrounding the garden, engraved with both their names. Anthony Acton and Diana Acton. More than brother and sister, less than brother and sister. May they rest in peace.

Perhaps the inspector was right, I thought, as I looked down at the stone. Perhaps Acton and Diana did belong together. Perhaps this was the only peace Diana could ever have hoped for.

'It's very beautiful here in the summer, when the roses are out,' the woman in black was saying. 'And in the spring, when the orchards are in blossom, the view from here is quite breathtaking.'

The lawn beyond the rose garden was dotted with little orange flames. Crocuses. They were just beginning to open. And beyond them, against a wall, taller green shoots tipped with yellow had appeared – daffodils waiting to flower. Spring – it was here. I wondered vaguely if there were primroses yet in the woods down below.

'You should come back in a month or two's time,' the woman was saying. 'The flowers then – the colours – it will all be quite lovely.'

I thanked her and returned to the car. I sat there for some moments before driving off. I wouldn't be coming back. For Diana, for Acton, for me, it was all over, and I knew that I had to go home now and try to make a new start. Leave them here with each other as the daffodils came out, the orchards blossomed and the roses flowered.

Acton and Diana had destroyed each other, as perhaps they were destined to, but at least I had survived. Diana had made sure of that.

It was a last gift from her, and I had to make the most of it.

A new start. I thought about it as I drove back to London that afternoon. It wasn't such a bad idea. I'd begin by clearing out the studio. It would be a simple enough task. Burn the unfinished pictures in the woodstove. Stack the easels away between the bookcases. Put the scattered books back in the case. Throw out the magazines, newspapers, beer cans and wine bottles. Wash up the unbroken cups and glasses and plates.

I could go away for a while. A long holiday. Yes. Somewhere warm and dry. Travel light; pencils and watercolours. Get back to work. Yes. That was a good idea. I'd do that. I smiled. The road ahead was clear. I'd soon be home.